PRAISE FOR *THE*

"The precise, savvy prose of David Davis t... compelling as to be absurd, realistic—and hu... sophisticated, bookish, middle-aged widower finds himself 'enthroned' among beneficent, highly advanced, though controlling, Alien visitors to our planet, the difficult literary objective becomes . . . *believability*! . . . Davis's hero, Hal Southerland, achieves it! We care about his fate as he negotiates his way through a network of Alien involvements; and as the visitors try to establish themselves in their adopted earthly home, the dramatic effect of *The Mistakes* lingers well past the final page . . ."

> —R. CARY BYNUM, Former Publisher, Author, *Night Streetcars, Woodhall Stories,* and *Reunion In Thera*

"It all started with a mistake—and no, I don't mean the universe, although that's debatable. The mistake in this novel was Hal Southerland opening his big dumb mouth to James Gilly about a possible alien spaceship heading to earth. From that one seemingly innocuous slip of the tongue, one mistake after another builds up to a bizarre and exciting boiling point in this hilarious sci-fi satire in the vein of *Catch 22* and *Hitchhiker's Guide to the Galaxy*. David Davis crafts a delightful tale about human incompetence mixed with a golly-gee optimism that leaves the reader laughing at, while also feeling strangely hopeful about, humanity's future. Can we coexist with Aliens? Well, as one character points out, 'humans have a very bad history of getting along with "the other."' But perhaps Hal can overcome his own mistakes and show us all the way."

> —DANIEL GUYTON, MFA, Author of *Three Ladies of Orpington* and *The Mother of God Visits Hell*

"David Davis invades readers imaginations as we follow his protagonist and widower, Hal Southerland, and the entire planet's surrender to the 'too slow to be scary' invasion. Prepare for your mind to be invaded, by Hal's unanticipated, unexpected leadership into a deal for a new earth."

> —VALETTA ANDERSON, Member of Dramatists Guild, Merely Writers and Working Title Playwrights, Served on Boards of Decatur Arts Alliance, Georgia Assembly of Community Arts Agencies and Working Title Playwrights, Former Executive Director of DeKalb Council for the Arts and Teaching Artist at the Alliance, Fox and Horizon Theatres, Former Adjunct Professor of Playwriting at Spelman College

THE MISTAKES
by David Davis

Published by

 köehlerbooks™

210 60th Street
Virginia Beach, VA 23451
800–435–4811
www.koehlerbooks.com

THE MIST▲KES

DAVID DAVIS

VIRGINIA BEACH

CAPE CHARLES

To K. and E.

CONTENTS

1.

THE BEGINNING

It all started at lunchtime. Hal Southerland was sitting in his little government agency office, eating his two slices of Milton's multi-grain, vitamin-enriched, high-fiber bread with nothing between them. At 125 calories a slice, it was still more calories than he wanted, but he needed the fiber. He was trying to lose ten more pounds to take a little pressure off his arthritic knees, but he couldn't seem to lose those ten pounds without stopping eating altogether.

So, he chewed well and surfed the net a little while he ate. He clicked on an amateur astronomy website he checked now and again. One post was asking if someone else would check on some star—so obscure it only had a number (CCM J02318+8916), not a name—that was high in the north sky, near Polaris, almost on the Earth's axis of rotation. Something seemed to be blocking the view of the star, and whatever the obstruction was, it didn't seem to reflect any light itself or move. It just seemed to be getting bigger, to the point it had started to eclipse a nearby galaxy as well.

Now, Hal hadn't been the top physics major in his class in college—not even in the top two or three of a very small group. In fact, that C in quantum mechanics, his last class required to graduate, probably stood more for Charity than it did for Competence. But it hadn't been the physics part that drove him out of the field and into managing software development; it had been the math. He understood how things worked; he just couldn't do the calculations. By the time he got to calculus in the complex number system, with the square roots of negative one rotating things along the z-axis while limits shrank to infinite smallness, he had realized that his future as a physicist was going to be limited.

But he had graduated. He had hung in there and finished. His bachelor of science in physics diploma was in a file drawer at home, but he did have one. So while he couldn't figure how fast the object blocking the star was moving, he got the general idea. Something black, growing bigger without seeming to move, well above the plane of planetary orbits—yes, that was going to get a lot of astronomers' attention quickly. And change everything.

• • •

Later that afternoon he pulled into his driveway at home and stopped to pick up the mail from his mailbox. That used to be something his wife did, but a lot had changed in the six months since she died of a heart attack. He hadn't really changed anything until two weeks after the funeral, when he tossed out all the throw rugs in the house and started loading the forks in the dishwasher with the tines down instead of up the way his wife had. He knew it wasn't really much of a declaration of independence, but it was a start. Other things would come in time.

He missed her, but life was calmer now, quieter, more routine. There was some comfort in that. Their daughter was an administrator way off in the Oklahoma State Department of Health, and his mother way past senile in a nursing home in South Carolina, so except for a Skype call from Oklahoma City now and then, he was alone. That actually didn't bother him. He certainly had enough to do to keep him busy. It had taken months, doing a little each day, to deal with all the things that had to be dealt with following his wife's death: legal papers, her clothes and makeup, cooking spices he had no idea when to use. His wife had been a pretty good amateur artist, and he was just now finishing up the process of giving away art supplies, shipping some artworks off to his daughter, and boxing up almost all the rest for storage. Only a few favorites remained on the walls, and the rooms that had been studios and supplies storage were now empty, along with most of the closets and chests of drawers. The house was neater, cleaner, and a good deal more organized now, which suited his personality better. His wife had never been artistically tolerant of empty spaces, but now the house was full of them, which didn't bother him at all.

Just as he got to the mailbox, James Gilly pulled up into the cul-de-sac and stopped. James lived down at the end of the street, and Hal felt like James saw himself as a natural politician. He certainly seemed to have the personality for it, the glib tongue, the hearty but unoffensive story always at hand, all your family's names and birthdays memorized, a slightly flexible but always popular opinion on just about everything. Hal thought that if James had had even a bit of sense, he probably would have been elected to something by now, Georgia State Senate, Roswell City Council, something. Instead he was the kind of man who thought he knew what everybody wanted but, at least as far as Hal was concerned, was constantly wrong. Any conversation lasting more than a few sentences usually was long enough for James to reveal that he was just repeating things he heard on talk radio, and he really had no idea what was actually going on. So, instead of the state senate or the city council, James was the president of the Homeowners Association, a post so unwanted that they usually had to recruit some newcomer to the subdivision before he or she found out how annoying the job actually was.

James rolled down his car window.

"How's it going, Hal?"

"It's going, James."

"I know it's been tough, all that legal stuff settling the estate on top of everything else."

"I've about got it all taken care of."

"Great. Listen, I hope you'll have time to come to the Homeowners Association meeting this Sunday. This guy from the highway department is going to give a presentation on the traffic circle they want to put at the intersection just before the entrance to the subdivision. It could make a big difference to our property values."

"Oh, I don't think that will make much difference once the aliens get here."

He knew it was a mistake almost as soon as he said it. All he had wanted to do was say something that would get James out of his hair. But somehow his mouth had come out with words before his brain had time to study on the implications.

"Aliens? Like from Mexico?"

"No, outer space. Don't you ever read anything on the web? Don't worry, it'll be on the evening news in a few days."

Hal took his mail and climbed back in his car and drove into his garage, looking back in time to see James gape at him for a second, shake his head like Hal was getting senile, and then drive off. Hal went on inside his house, put down his briefcase, and sat in his armchair for a few minutes trying to decide if he wanted to do anything different now, like visit some place he had never seen or eat something special, before . . .

Nothing came to mind, so he opened a plastic tub of chicken salad from Kroger for supper, Skyped his daughter, and went to bed early.

• • •

Actually, it was only two days before Hal saw CNN pick up the story from a science news blog on the Huffington Post, and the day after that he saw an ABC evening news report of a strange object drawing astronomers' attention. All the real astronomers interviewed were very careful not to say "UFO" or "aliens" or "spacecraft," just "very unusual motion" and "something out of the ordinary that requires investigation." But it was pretty obvious from the way they looked on TV that none of them had slept for the past couple of nights. When Hal read the posts on various astronomy websites of hackers who broke into the e-mails that were flying around between the various observatories, he saw phrases like "has to be powered to get that path" and "Good God DAMN, maybe we got six months."

Within a few weeks it was pretty obvious even on the Today Show, which Hal watched while getting dressed in the morning, that something unnatural was coming. The famous Cosmos physicist, Neil deGrasse Tyson, they interviewed one morning admitted this was not some space rock coming to destroy the world and turn humanity into dust and dinosaurs. It was slowing down, and asteroids didn't slow down. This was something sent by somebody who was actually controlling it.

As the days passed, Hal read reports in the Atlanta Journal-Constitution of some people rushing to get married and spend as much time as possible with the ones they loved before the unknown arrived. Other stories reported on people running out to have as much sex as possible with as many different people as possible before the end arrived. Then there were reports of some people heading for the hills to hide, others driving to the coast to swim while there was still an ocean. Some people quit their jobs, others quit their diets.

And after three or four weeks of this, the Journal-Constitution reported that most people just went back home and tried to get things back to normal. After all, the six months before the calculated arrival of the alien object was a long time, and somebody had to keep the electricity on and food in the grocery store, so the banks had to keep electronically depositing those paychecks that people had to keep earning.

The government, including Hal, kept working, mostly. He had plenty of leave saved up and thought about flying out to Oklahoma to see his daughter, but things were actually pretty busy at work for both of them, with the various levels of government trying to get ready for anything and everything, if they could just figure out what anything and everything were. His branch chief was discouraging anybody taking leave, though a few people did anyway, leaving the others to take on extra work. So he settled for an extra Skype call or two and a few longer emails. In the meantime, he kept an eye on the internet reports to see if any information popped up that might make him change his mind and take leave anyway.

Speculation on the websites he checked ranged from Jesus, Muhammad, or Buddha (or maybe all three) coming back to save the world to giant bugs or octopi coming to kill all the humans and siphon off their oxygen and water. CNN reported that some Republican senators proposed sending rockets tipped with nuclear bombs to intercept the object just inside the orbit of Mars (which meant they didn't understand when the astronomers said it was coming in from perpendicular to the planetary plane); Yahoo News reported that a California representative proposed a worldwide day of focusing all of mankind's energy on communicating telepathically with the obviously mentally superior, transcendent beings. The BBC News website said most people just looked up into the wrong section of the sky at night and wondered what was going to happen when "it" got here. But the only fact was that the black thing was getting closer.

• • •

So it was, after a few months, when work preparing for whatever it was that was coming had calmed down because nobody knew what else to do besides what they had already done, that, considering what had happened when the Spanish arrived in the New World with all their alien germs, and considering that he worked for an agency responsible for disease control, Hal decided to retire. It wasn't like he was one of the medical staff that might get sent to deal with whatever outbreak there was, but he decided that if something did happen, he wanted to be in control, not subject to the whims of a branch chief or orders from higher up the chain. He realized there was an element of cowardice there, but he was prepared to accept that.

He had been eligible to retire for several years, but the money was good and the work not too burdensome. Over the years he had actually gotten good at it. While his wife was alive it had gotten him out of the house while she worked on her art and created enough space between them to keep them both sane. The commute seemed to get longer every year, and he certainly didn't have the energy he used to, but the job had gotten his daughter through college and grad school without too much student loan debt and had been making his life comfortable for the past few years. But now the situation had changed, and he thought it would be better to change with it. He had helped make the world less safe for a few germs; now it was somebody else's turn. He wasn't quite sure what he would do at home now that the estate was settled and the house cleaned, but he figured he had enough books stacked up to keep him busy until the aliens arrived. After that, well, he would deal with that when the time came.

So, he filed the various forms, quietly informed his branch chief, and came in on the weekend to clear out his office. Mostly he wanted the family pictures that filled every empty space on top of cabinets and files. All through his daughter's childhood there had been at least one school picture each year, sometimes more when she played sports of some kind, plus the pictures of all three of them taken for church directories or when they could get a coupon for a big discount at Sears Photography Studio. Most of the photographs were at home, but he had usually selected one eight-by-ten from the package, put it in a frame, and taken it to the office. He boxed those up, along with a few personal items and reference books he wanted to keep for sentimental reasons, and loaded them in the trunk of his car. The rest of his professional books he stacked just outside his office for coworkers to take if they wanted them. He dumped most of the papers in the recycling bin, downloaded his files to a thumb drive, sent out an email to the branch announcing his retirement but not providing any contact information for his home (his branch chief had that if anybody really wanted it, which he doubted), and left his office clean, neat, and empty, as if no one had spent twenty-five years there doing whatever was asked of him. Now he just had to wait for the big black thing to get there and then watch the world as he knew it end, one way or another.

2.

AND THEN NOTHING

The problem was that when the big black thing got close to Earth, it didn't do anything. This, of course, just made everybody more anxious. Some reporter at the Journal-Constitution started calling it the Sphere of Damocles because photographs from the International Space Station showed it to be a black sphere, a little less than a third the size of the moon according to NASA. It came in slowly, making no noise on any frequency anybody could pick up, took up an orbit inside the orbit of the moon but above the International Space Station orbit, dropped off two much smaller spheres in the same orbit equidistance apart, perhaps so they could see or hear or scan or whatever the entire surface of the Earth, and then just sat there. And sat there.

For months.

This waiting made Hal even more uncertain about what to do with the rest of his life. He did fly out to see his daughter for Christmas, and had a good visit, but she had her own friends and social life, so when she went back to work at the health department after the holidays, Hal flew home and resumed his days of reading, taking walks, and keeping up with the nothing happening in space.

Over the months, as Hal watched on TV and the web, the various governments and space agencies and ham radio operators all reported trying to communicate with the sphere in various ways, from lasers and all radio frequencies to giant lines on the ground in various deserts formed by running dune buggies in carefully planned patterns. Nothing. It was if Earth had acquired three extra moons that were just for decoration. Finally, though the main object's orbit was well above the low earth orbit range of most of the rockets built to carry humans, the major powers got together and clamped some American solid boosters onto a Russian heavy-lift rocket, and topped the jury-rig with a refurbished American space shuttle, which contained a Soyuz capsule and a new private, experimental two-man space plane in the cargo bay. They stacked it all up on a launchpad in Kazakhstan but, try as they might, could not get the candle to light. The pinnacle of human technology just sat there on the pad, as inert as a rock, and did nothing. Sitting at home, watching it all not happen on TV, Hal knew they were in trouble.

And so nothing kept happening over and over until it seemed everybody thought nothing was going to keep happening, at least in their lifetimes. After another six months of nothing, regular television programming resumed, churches stopped having extra prayer services, and music videos that had nothing to do with aliens resumed being released.

And then something did happen. Hal got an email from the aliens. And he wasn't the only one. In fact, it soon became obvious from the reports that everybody in the world got an e-mail from the aliens. Or a tweet, or a text, or a voicemail on a cell phone, something. If you were old enough to read, you got something, even if it was on your neighbor's cell phone and they had to take it to you so you could receive the message.

The messages were basically all the same as Hal's except for the details. Go to a certain place at a certain time and pick two people to speak for your group. As best the Journal-Constitution and all the other news groups could figure out, the entire population of the world had been divided into groups of 100 adults and sent to some meeting place to elect their representatives. For Hal, the message said to go to the community room at a gym complex at the city park down the road on Sunday afternoon at 3:00 p.m. Hal thought about not going. He knew he didn't function well in groups. He couldn't pick out individual voices when there was other conversation in the background and knew he frequently said stupid things because he didn't understand what was being said to him. He also wasn't sure he liked being told what to do and when to do it by a bunch of aliens that he had never even met. On the other hand, he didn't know if anybody would take roll and what would happen if he turned up absent. So far the aliens hadn't done anything terrible, but offending them by not showing up might not be a good idea. And, of course, if he didn't go, he might not know what really happened at the meeting. So he went.

He had never been to this gym before, but the community room was basically a rectangle with a bunch of folding chairs all facing the same direction. He got there early enough to move one of the chairs back beside a table along the back wall. Other people drifted in, in little groups, talking among themselves. James Gilly came in with his wife and several other couples, and James managed to wave at him before going down to the front with the rest of his group.

Eventually somebody he didn't recognize called for order and got people to quiet down.

"OK, OK, let's get started. There's another group that has the room in an hour, so we need to get started. Most of you know me, but for those who don't, I'm Bill Williams, head of the Parks Department, and I got an e-mail telling me to moderate the meetings that are held here. Basically all we have to do is pick two people as representatives of this group. Nobody knows why or what they are supposed to do or what would happen if we didn't or what kind of people we're looking for, so let's not waste time asking questions nobody knows the answer to. This is the fourth group I've moderated today, and nobody knows anything, so let's just do it and go home."

"Who do you report the names to?"

"I don't. We just agree on two people and then we all leave."

"So how do they . . . ?"

"I don't know. Nobody knows."

"Which means they're listening."

"Maybe. Now, anybody got any nominations?"

That was when Hal's first mistake came back to bite him. James Gilly stood up.

"I want to nominate Hal Southerland. He's lived a few houses down from me for years. He knew these aliens were coming three full days before it was on the news. He has a degree in physics and lots of experience with computers and working with the government, so I think he would be better at this than people without his science and technology background."

Someone Hal didn't know stood up.

"How the hell did you know they were coming before anybody else did?"

Hal stood up slowly, feeling like a defendant standing before a judge who had just declared him guilty.

"I monitor a little astronomy website now and then. They were reporting something blocking light from a star and getting bigger, something well above the orbits of meteorites. I don't think I was the first one to put two and two together."

"Still, that sounds pretty smart. I second the nomination."

Hal was standing there trying to figure out how to decline when one of the women who had come in with James stood up.

"I think this gentleman would make an excellent representative, but I think the fact James Gilly knew about his expertise and has served us so well as the president of the Homeowners Association means that he would be excellent as the second representative, so I nominate James Gilly."

"I second" came from the general vicinity of James's wife.

"OK, that's two nominations; any others?"

There was one of those long pauses when everybody else in the room realized that two patsies were all that was needed and if everybody kept their mouth shut, they could all go home and avoid whatever fate awaited these two.

"Move the nominations be closed."

"Second."

"Move Hal Southerland and James Gilly be elected by acclamation."

"Second."

"All in favor?"

There were lots of "ayes."

"Any opposed?"

There was lots of silence.

And it was done. Hal just stood there as people he sort of knew and lots he didn't came up to shake his hand and thank him for volunteering and wish him luck and generally treat him like a Spartan about to go into battle. Finally, James came by to shake his hand.

"Well, Hal, looks like we're in this together, whatever it is."

"I'm not sure what to say."

"Not much to say, I guess. We just go home and go about our business until we get another email from the aliens."

"I guess."

So they did.

• • •

The next email came two weeks later. Just another time, date, and location to go to. James called a couple of hours later to make sure he and Hal were going to the same place, and told Hal he had called around and confirmed this was a meeting of the representatives from all the little groups in the area. Hal declined a ride, feeling like James had already gotten him into trouble and not wanting to associate with him any more than he had to. He thought again about not showing up, but couldn't think of any reason to avoid the aliens yet and felt a little obligated to the innocents who had elected him. He still had a bad feeling about this, but found himself going anyway.

The next meeting was in the biggest high school basketball gym in the area. Hal had gotten there early, but so did almost everybody else. Hal didn't know what the seating capacity was, but it must have been in the hundreds, maybe over a thousand, and it was full. If every person there represented about fifty others, this group must represent a pretty big section of town, Hal figured. He looked around for James and saw him talking to somebody in the first row on the left, so Hal turned right and climbed the risers to find a seat high up and away from the podium down on the other end of the basketball court.

Two women, one black, one white, shifted over to make room for him on the bleacher. Then a black woman came up to talk to the two women. Hal could not help overhearing their conversation.

"Quite a crowd."

"Yeah, those aliens are pulling our strings pretty much."

"At least it doesn't look like they are going to kill us since we're going through all this trouble."

"Maybe. Or they're going to herd us like cattle before they lead us to slaughter."

"Nah, I think we're just going to be slaves."

"Could be."

"What do you think they look like, anyway? Like those sci-fi monsters in the movies?"

"More like something we never dreamt of, breathing methane and with tentacles instead of fingers or something."

Hal wondered if anybody read the newspaper anymore, even

online. This kind of lack of logic had been pretty well rejected already. He couldn't help himself: he spoke without thinking. Another mistake.

"Oh, I suspect they look pretty much like us."

"And why would you say that?"

"Wherever they came from, they came an awful long way. Decades, maybe centuries to get here. In a spaceship that must have consumed a good share of a planet's resources to construct. And they could have gone anywhere in the galaxy. But they came here. So they were looking for a planet with water and oxygen, that had about this gravity, was about this warm, and had a magnetic field to keep the radiation down. They were looking for a planet that could support the kind of life this planet can support, which, to my mind, means they probably aren't that different from us, at least physically. Now, culturally, that's a different matter."

"Well, that's an interesting way of thinking about it," said the black woman, "Mr. . . . ?"

"Hal Southerland."

"Nice to meet you, Mr. Southerland. I'm Grace Corbin."

Hal suddenly had a bad feeling in the pit of his stomach.

"But I better get back to my seat. I think we're about to start." She walked down the bleacher steps and across the basketball court to a table behind the podium, where Hal watched her whisper to a man sitting behind the table and gesture up in Hal's general direction. The man did something with his computer and showed the screen to her. Hal wondered if he had time to move, but the guy at the podium was gaveling for order.

After that it was like déjà vu all over again. The moderator called for nominations for two representatives for the next level. The woman, who Hal later looked up online and turned out to be a power on the city council, nominated Hal. James leapt up to second the motion and make a short speech about Hal knowing the aliens were coming that was almost bad enough to save him, but in the end Hal was standing there beside some woman he had never met who had been picked as the other representative, shaking hands with all these people he didn't know and wondering if there was any way to resign from a position that had no known rules or responsibilities.

3.

WORSE THAN
NOTHING

Despite Hal's dread, nothing happened right away. No e-mails from aliens, no meetings of the representatives. James called him a few times to see if anything was going on, but after a few weeks, even the phone calls stopped. The retirement checks kept getting automatically deposited, his daughter Skyped every once in a while, but he never got around to telling her about his adventures in the meetings, and there were enough books to read and chores to do to keep him occupied, though he was getting toward the bottom of his stack of books. He was almost finished with a book on the ancient Greek Pythagoreans and how they thought mathematics and religion were pretty much the same thing. After that he had an old Terry Pratchett Discworld novel he had somehow missed years earlier during all the hubbub of being a parent, husband, and projects manager. The last book on the stack was Jared Diamond's Guns, Germs, and Steel on why some cultures came to dominate other cultures, which he had been trying to read for years but had never gotten to.

After that he would need to rebuild his stack. He wondered if the Barnes & Noble near the mall was still open. In college, in between the science and math classes, he had taken a lot of history courses, mostly as a way to relax but also to keep his grade point average up. He had kept the habit throughout his life of having a book on hand to read whenever he had a few spare minutes. Now he wondered how many more books he would get to read before whatever was going to happen happened.

And then the aliens landed, sort of. The big black sphere stayed were it was, but another black sphere, somewhat smaller but still pretty big, was birthed and slowly settled straight down, so slowly people had time to start betting pools on where it would end up. The odds quoted on the BBC News website suggested most people predicted some big, empty spaces: the Asian tundra, the Sahara, Montana. Others figured close to a major city: New York, Paris, Moscow. If anybody had bet on the high plains of Ecuador, they would have cleaned up. Because there it was, right on the equator. And there it sat, silent and alone, with everyone who was curious enough to walk up to it changing their minds as they got closer. Sometimes, at night, there were reports that smaller black spheres emerged and flew off, but they were black, it was dark, and radar didn't seem to work. And again, nothing happened for ever so long.

After so long that the Georgia football games had returned to being the lead story on the local news, Hal got another email. This time it was a plane ticket to New York City, with an open return date, and a reservation at some fancy hotel that wasn't even a chain. He kept expecting James or the other representative to call, but they never did, so he assumed he was on his own for this one.

He closed up the house as best he could; called the police vacation watch number and spent five minutes explaining that he had no pets, no alarm system, and no return date; and packed a carry-on bag with just the basics. Since he didn't know when he would be back, he locked his car in the garage and called a cab to the North Springs subway station and took a MARTA train to the Atlanta airport.

Landing at La Guardia, he was met at the gate by a woman in a chauffeur's uniform who somehow recognized him as he got off the plane. He realized this was not the normal procedure. He also realized the woman, despite the uniform, did not look like a regular chauffeur. She was tall, well built, pale, somewhat reminiscent of Marilyn Monroe, with wild blond hair that seemed to stick out from under her chauffeur's hat in ways that defied both gravity and any style he was familiar with. But she took his bag and led him through the airport to a limo, saying almost nothing before depositing him at the front desk of the appointed hotel in Manhattan. There the bellhop took a key card and envelope from among several laid on the check-in desk, picked up the suitcase, guided him to the elevator and then to his room. The bellhop put his bag on the bed, handing him the key card and envelope, and not even waiting for a tip before leaving without comment.

Hal realized that this was really not quite the normal way things worked in New York. He glanced out the window—the old-fashioned kind, a real window—and saw the street ten floors below. Traffic and pedestrians seemed to be passing by normally. He slipped the card key in his shirt pocket and looked at the envelope. His name was on the front, so he opened it.

"Welcome to New York City. You are congratulated on being selected from among the representatives. Please remain in the hotel until our business is concluded. This may take a few days. Meals will be provided at the hotel restaurant on the first floor. Any other items you may need are available at the hotel gift shop or on request to the staff. All charges will be covered by The Aliens. Enjoy your stay."

Hal read it three times. It never did say what he was selected for, or what the business that might take days was, or how many others had been selected, or what might happen when this was all over. He decided the chances of enjoying the stay were pretty slim.

• • •

After unpacking a little, he went down to the lobby, found the gift shop, selected a New York Times newspaper, looked around for somebody to pay, checked at the desk and was told anything in the gift shop was free, went back to the gift shop and added a New York Post, selected a chair where he could see both the entrance and the front desk, and read the papers while also peeking over the top of the paper to see what was really going on. There seemed to be at least half a dozen other people sitting around the lobby doing the same thing. A woman wearing a hijab was brought in by a male chauffeur with blond hair sticking out from under his hat. A man whose turban identified him as a Sikh was brought in by a female chauffeur that looked a little like Daryl Hannah, only with a blond Afro under her hat. Just like him, they were handed a card key and an envelope at the desk and escorted to the elevator.

A man wearing what looked to Hal like a European-style and very expensive suit came out of the elevator, crossed to the gift shop, selected a candy bar, looked for a clerk, gave up on finding one and slipped the candy bar into his pocket before going back up the elevator. A black man wearing a suit with a tie that Hal thought had the colors of the Pan-African flag came from the elevator, looked around the lobby, and crossed to the restaurant. This prompted Hal to check out the restaurant, which turned out to be just off the lobby, facing the street, with one wall of plate glass allowing a view of the sidewalk just outside the hotel and then of the street and the buildings across the way. Hal glanced out that window and saw the people of New York City passing by as if nothing unusual were going on, as if a mini–United Nations being convened by aliens in one of their hotels was just business as usual. And for NYC, maybe it was.

As he resumed his seat in the lobby, one middle-aged woman in a sari came out of the elevator and crossed directly to the entrance door. She was intercepted by a bell captain in a uniform so gaudy it seemed impossible, reds and purples and yellows in a pattern that resembled a military uniform in the way a clown suit resembled a Brooks Brothers ensemble. It was topped by a hat that reminded Hal of a Russian officer's hat, only higher in front, with very nonmilitary blond hair sticking out in all directions from under it.

"I'm sorry, ma'am. All the guests have been requested to remain inside the hotel for the time being."

"I've never been to New York before. I just wanted to see the Empire State Building. I understand it's not very far. I won't even go up it; I just want to see it."

"I'm sorry, ma'am. Perhaps afterwards."

She seemed to consider making a break for it or maybe kneeing the bell captain in the groin and walking calmly out the door, but after a moment the determination appeared to drain out of her, and she slowly turned and walked back to the elevator. Everyone else in the lobby and at the desk had been watching this, of course, and gradually returned to their business of looking like they were doing something when they were all just watching each other.

• • •

The next morning Hal was sitting at a table in the restaurant eating what the restaurant claimed was an omelet made with egg whites and generally healthy vegetables. It actually tasted more like stale tapioca. He was by the plateglass window, watching people hurrying by on the sidewalk, remembering why he generally avoided eating in hotel restaurants, when something fell from the sky outside, hit the pavement, and did not bounce. Hal's first thought was that somebody had fallen from a hotel window. His second thought was that whoever had fallen was now very dead. His third was that it was the woman in the sari from yesterday who had tried to leave the hotel. As Hal watched, a few people walking by on the sidewalk rushed to the body to see if there was anything that could be done. The sensible ones moved under the awnings and overhangs in case there was glass or other bodies also on the way down. Everybody else just sort of stood and gaped, noticing, like Hal, the bones sticking out of the body and the blood running to the sewer.

Then there were sirens coming, police running up, and people on the sidewalk evidently deciding they couldn't be late for work after all. Hal sat watching the scene and wondering if the woman in the now bloody sari had seen the Empire State Building on the way down. As the ambulance pulled away, he looked down at his now cold egg-white omelet, called the waiter over, and asked for an order of pancakes with blueberry syrup.

• • •

The rest of the day was quiet. He sat in the lobby reading the New York Times, the New York Post, The Washington Post, The Christian Science Monitor, USA Today, and even the National Enquirer, but saw nobody else try to leave. He tried to figure out what would cause a woman who wanted to see the Empire State Building to leap out a hotel window. He was not an expert on Indian religions and couldn't tell from her sari or jewelry which religion she was anyway, but he seemed to remember that all of them considered suicide as bad karma. He looked in the gift shop for a paperback novel to distract him, but somehow the science-fiction novels didn't seem appropriate anymore, the romance novels were not his thing, and the murder mysteries seemed pale compared to what he was living through. Finally he watched the local, network, and cable news, which told him a lot by not mentioning any alien meeting in New York or suicides from hotel windows.

• • •

The next morning he was back at the same table in the restaurant, having compromised this time on a Denver omelet using real eggs, when it happened again. This time it was a man in a business suit, but just as dead. Hal thought he remembered him from the lobby, maybe speaking Spanish to someone. This was getting to be a pattern that Hal didn't like, especially since he assumed he fit in it somewhere. This time he took the newspapers back to his room and searched through them for any reference at all to people landing on streets in Manhattan but found nothing. There seemed to be no news of anything that was actually happening.

• • •

That afternoon, the phone by his bed rang.

"Hello."

"Please come up to the penthouse suite. Just push the elevator button for the highest floor."

Whoever was on the phone hung up. Hal decided it would be wise to use the bathroom before he went up, then made sure his key card was in his shirt pocket before heading for the elevator, which just happened to be waiting for him with the door open. At the top floor, the elevator opened into a hallway, but directly across from the elevator was an open door. He peeked into the room behind the open door and saw it was empty. Totally empty. No furniture, no people, not even any fake paintings on the walls. He backed up and decided to try the other doors. All locked. He knocked on a couple of doors, but no one answered. Finally he came back to the empty room. This time he took a couple of steps into the room.

"Hello. Anybody home?"

The door closed behind him. A woman entered from a door at the other end of the room. Hal thought she reminded him of someone, but at first couldn't figure it out. Then it struck him— Margaret Thatcher on a bad hair day. He was beginning to wonder if this hair thing was a style or part of their DNA, assuming they had DNA. She wore a modest white shirt and a tweed skirt, just below the knees in length, with black shoes.

"Good afternoon."

"Good afternoon."

"I have been working on my English, but sometimes I'm not quite sure I have all the subtleties mastered. If you think you are not understanding something completely, please ask for clarification."

"You seem to be doing fine so far."

"Thank you. You understand that I am not, as you say, from around here."

"You arrived in a big, black spacecraft from a planet in another solar system far, far way."

"Yes. But we are not so different, you and I. We both breathe the air and drink the water. Parallel evolution, you would call it. We arrived at basically the same form through slightly different steps because we live in basically the same environment and occupy basically the same niche."

"OK."

"So we have a lot in common. Even more than we expected. So, Hal, we want to share this planet with you and your kind. There are not so many of us. We have certain technological advantages over you, but we don't want to cause any more problems for you than we have to."

"I'm sure we would appreciate that."

"But there is a little problem we have found. Something we want you to help us with."

"That doesn't sound good."

"We have been studying you for a long time, your kind and your planet."

"I sort of figured that."

"Remote sensing long before we left our planet, then more and more detail as we got closer. All those months in orbit when we wanted nothing more than to feel the soil beneath our feet, listening, studying. We were pleased by how much like us you are physically. There is much to admire about your kind. Your ways of settling disputes still leaves something to be desired, but I suspect you know that."

"We do seem to have a problem with that."

"We decided we really wanted to live with you, to share the planet, to learn from each other."

"I'm glad to hear that."

"There was just this one little problem."

"Yes?"

"Do you know what phytoplankton are?"

"Very small little plants that live in the ocean."

"Very good. And do you know what they produce?"

"Lots of oxygen."

"A very high percentage of all the oxygen on this planet. And do you know just how rare and precious that oxygen is? Not just here, but in all the galaxy?"

"I suspect that may be one of the major reasons you are here."

"That is true. Are you also aware that the phytoplankton and several other living things keeping the oceans alive are about to undergo a population collapse, drastically reducing the amount of oxygen on this planet?"

"No, I was not aware of that."

"None of your kind seem to be aware of that. And even if they were, I'm not sure your kind could do what needs to be done to prevent it."

"Which is?"

"It's a very complicated system, you understand. And the times when easy solutions could be applied are long past. They were long past even before we arrived. Now we are down to desperation measures."

"I see, I guess."

"What has to be done is not pleasant. Certainly not how we wanted to start our life on this beautiful planet. But we have learned from our own bitter experience. The alternatives would be much worse."

"I'm sure you have studied the situation carefully."

"We have to make four billion humans Disappear within a month. To very quickly reduce the environmental and pollution pressures on the planet."

"Excuse me? I'm not sure I got that."

"Four billion of your kind have to have the atomic bonds in their bodies broken so that they disassociate into their basic elements, falling to the soil as dust and evaporating into the air as humidity. They just Disappear. It is a painless process, we think. That's a question to which there is no way to get a definite answer. But it is very quick and no one screams. We can conduct the disassociation remotely from the main ship in orbit. That is not your problem. The place where you come in is deciding which four billion people."

Suddenly Hal realized why two people had jumped out the windows.

"I'm not the first person you've talked to about this, am I?"

"Sadly, no."

"You understand that killing four billion people is not the best way to win friends and influence people."

"Yes, we understand. In the long term even more will die, many very unpleasantly, if we do nothing."

"So why do you need me? Or the first two people you talked to?"

"We need you to decide which four billion."

"Why? What does it matter which four billion?"

"It could matter. Depending on how they are chosen. Surely you can see the possibilities."

Then it hit him.

"You don't need me to choose; you need me to take the blame. It's transference, like those people who blame the police instead of the terrorists for a terror attack. You do the killing, but since I decide who dies, everybody blames me when their wife or daughter or mother or son or whoever disappears right in front of them one day. I get the blame because I'm the one who decided. Honestly, lady, you understand us a whole heck of a lot better than you pretend to."

"It is difficult. There is so much variety and diversity. But whatever our reasoning, as straightforward as wanting to employ your understanding of your own kind or as devious as shifting as much of the responsibility as possible, we are offering you a deal. We can make the rewards very substantial."

"Rewards? Are you crazy?"

"Just the traditional ones—money, power, and, in your case, fertile females."

"I wouldn't live long enough to collect on any of that. Half the people who survived would be out to kill me for picking their loved one to die."

"Disappear."

"Whatever."

"We can create a situation in which you would be protected."

"Somehow I doubt that."

"Nevertheless, Hal, we are offering you a deal. I believe the term is a deal you can't refuse."

"I can think of two people who found a way to refuse."

"Yes. We tried to select people with a strong desire to survive, a certain dispassionate objectivity, and the flexibility to adjust to new circumstances. But perhaps we do not understand human beings on the individual level as well as we hoped we did."

"No kidding."

"Nevertheless, as I was saying, we are offering you a deal. Pick four billion people. Bring us a list tomorrow morning. It can be any four billion as long as they are recognizable by a physical characteristic. Race, age, gender, height, shoe size, bacterial or viral disease, even genetic characteristics as long as they are expressed. No recessive genes. No political party affiliations, no religions; it has to be something physical our remote scanners can detect. And in return we will make you king of this planet. Almost unlimited riches, power beyond imagining, women like your wildest dreams."

"Lady, if you don't mess up the government retirement pay or the whole financial system, I already have all the money I need. I learned a long time ago that I really don't need a whole lot just for me. Food, a few books each month, doesn't cost a lot. As for power, I have had a little power at times during my career, and generally I messed it up. I am not good at telling other people what to do or how to do it. I don't enjoy it and I usually just end up hurting other people.

"As for wild women, well, to be honest, forty years ago that would have been really tempting. Heck, even twenty years ago. These days, well, my wife has been dead for more than a year, so I'm not saying I haven't thought about another woman or two; I'm not that old. But these days it's not the force it used to be. Somehow I don't think I'm ready to kill four billion people just to get laid. Assuming you could find a woman who didn't want to kill me because I decided her father would die."

"Disappear. We say they Disappear. We think it captures the process better since there's no body left."

"Whatever."

"There are other factors to consider."

"Such as?"

"There are reasons the two people before you decided jumping out a window would be a preferred alternative to coming back in this room without a list."

"So humans are not the only ones who have problems resolving conflicts."

"It is not what you are thinking."

"No?"

"No. If you do not provide a list, you will be asked to remain in your room until the Disappearances are complete. You will be exempt from Disappearing. When it is all over, you will be sent home. There you will find out who Disappeared and who didn't. And you will live the rest of your life knowing that it could have been different. That you could have decided differently. That you had the opportunity to determine the future of your planet, and left it to some stranger that you know absolutely nothing about. That when your moment came, you turned and ran."

"I have been a coward before."

"Tomorrow morning, Hal. Tomorrow morning. This is your one chance. Don't mess it up."

And she turned and walked out the door behind her. After a moment, the door to the hall swung open and the elevator was waiting.

• • •

That evening, Hal stood by the window in his room and tried to watch the sunset, but there were all these tall buildings in the way. He remembered a visit to Arizona and the vivid sunsets there, dust in the sky turning all shades of red and not even a tree to block the view. Now concrete and steel was all he saw. He opened the window and looked out. His daughter would miss him, but she might not be around much longer either. His mother was so far gone she wouldn't even know anything had happened to him. It would be easy.

Then he wondered who was next in line. He was sure the aliens would keep going until they found someone who took their deal. Who would it be? What would they decide? He knew there was a reason he managed computers and not people. Actually, lots of reasons, most of which he didn't fully understand. He just never quite "got" people. Never quite fit in with them. He never quite figured out how his wife put up with him. Or why. Surely he was the last person who should decide who lived and who died. Or was it "Disappeared"? Dust to dust, as they say.

He certainly didn't want to be king of the planet, whatever that meant. Kings were usually bad news as far as he was concerned. Still, could he live with not deciding, passing the buck? He thought he knew what the last thoughts of the two people who ended up on the pavement were. Were they the cowards or the heroes? That seemed an open question right then.

And if he did decide, what would he decide? It wasn't like he could decide to kill all the bad guys, even if he could find four billion bad guys. It had to be physical traits. Kill all the blonds, that kind of thing. He didn't think being mean or cruel was a physical trait, unless he could tie it to some genetic thing a scanner could pick up. Even Star Trek scanners had limitations. They could read diseases, not personalities. So how could you decide? He sat down and opened his laptop, wondering if this was a mistake or not.

4.

AND THEN

The next morning he went back to the empty room, carrying his laptop. The door closed behind him. There was a long, narrow screen of some kind set in the back wall. On it was a number. The number was zero. Margaret Thatcher the alien entered as before, hair slightly wilder than before, as if she hadn't had time to comb it this morning, wearing the same white shirt and tweed skirt. With her came another woman, the one who had picked him up at the airport, not in the limo driver uniform but rather a white dress like Marilyn Monroe wore in that famous poster. In fact, now she looked a lot like Marilyn. He wondered if they were dressing to look like what they thought he expected or if he was reading too much into their understanding of the subtleties of appearances.

"You have a list?"

"I have a question."

"Yes?"

"If I ask you to disappear all the people with a certain disease, but there is an animal or something that is a carrier or reservoir of that disease, can you also disappear all those similarly infected animals so the disease also disappears?"

"We can Disappear everything that contains the same bacteria or virus."

"Will you, as part of the deal?"

"That is hereby added as an amendment. If it is possible, the diseases you specify will be exterminated from humanity forever."

"Thank you."

"So you have a list."

"I have a list."

"The screen will show the total number of your kind with the physical characteristics on your list as you read them out. You have to keep going until it reads at least four billion."

He opened his laptop and called up a file. "Everyone infected with HIV."

"And the apes and monkeys also infected."

"Yes."

A number, thirty-four million and some thousands, appeared on the screen.

"Everyone infected with tuberculosis."

"There will be some overlap among those groups."

"I understand."

The number grew by a little more than ten million, less than he had hoped.

"OK. Everyone infected with gonorrhea."

That got nearly another forty million.

"Chlamydia."

A big one, more than one hundred million.

"You don't have to do this one disease at a time if they are somehow related."

"OK. Syphilis, Chancroid, lymphogranuloma venereum, granuloma inguinale, and trichomoniasis; hepatitis B or C; human papilloma virus types 1, 2, 6, 11, 16, 18 or other strains that cause cancer."

That combination jumped the number by a billion and a half. Almost halfway there.

"Lassa fever, Ebola, Marburg, or any other hemorrhagic fever. Just to be sure, any polio, smallpox, leprosy, or Black Plague. Guinea worm, spotted fever, Lyme disease, including the worms and ticks."

"Of course. That is in the deal; you don't have to specify."

Now he was over two billion.

"OK. Malaria, yellow fever, typhus, cholera, rabies, dengue, Zika."

Another three hundred million plus were added. He checked his list. The numbers were not increasing fast enough. There were evidently more people with more than one disease than he anticipated.

"Genital herpes."

That got a big jump in the number, another half a billion plus. But he was still short. He began to get desperate.

"Anybody more than one hundred years old."

Not much effect, not even a million.

"Anybody more than ninety years old."

About twenty million. That would include his mother, but she had been wanting to die for months now, when she was lucid enough to want anything, so he was sure she wouldn't mind.

"Anybody with a terminal and incurable illness."

"You mean like cancer, Alzheimer's, dementia, that kind of thing?"

"Yes, if there's no treatment left."

"That requires an exercise in judgement that our scanners can't do. It's an either-or thing."

"And millions of people have cancer that could be cured."

"Yes."

"Damn."

"You still need millions, if that's the way you want to go."

"No, no. Let's see. OK, OK, damn. Sickle cell, thalassaemias, cystic fibrosis, Tay-Sachs, fragile X syndrome, Down syndrome, double Y syndrome, Huntington's disease, Edwards syndrome, Patau syndrome, trisomy 22, triple X syndrome, muscular dystrophy, Lesch-Nyhan syndrome."

"We can't always pick up the carriers for some of those."

"Do what you can."

That got more than half a billion. But the total was still a little short. He searched his list on the laptop again, hoping he had skipped something accidentally. Damn, no; he had used up every possibility he had thought of. He looked up at the aliens.

"May I suggest the rest of the tick-borne diseases?"

"Yeah, sure."

The number inched just over four billion. He stared at it and wondered if that was good or bad.

"Thank you, Mr. Southerland. That will suffice."

"May I go now? I believe I left my window open."

"Allow me to introduce Angelina Winston."

"Please, call me Angie."

"Angie will be your new aide."

"Aide or guard?"

"Let us say a little bit of both. She will now escort you to the Royal Suite."

The door behind him opened, Angie walked to it and gestured for him to go first. He closed his laptop and walked out the door and into the elevator. He was about to push the button for his floor when Angie intervened and pushed the button for one floor down.

"You have a new room now, Your Highness."

"Please don't call me that."

"But you are the king now. It was part of the deal."

"I'm willing to forget that part of the deal. I don't want it. You got what you wanted. Just let me go home."

"I think you will find that we aliens always keep our part of a deal. We try to be honorable that way."

The elevator door opened onto another hall with the door directly across open. Angie gestured for him to enter. It was indeed a royal suite, plush and luxurious, two bedrooms with king-sized beds and their own bathrooms, a small kitchen, separate sitting and media rooms. He wandered throughout the rooms, noticing the fine furniture, the original paintings, the expensive fabrics, and the total lack of windows. Solid, unopenable glass instead.

"I will have your things brought up from your previous room. There is some food in the kitchen, but we will mainly order from room service for the time being. The menu is the same as in the restaurant."

"And how long is 'the time being'?"

"It takes a little time to get everything ready. The Disappearances will start when deep night reaches the middle of the Pacific Ocean tomorrow night, occurring about two o'clock in the morning local time in each place. Most people will be asleep when it happens, so it will be very peaceful for most of them. Then it will take twenty-four hours to go completely around the globe. Afterwards there will be a period of adjustment of at least several days."

"No kidding."

"Your cell phone has been disabled except for receiving texts or other incoming information. Nothing outgoing. Same for your laptop. You understand."

So much for a call to his daughter.

"Unfortunately, I guess I do."

"Less panic and all that."

"Word is going to get out after people in the Pacific Islands start waking up and finding half the population gone."

"I think people are going to find it very hard to communicate other than face-to-face for the next couple of days."

"Ah, yes. And planes suddenly won't take off and cars won't start and trains will just sit on the tracks for a while."

"Something like that."

"Tell me, Angie, how do you feel about all this?"

"It is regrettable, but necessary. You have no idea just how precious this planet is, to your kind and mine. It must be taken care of, no matter what."

"I see."

"You must be hungry. Let me order some lunch."

"And so the condemned man ate a hearty meal. I guess I really don't need to worry about my diet anymore, do I? Would it be possible to get a pizza? A real New York pizza, with pepperoni and ham, double cheese, and maybe a few anchovies?"

"Let me see what I can do."

She went out the door for a moment, revealing that there were now two "doormen" in the hall. She spoke to one, then stepped back inside, closing the door.

"It will take about half an hour."

"That's fine. I really didn't have anywhere to go anyway."

He turned and walked into one of the bedrooms, closing the door behind him. He sat on the end of the bed, looked at what appeared to be a real Impressionist painting of waterlilies on the wall across from the bed, and wondered what he was supposed to be feeling right now. Whatever it was—guilt, regret, satisfaction, victory, fear—he wasn't feeling it. He wasn't feeling much of anything and wondered why.

• • •

After the pizza, the sleepless night caught up with him, and he slept most of the afternoon. For supper he reverted to type and went with the tuna salad. Then he asked Angie to leave him be for a while and spent a few hours watching the cable news channels, which obviously had no clue about anything, especially what was about to happen. Finally he decided that deep night in the Pacific would be about early morning in New York and went to bed.

• • •

The next morning he settled for a couple of breakfast bars and some orange juice from the kitchen, then resumed his post in the media room as they reported problems contacting Hawaii, and then one by one the channels went dark. Later that morning Angie came in with another alien, this one dressed in a white lab coat and scrubs with a small black bag, with black hair and a short beard, both very curly and unkempt. Angie was now wearing sneakers with no socks, tight blue jeans, and a white T-shirt with "Alien Power" printed on the front.

"This is Doctor Harvard, the royal physician. He's going to give you a quick physical exam. We have to take care of the king."

"Yes, I have to be healthy when somebody shoots me."

"Please just stand still, Your Majesty."

"Please don't call me that. If you're going to be my doctor, call me Hal, or bumbling idiot, or stupid clod, something familiar."

The doctor took something that looked to Hal like a Star Trek phaser instead of Bones's medical scanner out of his bag, and passed it slowly over Hal from his head to his toes, stopping at his ears, eyes, heart, gut, groin, and knees.

"Those knees must ache sometimes."

"Once in a while, if I don't do my stretches every day."

"Well, let me see if I can give you something to help with that."

Another black gismo came out of the black bag, got pressed to his neck and held there for a second. Then he was handed two pills and Angie provided a bottle of water.

"Just a little something for aches and pains. No side effects. One size fits all."

He swallowed the pills.

"I think you will feel much better in a little while. Angie will let me know if anything else is needed."

And the doctor packed up his little black bag and left.

"So, you have figured out human anatomy down to the cellular level, I take it."

"Something like that. Physically we are not that different."

"That's what I keep hearing."

· · ·

Later, as he was sitting in an armchair staring at a TV screen full of static and Angie was stretched out on the couch, he finally got a little bored.

"Interesting T-shirt."

"You like it?"

"So, you're calling yourselves 'The Aliens?'"

"Just going with the flow."

"You realize it isn't a compliment."

"Sometimes it's better to just embrace an insult and transform it. Like 'Yankee Doodle.'"

"OK. I get the reference. So what do you really call yourselves?"

"What do you mean?"

"Well, we're 'homo sapiens,' or 'human beings,' or just 'humans.' What's your term for what you are?"

"Ah. There's not an exact equivalent, but the best translation would be something like 'the People.'"

"OK. Makes sense."

"Could get confusing if you're 'the Humans' and we're 'the People.' Being 'the Aliens' works for us."

"Does that go for individuals too? I take it Angelina is not your real name."

"Let's say it is sort of a rough English equivalent to what my name means in my language."

"So you have the idea of angels in your culture?"

"Well, not exactly the way you mean it. Actually, my name literally means beautiful little light in the night sky. I guess Star or Estella would have been a more literal translation, but Star seems so much like a name an alien would have, and I like the sound of Angelina more than Estella."

"Well, you seem to speak English well."

"It's a tricky language, but I've been working on it for more than a year. All those TV broadcasts actually do make it past Pluto. And in some ways it's very similar to our language in that they are both composites of several other languages. But in our language the pitch and change of tone also matter, sort of like Chinese. Very musical."

"I see. So what is your name in your language?"

She made a sound that reminded him of a bit of recitative from a French opera.

"OK. I think I'll just call you Angie, if you don't mind."

"Definitely the way to go."

Suddenly the static on the screen began to clear. Some talking head he had never seen before appeared behind a desk in a news studio. He looked like an intern who had been assigned to sit there while the real reporters ran around trying to find out what was going on.

"Are we on? Is it working?"

There was a pause while the intern looked around at monitors and probably dozens of people running around behind the camera.

"Uh, OK, uh, welcome back. This is Harry Waters reporting. All electronic communication appears to have been disrupted for over twenty-four hours now, but we think we are back on the air. Here in New York there have been reports that hundreds, perhaps thousands of people vanished in the middle of the night. This may not be limited to New York City because the communication disruptions started in the Pacific Islands and quickly spread around the world. We don't know what has happened in other places, but here everybody reports knowing one or more people that just don't seem to be here anymore. We have reports of people waking up in empty beds when they had gone to sleep with a husband or wife. Others report parents or children missing from their homes. We hope to have more information now that the phones and e-mails seem to be working again, but—"

The static came back for an instant; then the face of the Alien that looked like Margaret Thatcher appeared on the screen. This time she appeared to have Phyllis Diller's wig on.

"Fellow inhabitants of the planet Earth: We regret that it has been necessary to cancel your communication for a while. This was necessary to prevent panic while we made certain emergency adjustments to the environment. When we arrived here, we found this planet very beautiful and bountiful, but very close to a collapse of certain key species. After serious study and consultation, we determined that drastic measures were absolutely necessary to preserve life on the planet, both yours and ours.

"It was necessary to drastically reduce the stress on the environment by reducing the human population significantly, among other steps. We had the capability to do that, but we did not want to be the ones to determine who would Disappear. For that, we turned to one of you, the king of the planet, who provided guidance on how to determine who would Disappear. We followed that guidance, and many of your friends and family have Disappeared so that the planet can live. Do not bother to look for these people; they are gone. We regret any sorrow this may cause you, but, as I said, it was necessary, and who Disappeared was determined by your king. Further information will be released as we settle into the new normal. We return you now to your regularly scheduled program."

There was a bit of static again, then the intern reappeared.

"Are we on again? Uh, we seem to have just had a message from the Aliens saying that some king of the planet has decided that millions of people had to disappear in order to save the environment. We will try to get more information on this king, but right now we want to go to one of our reporters down on the plaza."

Hal turned the TV sound down and stared at the screen.

"I am so dead."

"Not to worry."

"I am going to be the most hated man in the history of the world."

"Well, we still like you."

"Oh great, I'm Patsy of the Week in Alien Times."

Suddenly his smartphone beeped, signaling a text message.

"There are millions of texts going out right now, system is totally jammed, but we made sure yours got through. It's good to be king."

He looked at the screen, and the lump in his throat was bigger than he expected it would be. Tears leaked from both eyes.

"Daddy?"

His hands shook so bad it took him almost a minute to type the reply.

"I'm OK for right now. In NYC. Lay low and watch the news with a grain of salt. Love you. Dad."

He slipped the phone back in his pocket.

"Does your protection extend to the daughter of the king?"

"It does, though in a different way. We don't want to draw any attention to her right now. But she is being watched over. She will be fine."

"Thank you."

"That's what I'm here for."

He turned the TV off, got up and walked into his bedroom, closed the door behind him, lay down on the bed, and stared at the ceiling for a very long time, trying to turn his brain off.

5.

THE ISLAND

The next week was a blur in his memory: Hal watched TV news coverage and monitored online news posts as, at first, people ran around like chickens with their heads cut off, trying to find out which of their family and friends were still here and which were gone. After the first few hours, the TV reported riots against the Aliens, but that sort of fizzled out when people realized the only Aliens they knew about were off in space or in a sphere in Ecuador and didn't seem to react no matter how many police cars got turned over. Soon the riots started up again, only this time against governments that hadn't protected their people from the Aliens. The governments stopped those riots by announcing they were all uniting to attack the Aliens, prompting rioters to drop the rocks they were throwing and rush to join one army or another. Of course, that got absolutely nowhere since any weapon that had so much as a computer chip didn't work at all, and the people and bullets in Ecuador couldn't seem to even get close to the sphere.

The CNN reporter on site said this left people there discouraged.

Within a couple of days there were television shows and newspaper stories analyzing the patterns of who Disappeared and who didn't, and always getting it wrong. Hal noticed speculation in social media about who the "king of the planet" was; then his name was figured out by somebody, followed by speculation about where he was hiding, at which point Hal stopped following what was trending. With the riots dying out, local governments started reasserting some control, mainly because nobody could figure out what would get a rise out of the Aliens safe in their spheres, not realizing there were also a few sitting around a hotel in Manhattan. Another day brought long, speculative articles in special online editions of Time and Newsweek on the potential impact of four billion fewer people on the environment and the economy, along with articles in People about which movie stars had Disappeared. Governments quickly enacted some emergency measures to stabilize the economies and keep the infrastructures functioning, most of which actually worked, prompting accusations the governments were getting guidance from somewhere.

A couple more days brought some grudging scientific support, in the more serious media Hal read, for the data the Aliens released supporting their action, though that cost some scientists their careers. Some editorial writers began to rationalize about who was really in charge now and how people had to adjust their expectations and accept the new reality, and these writers were then promptly accused by other editorial writers, who proclaimed their own eternal resistance to the Aliens, of just wanting to be on the "winning" side, no matter how brutal. The result was cautious deference to and passionate hate for both the Aliens and the king in almost equal measure flying through the media.

But after a few days Hal noticed a subtle shift of the focus from blame and damnation to recovering from the trauma and adjusting to the new situation, whether they liked it or not, and even a few tentative hints of acceptance. As Hal read it, the consensus in the media was coming around to the idea that there didn't seem to be another immediate threat, nobody could think of anything to do to the Aliens that would actually make a difference, and the humans left had plenty to do to get life settled into a new normal. As some Twitter user tweeted, "Aliens Suck; Deal With It." After all, what else could they do? It was plain who was really in charge. And it was just as plain that humans couldn't do a damn thing about it.

Eventually Hal stopped watching the TV news and reading online news sites every waking hour and started dealing with getting on with what was left of his life in his new reality. He wrote a long letter to his daughter to be delivered after his assassination, putting it through several drafts, and storing it electronically and in hard copy. He also ate omelets and pizza till he got tired of it.

Then, twenty days after the Disappearance, Angie walked in and announced, "We're moving. We'll take care of your stuff. The transport is on the roof."

"Why? Where are we going?"

"You'll see. Come on, you get to be the first human to ride in one of our transports."

He followed her out the door to the stairs behind the fire door, up two flights, and out on the roof. It was the first time he had been outside since before he made his list. On the roof was a black sphere about the size of a UPS truck with an opening just big enough to walk through where the sphere touched the roof. What kept it from rolling over he had no idea.

Angie walked to the door, then stepped aside to let him enter first. Inside were two seats that looked like a cross between first-class airplane seats and bucket seats from some fancy sports car. Beyond that was only blackness. He sat in one seat and Angie took the other. He looked for a seat belt to fasten, but couldn't find one.

"Do I need to strap in or something?"

"We won't let you fall out."

He wasn't quite sure if that was good or bad. The door closed and a dim light came from somewhere, but there were no windows or viewing screens. He waited.

"When do we take off?"

"We've been up for almost a minute."

"Oh. Smooth ride."

"We would have the stewardess serve drinks, but it won't be that long a flight."

"Oh. Did you just make a joke?"

"I'm working on a sense of humor, but I'm not sure I've got it yet. Learning a language is almost easy compared to learning a culture. Learning another species' sense of humor is really tricky. If I get it wrong, let me know."

"I'll try to remember that."

The light dimmed as the door opened.

"After you, Your Highness."

He got up and stepped out. Off in the distance he could see the Statue of Liberty. Looking around, he saw the skyscrapers of Manhattan across the water in one direction, a big bridge off to one side.

"I recognize this; Governors Island. It used to be a Coast Guard base right in the middle of New York Harbor. Then it got sold to the city or the state or somebody."

"Very good. We've sort of taken over here. It's close to everything, but we can control who actually gets here."

There were several flashes from some of the skyscrapers.

"Just ignore those. Snipers can shoot that far, but we don't let the bullets through."

"Well, that's comforting."

"We just think it's better to let them blow off a little steam."

"Probably wise."

"All those buildings over there are for us. The Aliens' offices. You get these two. The smaller one is your castle, the bigger one is the seraglio for your harem. I admit it doesn't look much like a castle, but you have the East River and Buttermilk Channel as your moat, and the inside has been renovated—"

"No, wait; go back to the harem part."

"That was part of the deal, remember? Fertile females. One hundred of them, from all over the world, aged eighteen to twenty-four, very beautiful."

"Yeah, how many of them have a shiv up their sleeve to cut my throat the first time they get close enough?"

"It was made very plain to them that any attack on you would result in very bad things happening to their parents, their siblings, their other relatives, their friends, their classmates, their entire community. But we are not expecting any problems since they all volunteered. Actually, they are rather eager to have sex with you."

"Where in hell did you find one hundred women who want to have sex with an old man like me?"

"Well, in addition to you being rich and powerful, which human women seem to find attractive, we offered them a little incentive."

"Incentive?"

"They come here for a year. They get free room and board, an expense account on the internet, and free online classes for college credit. If they don't have sex with you during the year, they get a plane ticket home. If they do have sex with you, they get a full scholarship to any university they choose for undergraduate and graduate study after their year is up. If they get pregnant by you, they get the scholarship plus a trust fund for them and the child that will let them live well and educate the child in the best schools. So, I expect most of them are anxious to catch your eye for a sensual evening in the castle. Then after a year we get a different one hundred women who want to please you."

"You're kidding. This is your new sense of humor, right?"

"No. Very factual. No irony. We have one hundred women in that building who want to have sex with you. Would you like to meet them? I can have them line up for a review. Would you like them clothed in their native dress, topless, or nude?"

"I think I would like to deal with them later. I think I need a little time to adjust, mentally. Just the idea of them all lined up boggles the mind."

"Fine. Then would you like to see your new home?"

"Yeah, let's do that—tour the new digs."

She led him across the yard, up the walk, and onto a large porch that went around the two-story, white house with green shutters on the windows. It had probably been a Coast Guard office building when it was originally built more than a hundred years ago, but he doubted if any of the original building was still part of the structure as it seemed to have been renovated several times. All that was left was the general shape and size of the first building. By the door was a plaque that read "King of the Planet. Please knock."

Angie chose to ignore the sign and opened the double wooden doors, then stepped aside again to let him go first.

"Your Highness."

"Stop calling me that."

"Well, I don't think 'Your Lowness' is going to work."

"Might be worth a try."

He entered the entrance hall and recognized a painting on the wall. His wife had painted a portrait of him years ago.

"I see you have been to my house."

"We managed to get all your belongings out before the mob burned it down."

"They burned my house down?"

"Once they figured out who the new king was, some people got a little out of control."

"Oh, great. Guess I am stuck on this island until somebody finds a way to kill me."

"You will find everything personal in the living quarters on the second floor. We did put a few of your wife's paintings in the rooms on the first floor, the dining room, the conference room, the throne room."

"Throne room?"

"You are a king. The king, in fact. The only one."

"With, like, a real throne?"

"It's just a big chair, well padded. Should be very comfortable. No gold or diamonds though."

"Thank goodness."

"Would you like to see it? Your staff is waiting to meet you in the conference room, but we could detour through the throne room."

"My staff?"

"You didn't think I was the only one, did you? I'm your personal aide and liaison with the Aliens, but you also get a press agent, a translator, two political advisors, one financial advisor, a butler, two cooks, and two maids. Plus the harem."

"Oh yes, can't forget the harem."

"So, do you want to see your throne first?"

"No, let's do the staff thing first. I know I don't like to be kept waiting."

Angie opened a door on the left side of the entrance hall and led him into a large room that had been furnished as a waiting area, chairs around the walls with a few coffee tables covered with magazines. She crossed through to a door on the other side, opened that door, stood back, and announced, "The king of the planet."

Hal heard a scraping of chairs as people stood up. He walked into a room with a long conference table in the center, seats for ten around the table, and more chairs along one wall. The walls on two sides were mostly windows, with French doors that opened onto the porch as it wrapped around from the front to the side. It looked like the conference rooms he was used to in his old government office building, only nicer and newer, with a real wood table and chairs not made by prisoners from some federal pen.

The second thing he noticed was that two women were wearing

French maid uniforms like you saw in catalogs for Halloween costumes, with the skirts so short they were more decoration than covering. There were two men in white, double-breasted chef's uniforms with chef's hats at least two feet high. There was one guy in what Hal figured was supposed to be a butler's uniform, but came closer to black tie and tails. The other three men were in variations of the dress business suit, if you assumed that beige polyester was still acceptable business dress fabric for one of them and that a white zoot suit had ever been business attire for another. For the two women, one wore a power-red tailored pantsuit and jacket over a white blouse, and the other had opted for a basic little black dress that would have needed another yard of fabric to even come close to reaching her knees. Even the chef's hats could not conceal that everybody in the room except Hal badly needed serious attention from a barber or hairdresser, though some of them at least seemed to have made an attempt at getting a comb through their hair.

"Allow me to make the introductions. Your Royal Majesty King Hal the First of Planet Earth, this is your media consultant, Mr. Dale Carnegie."

The zoot-suit guy made a little bow.

"Your translator, fluent in the most common twenty-six languages on the planet, Dr. Eliza Dolittle."

That turned out to be the red power suit.

"Your political consultant favoring hierarchical, individualistic political views, Esquire Strom Thurmond."

The polyester guy acknowledged his introduction.

"Your political consultant favoring community-focused, disseminated political power, Dr. Golda Meir."

Shockingly, this was the little black dress, who tried to curtsy without removing any mysteries about underwear. She also had dark-black hair and olive skin, like the man standing next to her, but unlike all the other pale blonds in the room. However, both their hairstyles were just as wild and unruly as the others'.

"Your secretary of the Royal Treasury, the Honorable Sir Milton Friedman."

The honorable sir turned out to be the one who was actually wearing a normal suit, if you didn't count the chain locked to his belt that held on to a wallet so big it stuck out of his back pocket and kept his jacket askew.

"Your royal butler, Mr. Jack Nicholson."

"Your Highness."

"The two royal chefs, Arby Rogers and Moe McDonald. And the two royal maids, Beverly Hills and Marilyn Mounds. The chefs and maids will alternate so you always have a chef and a maid on duty, but will all help prepare for large dinners or other special events."

"I see. Well, it's a pleasure to meet you all. I'm very new to this king stuff, so I'm not sure of the correct protocols. Please excuse me if I do something wrong. I really don't have anything else to say right now, but I'm sure we'll have an opportunity to talk more later. Right now I'm sure you all have things you need to do."

The butler, chefs, maids, and the translator took the hint and exited out a door at the end of the room as gracefully as possible. That left the public relations guy, the two policy wonks, and the money man.

"Yes?"

"Your Highness, forgive me, but when you have the opportunity, we need to discuss rehabilitating your public image."

"Ah. Well, you see, I've never had a public image before, so I'm not quite sure what to do with one. I'm also not sure how you can spin choosing four billion people to Disappear and make it sound like a good thing. Tell you what, let me think about that for a few months, and I'll get back to you, if I'm still around."

Mr. PR hesitated, appeared to run several possible responses past his better judgment, settled on "At your convenience, Your Highness," and backed out the door. Hal turned to the two policy wonks.

"Next."

After an exchange of glances, the little black dress spoke.

"Your Highness, there are several policy issues that have been referred to you for discussion. They relate to cultural issues that we Aliens are not sure we fully comprehend."

"It is becoming obvious to me that there are a lot of cultural issues that the Aliens do not fully comprehend. But I have been locked in a hotel room for the past few days, so I'm not sure I'm up to speed on cultural issues except Disappearances. Is anybody going to die if I don't decide any of these issues today?"

"Uh, not that we know of."

"Fine. Why don't you send some briefing papers on these crucial issues to my personal assistant and ask her to schedule some time in my busy schedule after I have had a chance to review all of my options."

"Uh, sure, yes sir. We will prepare arguments for all sides of each of these issues. Thank you, Your Highness."

There was a grabbing of briefcases followed by an exit, leaving only Angie and Milt the moneyman.

"And?"

"This is a little more personal, Your Highness. The first deposit of your billion-dollars-a-month salary has been made to your account, and we need to discuss how these funds are to be allocated to various investments and expenses. Even after deducting for staff salaries and expenses, that's still a lot of money that could have an impact on the various markets depending on how—"

"Wait. Hold up. Go back to 'first deposit.'"

"Uh, you have direct deposit of your monthly salary to your checking account, sir. It's the same account your retirement checks go to. I mean, it gets a little interest, but really, leaving a billion dollars in a checking account is not the best use of the money."

"Are you saying billion, with a B?"

"Yes, Your Highness. With a B. Every month. Didn't they tell you?"

"No, that seems to have been left out of the fine print."

"Well, that is your salary, Your Highness. Of course, you have certain expenses that will be charged against it. The salaries of your staff will be deducted, and I must say you are very generous to us. Not totally out of line for the jobs, of course, but above average."

"I'm glad to hear that I'm such a great guy."

"And there will be deductions for food and clothes, electricity, water, that kind of thing. Plus whatever else you choose to buy, of course."

"Of course."

"But it's still a lot of money to leave in a checking account."

"Yes, I see your point. Tell you what; can you set up a trust fund for my daughter in such a way that nobody knows it came from me, no matter how deep they pry into the financial record?"

"Yes, of course. It may take a few days, using multiple channels, setting up some private accounts, going through various currencies and businesses, maybe a shell corporation or two, moving some bearer bonds manually."

"Why don't you work on that for right now. Set her up for half a billion. Then put a quarter billion in my savings account and leave the rest in checking to pay all these bills, if that will be enough."

"Uh, yes sir, that will more than suffice."

"And send me your recommendations for how to handle next month's billion in a couple of weeks, OK?"

"Yes, Your Highness. Thank you."

"OK, off you go; you have money to launder."

And with that it was him and Angie again.

"I'm not sure, but I suspect you were not really being nice to them."

"Do I really have to make decisions about stuff?"

"The deal was money, power, and fertile females. That has been translated to mean a billion dollars a month, decisions affecting the entire planet where we are not sure exactly how things should go, and one hundred sexy women. You got a problem with that?"

"Can I abdicate?"

"No."

"Can I jump in the river and swim out to sea?"

"No."

"What can I do?"

"You can let me show you the rest of the house."

So she did.

• • •

The rest of the house turned out to be a display of a hundred uses for all known types of wood. Wood floors of pine, walnut, and maple. Wood paneling on the walls, dark in the dining room with an oak dining table and ten chairs as in the conference room, light wood in the throne room, which was empty except for a large, straight-backed chair on a raised platform. There was padding on the seat, arms, and back, but it took him several minutes of close examination to realize the chair was cypress wood, the grain carefully matched for symmetry. The back of the first floor held the kitchen, pantry, and a small break room for the domestic staff.

Upstairs was the master bedroom with, what else, a king-sized bed, a four-poster of African ebony, with the pictures and personal items from his old house now displayed on various bedside tables, chests of drawers, and other furniture of woods he didn't even recognize. All he could figure was that for people who had just spent heaven knew how long in a spaceship, wood would be the ultimate luxury item.

Just inside the large window with a view of the Statue of Liberty was a little sitting area with a giant TV. The bathroom had a whirlpool tub big enough for three or four people, plus a separate, walk-in shower with ten nozzles and room for half a dozen bodies of one kind or another. Hal wondered what the water bill was going to be. There was also a huge walk-in closet that had all his clothes from his house, plus dozens more suits, shirts, pants, and coats that he did not recognize, not to mention a rack of several dozen pairs of shoes.

Beside the master suite, there was a bedroom with the things from his daughter's bedroom at home, placed as if she had just left for college and would be coming back any day. Next door was a room with the things from his old guest room, only this room, like all the others, came with its own bathroom instead of having to share a bathroom on the hall with his daughter's room, as in his old house. There was a library, with floor-to-ceiling bookshelves on all four walls, almost full with the books from his home, from his wife's cookbooks to his college physics textbooks he had saved, carefully arranged according to the Library of Congress cataloging system. In the middle was his old desk, with a new computer, and several chairs, some old, some new, arranged to catch the sunlight for easy reading or set beside a lamp of some sort. At the back on the second floor was a storage room with all the things from his old house that had not fit in the new lodgings, carefully spaced on shelves three feet deep, with number tags attached and an index of items placed by the door. And at the front was another room that Angie ignored, simply saying "And this is my room" as they passed by the door.

"I need some time by myself."

"I'll go check with the cook on the menu."

Hal wandered into his daughter's room, examining the basketball trophies and honor roll certificates, the Harry Potter posters and pictures of him and her mother. Then he crossed the hall into the master bedroom and looked out the window at the Statue of Liberty off in the distance. He started to consider the irony, but decided that was a dead end. He instead started to wonder about Aliens who seemed to have mastered very advanced technology, but were having trouble sorting out the fine points of modern human civilization. That led him to wonder just how well he and Angie and the other staff would be able to understand each other. That led to wondering if they really expected him to have sex with 100 women every year. The image of an endless line of naked women was forming in his mind when out of the corner of his eye he saw a series of flashes from the tip of Manhattan. Shifting to another window, he saw hundreds of flashes, big and small, followed by various fireworks just off the shore of the island as bullets, mortar shells, and other non-computer-based weapons were blocked by whatever the Aliens were using for protection.

"Well, I guess they know I'm here," he said to nobody.

6.

AND SO

He watched the fireworks for a while, then watched the sun as it set over New Jersey. Somehow it was still beautiful, even with all the harbor cranes and storage tanks along the coast across from the island. Then his stomach growled and he wandered downstairs into the dining room. Jack the butler was standing there, waiting for him with a single place setting on the large dining table. Jack pulled out a chair for him, so Hal sat down. There was a large goblet of red wine and a glass of water, plus all the silverware for all possible known uses of eating utensils.

Jack stepped into the adjacent kitchen and returned immediately with a bread plate with several slices of bread, a salad plate with a small salad, and a metal rack with several types of oils and vinegars. Hal ignored the wine, but sipped some of the water, picked up a piece of bread, realized it was some kind of French bread that was almost hard as a rock, and put it back on the plate. He scanned the oils and vinegars, selecting a plain-looking virgin olive oil and a white vinegar. He tried to apply them sparingly, but quickly realized he had been too liberal with the vinegar. He poked around looking for pieces of lettuce that had not yet been contaminated, but soon gave up and pushed the salad away.

Jack had been standing behind and to the side, and quickly stepped in to remove the salad plate and rack of oils and vinegars. He returned instantly with a large dinner plate containing a steaming slab of prime rib, a baked potato topped with scoops of butter and sour cream and a sprinkle of bacon bits, and a heap of little green English peas interspersed with pearl onions. Hal took a second to assess the situation, then scooped as much of the butter and sour cream off the potato as possible before they could melt and soak into the potato.

Hal then ate a few bites of the prime rib, just to see what it tasted like, ate as many of the peas as possible without getting an onion mixed in, then gave up and turned to the potato. Most of that was edible, with just a slight coating of butter and an occasional tang of sour cream, but there was still a good deal of food on his plate when he pushed it back and cleansed his palate with the tepid water.

Jack seemed to hesitate a beat this time, but removed the dinner plate and returned with a serving of what Hal at first took to be flan but soon realized was probably crème brûlée. He took a few bites of that since he was totally unfamiliar with it, then pushed it away with more than half left on the dessert plate. He finished the glass of water, waited as Jack cleared away the plate and untouched wine, and made his exit while Jack was in the kitchen.

At the top of the stairs, he glanced around, saw that Angie's door was closed, and went into his own bedroom. He sat in the sitting area to watch half an hour of Headline News, then wandered into the recreation of his daughter's bedroom. He sat at her desk for a minute, took out his smartphone, and composed a text.

"Moved to Gov. Is. in NY harbor. Safe for now. Lay low and disown me if needed. Love you."

He didn't even bother to sign it, just hit send and put his phone back in his pocket. Back in his bedroom, he saw that someone had been there long enough to put a Godiva chocolate on his pillow, turn down the corner of the covers, and place a carefully folded pair of red silk pajamas and some slippers at the foot of the bed. He turned back to the door and realized there was no way to lock it. Evidently privacy was not part of the deal.

He ate the chocolate, carefully moved the pajamas and slippers to a chair, took off his running shoes with the prescription insoles that were intended to take some of the pressure off his ankles and knees, removed his shirt and pants with the pockets still full, and hung them over the back of another chair. He moved into the bathroom and was happy to discover the electric toothbrush from home, evidently with fresh batteries, to use instead of the manual version he had packed for his trip so long ago. After the usual evening rites, he dumped his socks, briefs, and undershirt in what he hoped was the laundry hamper and crawled between the satin sheets on the bed. He wondered if he would be able to trade them for flannel sheets when the cold New York winter blew in across the river. He then stared into the dark at the ceiling for a while, then tossed and turned through various degrees of sleep.

• • •

He awoke when light was already edging around the curtains, considered his options, and got up anyway. It took him nearly five minutes to figure out the best combination of nozzles and settings for a simple hot shower, but he decided he liked having a shower big enough in which to do all the range-of-motion exercises he did every morning to keep the arthritis stiffness at bay. Here in the shower he could keep the sore joints under the warm water as he stretched to stay limber. Only then did it occur to him that whatever the Alien doctor had given him had worked pretty darn well and he hadn't had any significant pain for days.

At any rate, after the long shower and all the other bathroom activities, he emerged to see someone had been there to make the bed and lay out white silk boxers, a silk T-shirt, and silk socks. Beside those was a white Armani shirt and dark-blue suit, with a silk Jerry Garcia tie and a Gucci leather belt, and a pair of dress shoes with some Italian label he didn't recognize.

He slipped into the underwear and socks, then went rummaging around the walk-in closet until he found a pair of his old jeans, a plaid flannel shirt, and his favorite L.L. Bean jacket, which he figured he would need for the morning chill. He pulled the belt from the Armani suit and through the belt loops of his jeans. He started transferring the contents from the pockets of his shirt and pants of yesterday, realized he probably didn't need the car and house keys anymore, and dumped those in the drawer of his nightstand. Yesterday's clothes went into the laundry hamper, then the running shoes with the insoles were wrapped around the silk socks. At first, his feet slipped around inside the shoes, but he re-laced them from the bottom and got a firmer fit.

Going downstairs, he encountered Jack the butler pulling out a chair for him again at the dining table, but he went around him and into the kitchen. Angie and one of the maids, he had no idea which one, were sitting at a breakfast table by the window eating what looked like stacks of cinnamon rolls, one of the cooks (he thought it was Moe, but wasn't sure) was greasing up the griddle, and Jack came in from the dining room but stopped in the doorway. Hal crossed to the breakfast table, hung his jacket over the back of an empty chair, and opened the door of the commercial-sized refrigerator.

"We got any yogurt?"

Out of the corner of his eye, he saw the exchanges of glances between Jack, the cook, Angie, and the maid, and increasing looks of panic. Finally, the maid spoke up to save the day.

"Of course, Your Highness."

She crossed to the refrigerator and took out a plastic lunch bag, unzipped it, and took out two individual-serving containers of mixed berry yogurt and a plastic spoon.

"That looks like part of your lunch."

"Uh . . ."

"Tell you what, I'll trade you. I'll take the yogurt and you can have for lunch whatever the cook was going to fix me for breakfast. That work for you?"

"Yes, Your Highness. Sure."

Hal handed her the lunch bag and took the yogurts to the breakfast table. Jack the butler stepped forward finally.

"Uh, Your Highness, the cook has been—"

"You know, Jack, you are being a really good butler and I'm being a really lousy king. But since we're all pretending I'm really a king, you all are going to have to adjust to my eccentricities rather than me adjusting to your expectations. Which brings up something else. You all get to 'Your Highness' me once a day, the first time we talk. After that, it's 'sir.' Think you can live with that?"

"Uh, of course, Your . . . sir. Whatever you say, Your . . . sir."

"Thank you."

Hal turned and sat at the breakfast table, gesturing for the maid to resume her seat, which she did after getting a nod from Angie. Hal opened one of the yogurts and turned to face Angie.

"After you finish your breakfast, get a message to the finance guy from yesterday that I want to meet with him in the throne room in about an hour. Then grab a jacket; you and I are going to take a morning walk."

"Yes, sir."

Angie and the maid finished their cinnamon rolls about the time he finished his first yogurt.

"If we may be excused?"

"Of course."

As he opened his second yogurt, he glanced around to discover the kitchen was now totally empty. Just as he finished the second yogurt, Angie returned with a jacket over her arm.

"Any idea where the empties go to recycle?"

Angie indicated a bin, he lifted the lid and dropped the empty yogurt containers and plastic spoon in, replaced the lid, slipped his jacket on, and went out the back door and down the stairs, headed for the nearest shoreline. The wind was chill and he turned his collar up. He stood, watching the little waves break against the boulders carefully placed to prevent erosion. Angie came up and stood beside him.

"Is this our morning constitutional, did you have something you wanted to see, or is this some pathetic attempt to talk privately where the crashing of the surf will drown out any attempt to overhear?"

"Well, I can see you have your back up this morning."

"I'm not sure I understand that."

"Some animals, when they are angry or threatened, will hunch their back up."

"Ah. You could have been more polite to the staff this morning."

"I could have just stayed in bed."

There was a pause as they both watched the waves.

"So, was there something you wanted?"

"You know, when your lot first offered me this deal, I thought it showed a deep and profound understanding of human nature and the use of scapegoats. Now I am beginning to think it showed a deep and profound understanding of how little you understand human nature and modern cultures."

"Is there a question in there?"

"Probably a hundred questions. But the one I need an answer to right now is this: when you and I talk, how can we know we are really understanding each other?"

Hal watched as Angie stared out over the harbor, seeming to be seeing some shore that was farther away than he could imagine. The pause dragged on and on as she seemed to consider every possible reply and the implications thereof. Then there was a long sigh and a drawn breath.

"I guess the short answer is that we can't really understand each other, not totally. But that would be true if we were two humans or two Aliens. Surely you've been misunderstood enough by other humans to know how bad people are at understanding each other."

"I can relate to that remark."

"Now think what it's like when two people come from very different cultures. Think about the Pilgrims and the Indians. The Pilgrims looked at the Indians' cornfields, with the beans and squash plants mixed in with the corn, and didn't even realize at first that the Indians were actually cultivating them. It didn't occur to the Pilgrims that anyone would deliberately plant crops in anything but neat rows, in separate fields, with defined borders. And neither one of them would have understood a word if you had told them the bean plants were fixing nitrogen in the soil that the corn could use as fertilizer. Way beyond anything they could even conceive. And the Indians could never imagine how many English there were and how they would sail over, wave after wave, hundreds, then thousands, then millions. Words describing that would not have had any meaning to them.

"Well, Hal, you and I are as alike physically as the Pilgrims were to the Indians, but our culture and psychology and history and basic assumptions about what reality is are much further apart. It's a miracle we understand anything about each other."

"I see. Or I guess I see that I don't see."

"Let me try another metaphor. Say you took the faculty of Harvard University, gave them guns and lightsabers, and dumped them into Genghis Khan's Golden Horde way back when. Now, they could probably use the guns and lightsabers to stay alive, maybe even take over a little bit. Being smart people, they could figure out the language in a few months, decipher the basic power structure, recognize the symbols of authority. But even a year or two in they would still be making little mistakes in dress, in manners, in conversation. And an occasional big mistake in judgment. And it would still be a small group of college professors trying to find a way to survive in the middle of millions of Mongols who fight on horseback, live in yurts, and massacre entire cities."

"OK."

"We're doing the best we can here. You have a really crazy planet."

"I'm sure that's an understatement."

"And sometimes we need some human to help us out a little. All your various experts don't seem to agree on much of anything, and public opinion usually splits about fifty-fifty on most issues. So when we're really not sure what to do, we are going to come to you. We think you did a good job with the Disappearance stuff, so we think you can keep helping. You get money, power, and females, but you are going to have to keep earning it. And I am sure there are going to be misunderstandings, on both sides, that neither of us even realizes at the time. But we are just going to have to do the best we can and live with whatever mistakes get made."

"Well, damn."

"Yeah, damn."

"I told your Dragon Lady I wasn't good at this kind of thing."

"Dragon Lady?"

"Your boss. At the hotel. Who offered the deal."

"Oh. Yes. Her. I will tell her she is now officially the Dragon Lady. I think she will get the humor in that."

"Well, I'm glad somebody will be enjoying this."

A wind blew off the harbor, and Hal realized he was cold.

"It's cold out here. Let's go back inside."

He turned and headed back to the house.

"So I'm stuck with all this, am I?"

"Sure as shooting."

"Including the women?"

"Yep."

They walked silently until they got near the porch.

"What's the cook's name?"

"The one this morning?"

"Yeah."

"Moe McDonald."

They walked up the back steps and took the door into the kitchen. The cook was there, chopping carrots.

"Hey, Moe."

"Yes, Your . . . sir."

"Let's try this. Draw up the menus for the next two or three days, give me a few options, and I'll get back to you with my preferences and maybe a few comments. Maybe we can get to know each other's tastes without having to toss out much food."

"Yes, sir. I'll send the menus to Angie."

"Sounds good."

They passed through a couple of other rooms and ended up in the throne room. Milton the moneyman was already there, standing awkwardly. Hal took off his jacket and hung it on one of the planks making up the throne, then sat down.

"Milton, wasn't it?"

"Yes, Your Highness."

"OK, new rule is one 'Your Highness' per person per day. Just 'sir' after that."

"Yes, sir."

"OK, Milt, you know, I got to thinking last night, and I was just sort of wondering where in hell you are getting the one billion dollars a month you say you are paying me."

"Oh. Well, it's part of the service fee we collect."

"Service fee?"

"One dollar per person per month."

"OK, give me the long version."

"Yes, sir. Well, let's see. You know after the Disappearances we divided the population of the world into hundreds, then thousands, then ten thousands, then millions, and so on."

"I sort of got an idea it was something along those lines."

"Well, we sort of grouped those various groupings along existing governmental lines—state, province, nation, that kind of thing. I mean, we did make a few adjustments, mostly in Africa, the Balkans, and the Mid-East to sort of lump ethnic groups together a little better, put a few of the smaller nations together for administrative purposes, that kind of thing. The Vatican is now part of Italy as far as we are concerned, for example."

"And got it down to one hundred nations, I bet."

"Uh, yes, sir."

"Your homework assignment is to send me a report on the Aliens' fascination with multiples of ten, but get back to the service fee for right now."

"Yes, sir. It's sort of a holy number—"

Angie interrupted.

"Back to the point, Milton."

"Yes, Miss Angie."

"Miss?" asked Hal.

"Poor translation of a cultural concept with only surface similarities."

"Uh, as I was saying, we grouped the populations to keep the national governance units largely intact. It gave us somebody to work through. So, while you were hiding out, or, should I say, avoiding public appearances, we went to these national governance units with a deal."

"A deal they couldn't refuse, I assume."

"We thought it was too good a deal to pass up."

"And?"

"We told them we would save them billions of dollars by making their defense budget unnecessary; making all bombs and missiles, war planes and warships, tanks and armed drones inoperable. Any electrical weapon."

"But you had already done that."

"Yeah, but they didn't know it was permanent. We also pointed out that they would be saving billions on national health service costs and things like that after so many sick people disappeared and that there would be other savings, in education with fewer students, in environmental protection with much less stress on the environment with fewer people driving and eating and breathing and that kind of thing."

"Yes?"

"So we asked for a little service fee for all the ways we were saving them money. A dollar per person per month. For almost all the nations it was a good deal. For the big nations with big militaries it was a major bargain. A few of the little guys who weren't spending much to begin with had to stretch some, but we're not pushing them very hard. Anyway, we end up with a little over four billion a month, starting as of about three days ago, and you get a billion of that."

"Ah. My fee for services, so to speak."

"Yes, sir. So to speak."

"Thank you, Milt. That will be all for now."

"Yes, sir, uh, there is still the matter of the distribution of your money, sir."

"Yes, but I had to know where the money came from before I could figure out where it should go."

"Yes, sir. Thank you, sir."

And Milton the moneyman left the throne room.

"You don't approve us getting paid for stopping wars?"

"I'm not sure yet. After all, you were stopping them for free."

"It requires a certain monitoring. And there are worse ways to get the money we need."

"No doubt. I'm just not sure I like being one of the big expenses you have to pay for."

"Look at it as us providing you the opportunity to provide funding for good causes or something like that."

"Yes, a billion chances a month to give money to the wrong

thing. I told the Dragon Lady I was not good at this."

"We can provide any information you ask for about various organizations."

"Let me think about it."

"OK. Do you want to think about lunch?"

"It's still a little early, isn't it?"

"Moe wants to know if you would prefer a Philly cheesesteak with fries or a half-pound sirloin hamburger with chips."

"Tell him that it's illegal to kill the king with cholesterol, or whatever translates best to get him to lay off the saturated fat. Tell him to look up egg salad sandwiches and Southern iced tea and get back to me. And grits, tell him to look up grits as a breakfast food."

"OK. I'm sure he will do what he can."

"Tell him I have great faith in his adaptability."

"OK, what next? You want me to get Strom and Golda in for a meeting? Or maybe Dale?"

"No, I need more time to think. I need to carefully consider my situation before I do something stupid. Or, to be more precise, when I do something stupid, I want it to be a carefully considered move, not something accidental, so that I can fully deserve the blame."

"How noble of you."

"I do what I can. No, I think the next thing has to be something with all these women you have stashed next door."

"OK. What?"

"What happens if one of them wants out of the deal, just wants to forget the whole thing and go home?"

"They aren't sex slaves, Hal. But if they leave before the year is up, all they get are a ferry ride, taxi fare, and a one-way ticket in economy class."

"OK, I want a line-up after lunch, in their national costumes, each one in the doorway to her room. I'll do a little walk-by. Is that doable?"

"I think that can be arranged."

"Then I'll leave you to it."

Hal left her there in the throne room and went upstairs to his bedroom and spent the next couple of hours staring out the window, trying not to imagine 100 naked women.

. . .

When lunchtime came, he went down to the dining room and found Jack the butler pulling out the chair for him.

"Is Miss Angie here?"

"She is in the kitchen eating her lunch."

"Ask her to bring her lunch in here and eat with me, please."

"Yes, sir."

While Jack was in the kitchen, Hal checked the table and found a glass of tea with three almost melted ice cubes floating at the top. A sip revealed it was about half tea and half sugar. He expected the sugar to precipitate out into crystals at any moment. There was also the glass of water, and he poured some of that into the tea to cut the sweetness a little. Just as he finished pouring, Angie entered carrying a plate with a sandwich and a can of Coca Cola, followed by Jack the butler with a plate for Hal. As Angie sat beside him, Hal noticed that her sandwich was about three inches thick.

"What in the world is that?"

"The sandwich? Pastrami and marshmallows on wheat bread."

"Marshmallows? With a Coke? You are going to get such a sugar rush."

"Marshmallows are a new thing to us. So far, they are the number one human invention we didn't already have. We're trying them on just about everything. We have something like Coca Cola, but your version is easier to get ahold of right now."

"Well, marshmallows work pretty well on sweet potato casserole, melted and mixed with Rice Krispies and butter, and in several candy bars, but after that you're on your own."

Hal decided it would be a good idea to inspect his own sandwich before taking a bite. He lifted up the top piece of bread and started working his way down the layers, pickles to tomato to lettuce to fried egg, with mayonnaise on both pieces of wheat bread. He slid the pickles off onto his plate and took a bite.

"OK, this isn't bad. Jack?"

"Sir?"

"As diplomatically as you can, tell Moe that this is a big step in the right direction, but next time let's boil the egg until the center is hard, then chop it up in little pieces and mix the mayo with the egg before putting it on the bread. Oh, and no pickles for me, please. And the iced tea is good, but fill the glass with ice before pouring in the tea and only about half as much sugar, please. But we're getting there."

"Yes, sir."

"Now, Angie, I'm sorry to take you away from your friends, but I wanted to talk to you before the walk-through of the girls' dorm."

"Yes, sir."

"What's the plan?"

"There are three floors, central hallway, rooms on both sides of the hall, elevator in the middle, stairs on each end, dining hall and sitting room on the ground floor. One of the house mothers, Donna Reed, will be there to provide introductions, and Eliza Doolittle, your translator, will also be there to provide any translation necessary. I thought it would be best to start on the top floor and work your way down so you could exit easily."

"And you will accompany me."

"If you wish."

"That was not a request; that was a royal command."

"Yes, sir."

"But there is something you have to understand about this little visit. This is not for me to meet the women. This is for the women to come face-to-face with reality. It is one thing to think they will get all these benefits if they have sex with the king of the planet. It is another to think about crawling into bed with an ugly man old enough to be their grandfather."

"I don't think you qualify as ugly, as humans go."

"Beside the point. No introductions, no discussions. I just want to make each of them look me in the eye and see what they are getting into."

"As you wish."

And so it was. Hal insisted they go up the stairs so there would be no doubling back. They started on the top floor and stopped in front of each woman. A few tried to bow or curtsy, but most of them looked him back in the eye as he stood staring at them. A few, mostly Asians, tried to keep their eyes downcast or averted in some way, but he snapped his fingers beside his face and they looked at the sound, then at him. Generally, he was able to keep his focus on their faces, at least until they got to the woman on the second floor who was wearing a grass skirt and flowers in her hair and nothing in between. He couldn't help glancing down, which made her smile. During the walk down the next flight of stairs: "I thought I said—"

"She's from Yap, one of the Pacific Islands. That is her national costume. All the other girls are jealous."

When it was over, they walked out the fire door by the stairs, and all Hal could remember was a sea of faces dissolving together into one cubist image that was both an ocean of temptation and a bobbing apple of warning.

"Let me know how many drop out."

"Yes, sir."

And he walked away to the breakwater, signaling Angie not to follow.

7.

AND SO IT GOES

He spent the rest of the afternoon doing some basic research on the internet, trying to get a grasp of macroeconomics, rather than the microeconomics he had dealt with on a personal level. He thought about ordering some real books from Barnes & Noble or Amazon, but realized he didn't know his mailing address, or even if he had a mailing address. He was used to being old-fashioned and out of date, but so much had changed in the past few days that he wasn't even sure the latest technology he hadn't even adopted yet wasn't already out of date and replaced by something new he hadn't even heard of.

About midafternoon he did get a text message from Moe via Angie proposing a supper of baked chicken; black-eyed peas; sweet potato casserole; a salad with lettuce, walnuts, and ranch dressing; apple pie a la mode for dessert; and lemonade. Moe seemed to be adapting quickly. Hal texted back his approval, sans the ice cream, and asked Angie in the same text for his mailing address.

Turned out it was "King of the Planet, Governors Island, New York, 10004." He thought about trying to fit that into an online order form and ended up just e-mailing Angie a list of books he wanted and went back to trying to find out as much as he could online about handling money counted in the billions. He was already getting the feeling that, like most newly rich people, he was really going to mess up what he did with all that money.

He ate supper alone, Jack telling him Angie was busy dealing with the harem. His only suggestions to be relayed to Moe were that the sweet potato casserole only needed one layer of marshmallows melted on top, not three, and that the lemonade did need a little sugar, not just squeezed lemons and water, though the amount of ice was just right.

The evening was spent with an online scan of the news and more research on economics. He was getting the idea that economics was not only the dismal science; it was the most confusing one. Mostly it seemed a way to try to explain what had happened in the past, not a very good way to figure out what would happen in the future if lots of money was used in certain ways. Not to mention that four billion people Disappearing overnight was a wild card there seemed no way to factor into any of the prevailing theories of how the economy should work.

• • •

When he came down to breakfast, there were two place settings at the table, and Angie came out of the kitchen to join him as Jack served them both scrambled eggs, bacon, and grits, with orange juice to drink. Hal decided to give everything a try and was pleased, even with the grits, though he limited himself to one piece of bacon. Angie ate a taste of the grits, but mainly stuck with the eggs and bacon. He wondered if she was an Alien Yankee.

"Three of the women in the harem left last night."

"Only three?"

"Evidently you are not as physically repulsive as you think you are."

"Is that what you were doing last night, persuading the others to stay?"

"There was some discussion with me and Donna Reed by a few others, but it was not a hard sell. We really don't want them here unhappy. The three that left will be replaced as soon as possible."

"I assure you, ninety-seven women are more than enough."

"Yeah, but you know us crazy Aliens and our fixation on multiples of ten."

"Someday you are going to have to explain that fixation to me."

"It goes way back. The origin is lost in the mist of time. Mostly it's a superstition now, but a strong one. Things just seem to work better for us in tens."

"OK, whatever rows your boat."

"That list of books you wanted . . . hardcover, paperback, electronic, or does it matter?"

"I guess electronic would work if you can get me a new reader. My old Nook gets heavy when the reading is heavy. Or maybe my hands get tired when the topic is heavy. But hard copy would work if something is not available electronically."

"Everything is available electronically."

"Everything except me. So far."

"Well, until then, we'll make do with what we have. On another topic, Milton Friedman wanted me to let you know that the trust fund for your daughter had been set up. Should he tell her?"

"That was faster than promised."

"He aims to please."

"Is she having any trouble?"

"A few of her friends have figured out that she is related to you, but none of them are blaming her yet. It's not public knowledge."

"Just let her know that she has some money she can draw on if she needs it. Don't tell her how much. Not yet."

"OK."

There was a pause in the conversation as they finished what was on their plates. Jack came in with a cup of coffee for Angie and a cup of hot chocolate for Hal, then cleared the plates.

"What's on the schedule for today?"

"What would you like to be on the king's schedule for today?"

"The king wants to fly down to Disney World and spend the day watching happy children."

"Disney World is closed for a few more days until they can train new staff to replace those that Disappeared."

"That figures."

"Perhaps some women from the harem could provide a little diversion. Quite a few asked last night when the sex was going to start."

"You mean Golda and Strom aren't begging for an hour or two to get me to decide the fate of the world, and Milton doesn't want me to set up a new monetary system this afternoon, and what's his name, the PR guy, isn't wanting to run by me his proposal for a media campaign to get me elected the next saint?"

"Well, I think Dale the PR guy is considering asking for a papal dispensation for you."

"No thanks."

"Doesn't hurt to ask."

"Yes, it does. It admits that you have committed a sin for which you need a dispensation. It's an admission of guilt, at least morally, if not legally."

"We get the basic idea of this 'sin' thing, but exactly what qualifies as sin and what doesn't is something we are having trouble nailing down."

"You and everybody else."

"But you think picking which four billion to Disappear wasn't a sin."

"I think that's yet to be decided, and not by the pope. Besides, it's not a good move to put him in that kind of position. If he forgives me, like a good Christian, half the snipers out there go to Rome and starting shooting at the Vatican. And if he doesn't, he violates his own oath as a priest to offer God's forgiveness to penitent sinners. It is not good PR to put the pope in an impossible position."

"I'll let Dale know to hold off on that one."

"Thank you."

"So, back to the schedule."

"If Golda and Strom have some position papers for me to read, I'll read them, but I don't want to talk to them until I have had time to read the issues first. Otherwise, I need to read a couple of those economics books before I talk to Milton again. And tell Dale not to do anything without sending me a written briefing first."

"Any suggestions I need to pass along to the house staff?"

"The food is getting much better, but let's keep running the menus by me ahead of time. It seems to avoid problems. And I think we can skip laying out my clothes unless there is some formal occasion. I prefer to pick out what I wear myself."

"OK. And the women?"

"Will have to endure their isolation for at least one more day while I try to figure out what to do with my next billion dollars."

"I'll have a new electronic reader sent up in fifteen minutes, with all of the books you requested already loaded."

"Thank you."

"Pimento cheese or ham sandwich for lunch?"

"Pimento cheese, on wheat bread, not grilled, just plain. Iced tea, lots of ice, not much sugar."

"A salad? Some sherbet for dessert, or maybe some Oreos and milk?"

"Just the sandwich. This was a big breakfast."

"Text me if you need me."

"Definitely."

• • •

Fifteen minutes later Jack knocked at the door to Hal's room and handed him a very thin and very light electronic tablet with ultra-high resolution that made the text look like very fine printing on the best paper. Hal wondered if this was something you could get at Best Buy or if he had something not made by human hands. Either way, it was very easy to figure out how to operate, even for him. So the rest of that day was spent poring through Economics for Dummies and other basic economics textbooks, even reading during lunch and supper (ham steak, mashed potatoes with red-eye gravy, Southern-style green beans, but no dessert in order to offset the calories in the greasy but delicious gravy). By evening he was convinced that he hated being king of the planet, he hated economics, and that he had no idea what to do with all that money.

8.

DECISIONS
DECISIONS
DECISIONS

T he next morning his fancy new tablet reader was flashing a little light when he glanced at it. Pushing a couple of icons revealed two new files—the briefing papers from Strom and Golda on the two questions they had for him. One had to do with a demand from Saudi Arabia, Qatar, and Yemen that they be allowed to require women to wear veils in public as part of their religion; the other had to do with riots in the Philippines and Poland trying to stop abortion. Working his way through those, on top of the economics stuff, took almost all of his waking hours for the next three days, interrupted only by silent, solo meals and hours spent staring out windows, pondering and trying to understand all the ideas in all the readings.

Finally, on the fourth day, Angie was waiting for him at the breakfast table when he came down.

"It's time to earn your keep. The full council will meet with you at nine o'clock."

"I need more time."

"You once asked if anybody would die if these questions weren't answered today. Well, with the riots and some other incidents, it turns out the answer is yes, people will die."

Jack entered with Greek yogurt and fresh blueberries (flown in from heaven knew where), orange juice, and wheat bread toast for both of them. Seeing the staring contest going on, he placed his load of food on the table and exited as quickly as possible.

"I do not respond well to pressure."

"You do not seem to respond well to anything."

Angie picked up her yogurt and juice.

"Nine o'clock in the throne room."

"Conference room."

"As you wish, Your Highness."

And she was gone into the kitchen. Hal stared at his breakfast, picked a few blueberries out of the yogurt, drained his orange juice, and went back to his room.

• • •

When nine o'clock came, he walked into the conference room. All five of them were there, Angie, Strom, Golda, Milton, even Dale Carnegie. They stood, and he waved them into their seats as he sat. He had to admit they were more appropriately dressed than before. Dale looked like some kind of Hollywood agent, blue blazer over a white wool turtleneck pullover sweater. Strom and Milton had somehow settled on almost identical navy-blue suits from some designer, differing only in the color of the handkerchief corners sticking out of the breast pockets of the jackets. Golda was now in a white pantsuit with gold trim, tightly tailored to her body. Angie had changed to a long, straight dress, calf length, brown silk with red threads woven in to make the colors subtly shift in the light, scoop neckline. Somehow she was getting her hair to almost hang down instead of sticking out, a trick none of the others had picked up yet.

"We can go in any order you wish, Your Highness . . . sir."

"I am curious as to why Dale is here. I was not aware of any topics on the agenda related to distorting my public image."

"I am here to be aware of what decisions are made so I can at a slightly later time propose ways to communicate those decisions in a way that reflects best on the king of the planet."

"Well, I suggest you just blame me for everything. That works for me."

"I'll try to come up with something a little better than that, Your Highness."

"If worse comes to worst, you could just tell the truth."

"I'll keep that in mind, sir."

"OK, let's get the money stuff out of the way first. I've been working on that the longest, so I'm sure that will be the worst decision. Milt, I want to start at the bottom and work up. Take out each month whatever we need for salaries and expenses, plus a little cushion. Then set up a series of foundations that provide funds for specific types of organizations. Start with organizations that promote prenatal health and breastfeeding. And tell Nestle and other baby formula manufacturers that they can only promote their products as substitutes when breast milk isn't available. No more of this trying to talk women into using formula as if it was better than nursing."

"Yes sir."

"Then move on to programs that train new mothers on how to take care of their babies, both in the hospital and at home, what they can expect of babies, how to deal with them, the importance of talking to their babies, singing to them, reading to them, that kind of thing. Lots of the socialized medicine countries already have some of this, but I want it all over the world, for everybody."

"Yes sir."

"Next on the priority list is daycare for children of working mothers. It needs to be affordable; not costing so much that it makes working financially not worth it. And the childcare workers need to be paid well, screened closely, given training, and monitored carefully. That may take two or three kinds of foundations and some lobbying for legislation to pull off."

"I think you will find that we Aliens are very effective lobbyists."

"Then the same kind of thing for preschool and kindergarten programs, available to all, affordable, trained teachers paid a very decent wage in order to get good people, effective student-teacher ratios, etc. Once all that is in place, let's start looking at how to pay for school fees, school supplies, uniforms in the places that require school uniforms. I don't want anybody not to be able to go to school because their parents are poor. Any questions?"

"I believe I get the idea. I'll draw up charters for the various foundations and run them by you."

"Thank you, Milt. And when all that is in place, if there is money left, we'll talk about what else we can do for elementary school education and then move up through the grade levels."

Dale spoke up. "I don't think I will have any trouble promoting this."

"Let's do this as anonymously as possible, Milt."

"Please, sir, give me a chance."

"Dale, you will keep my name out of this. I don't want anybody refusing any of these programs because I'm associated with them. Understand?"

"Yes sir."

"Milt?"

"Yes sir."

"OK. Moving along. What's next, suppressing women or killing babies?"

There was a moment of silence before Angie spoke. "You understand we are asking for advice and guidance on these issues.

You are not making the final decision. These are just crucial matters where we are not sure we understand all the implications and secondary effects."

"But I could be a convenient scapegoat again, the good old king of the Earth who Disappeared everybody."

"Technically, it's king of the planet."

"Whatever."

"We are just asking for your insight, from the point of view of a human who has shown the ability to think about things with a little more objectivity than most."

"OK, OK. Just remember that you don't always get what you pay for."

"We will take that into account."

The king of the planet stood and crossed to the window. The others started to stand, but he waved them back down. It was cloudy and looked cold outside, like snow was coming. It occurred to him that he was going to be stuck on an island in New York Harbor throughout a long, cold winter. He wondered if there would be ice on the rivers, then pulled his mind back to the first question.

"The thing to understand about forcing women to wear a veil in public, or any of the other coverings, is that they started before Islam, or any of the other major religions for that matter. They are customs, cultural traditions that were integrated into, validated, and then reinforced by the religion. If you look at them in the context of the entire culture, the restrictions on women's movements without male accompaniment, the arranged marriages, the way women who have been raped are devalued and blamed, and all the other ways women are treated both in Islam, Hinduism, and in other related cultures, it quickly becomes apparent that the veiling, etc., is an attempt by males to assure the paternity of their offspring by controlling the sexuality of the women, not some grand command from God Almighty.

"It has often been pointed out that a woman always knows a

child is hers because she sees it come out of her body, but a man is never absolutely sure a baby is his child. So, males are desperate to assure the paternity of their children. In the heyday of Rome, newborns would be placed on the floor in front of the husband. If he picked it up, he was accepting it as his. But if he left it and walked away, he was rejecting the baby as being fathered by someone else, and it would be put out on some hillside to die."

He paused when he heard Angie whisper to Strom, "Not the one near Atlanta—the Roman Empire, in Italy, two thousand years ago." Strom acquired a look of understanding and gestured for Hal to keep going.

"In a way, it makes sense. A man puts so many resources, money, effort, time, emotions, maybe risking his life or even dying, to raise and protect a child, whether you're talking primitive hunters who risked life and limb to get meat for their child or modern man who works two or three jobs to send them to college. They want it to be their child, bone of their bone, fruit of their loins, DNA of their DNA. So they cover their women up, keep them in the house, and do everything possible to make sure some other man isn't taking their place, so to speak."

He glanced over at the people sitting around the table. Golda seemed to be flipping through pages on her tablet computer, as if looking for some reference. Strom was typing something on his tablet, perhaps taking notes. Angie was listening intently, but frowning.

"The problem, of course, is what all this effort requires and what it does to women and to the relationship between men and women. In short, it turns women into commodities, guaranteed virgin baby factories to be bought for a bride price and locked away from any other possible exposure to sex. For all the claims of respecting them and honoring them, they are honored and respected only so long as they maintain their value as exclusive fertility providers. Anything less than that, and they are fallen women, no longer of the same value in the culture. Either way, respectable or fallen, they are not fully persons, with the full intellect and ability, the same level of humanity as a man.

"Where this really starts to fall apart is in a post-hydraulic age. Very few people seem to have fully realized how the very basis of the organization of society and culture has changed recently. Sheer physical strength is no longer the determining factor. It's not how well you can swing a sword or how deep you can plow a furrow with an ox and a wooden, or even a steel, plow blade. Even into the 1900s strength mattered. Try driving a truck without power steering or power brakes. That took a man's muscles. Now, even the tiniest woman can drive a semi with power steering and air brakes, or fly a jet for that matter. Now what matters is how smart you are, what you know, how well you can think. And to say that women are not as able as men in those areas flies in the face of all the evidence."

Both Strom and Golda had now abandoned their tablets and were strictly paying attention. Hal wondered if they were having problems with translation or cultural references. Dale Carnegie looked totally lost. Milton Friedman seemed to be keeping up, but was having to work at it. Hal glanced at Angie, but she gave him a slight nod to keep going.

"So, are we going to allow certain cultures to maintain customs, even if tied to a religion that, for all the verbiage, treats women as restricted human beings when physical strength is no longer a significant criteria for measuring worth? My personal opinion is that any culture that blocks half the population from fully participating in education, professions, and society is cutting its own throat. The males are just going to have to adjust to a culture in which women are more active, sexually and otherwise, and trust them to control their fertility and limit offspring to the agreed-upon male. If there's a question, let them demand a DNA test.

"Now, this is not to say that women in these cultures should not be allowed to wear veils, if they choose to as an expression of association with a religion or membership in a cultural group. But it must be the woman's choice, and there must not be legal or social punishment for women who choose not to wear a veil. The context should also matter. Even the religious women may choose to wear the veil or whatever to the market or the mosque, but toss it in the gym bag on the tennis court. And these roving gangs of religious enforcers have got to go away. No country is monocultural anymore, so the law has to be secular, not religious. Ministers can preach anything they want, but the law cannot impose the practices of the religion of one group on others, even the members of that group. The law has to be based on common values across religions, not the specific customs of one. So, veil if the woman wants, no veil if she doesn't, and no punishment or restrictions on participation in society or profession either way. Questions?"

There was a pause, then an exchange of glances between Strom and Golda. Strom spoke up. "That seems an admirable ideal, but not very practical to enforce when some people seem willing to go to war to maintain their religion."

"They are not maintaining their religion. They are attempting to enforce their culture on others using the religion as a sword. But I agree that religious fanatics and extremists, of whatever religion, are generally a problem. But they usually only cause wars when there is an underlying problem, a demographic shift, the clash of two or more cultures, or a serious economic problem, for example. In the case of the Middle East, we have all three: an explosion of young people, the clash with European cultures, and what, even with the Disappearances, is still probably an overpopulation compared to the declining fertility of the overworked land and the shortage of fresh water. You need to look at the religious conflicts as symptoms of the underlying problems, not the primary problems themselves."

"I see we need to bring our anthropologists more heavily into this, don't you think, Golda?"

"Yes, Strom, a longer and wider view may be the way to go here. Thank you, sir."

"Just my two cents' worth, even if it's costing you billions."

After a pause, Angie spoke up. "Perhaps we can move on to the issue of the abortion riots. Unless you would like a moment, or perhaps a break for cookies and tea?"

"No, let's get this over with. I hate being king, so let's not drag this out."

"Yes, sir."

Hal started to pace, then stopped himself and turned back to the window.

"The heart of the question about abortion is when does a clump of cells turn into a person, a human being. Answer that, and most of the other issues get resolved. In this case, there are groups calling themselves Christian who maintain that there is something called a soul, a nonphysical but essential element of being human, that enters the ovum at the moment of conception, rendering this single fertilized cell into a human being. Some other religions make the same argument. There are several problems with this argument. The first problem is that the idea of a 'soul' is not a Christian concept. It's Greek."

He glanced at Strom. "Classical Greece, five or six hundred years BCE up to the conquest by Alexander the Great; Socrates, Plato, those guys."

Strom said, "Thank you."

"The idea that a nonphysical entity that is the essence of a human being, with the personality and perhaps the memories of a person, exists after death, and maybe before birth, probably goes back to the original Indo-Europeans or earlier and is probably related to the idea of reincarnation and karma that was further developed in Hinduism. It certainly is not in Judaism before the conquest by Alexander the Great and the Maccabean period. Before that, if anything lived on after death, it was just a shadow, a shade, that went to Sheol after death and gradually faded away as the memory of that person faded away in the land of the living. Even in the Christian Bible, one of the differences between the Jewish Sadducees and the Pharisees during the Roman era is that the Sadducees did not believe in a resurrection of the dead.

"In the Jewish scriptures, life was breath; you weren't alive unless you were breathing. You can see this in the creation story of Adam and in the story of Ezekiel in the valley of the bones. The bodies weren't really alive until they had the breath of life breathed into them. You see the same idea in the crucifixion of Jesus in the verse usually translated as him 'giving up the ghost' that actually says he gave up 'the breath.' And the Christian theology in the New Testament is definitely that it is the body that gets resurrected, not some 'soul.'

"That's what all the stories about the resurrected Jesus were pointing out when they talked about Jesus eating and being touched. It may be a glorified or empowered body, but it is definitely a physical body, and that's why later parts of the New Testament talk about graves being opened and bodies rising into the air. They probably got the idea from Zoroastrianism while the Jews were in exile in Persia, but Christianity definitely comes down on the side of the resurrection of the body, not some nonphysical soul. The idea of a soul only crept into Christianity later, when people tried to reconcile Christianity with Greek philosophy. Do not ask me how this relates to resurrecting the people who were Disappeared and just got turned into molecules. That is beyond my theology."

Hal stopped to check on his audience. Dale looked like he had given up trying to keep up. Milton also looked a little lost, but at least seemed to be still trying to make sense of it all. Strom was probably compiling a list of cultural references to look up. Golda and Angie, amazingly, appeared to be getting the main points, though both had also made a note or two for future reference. Again, it was Strom who signaled him to continue.

"So, that's the first problem. The second is a little less theological. The evidence is that at least half, maybe as many as two-thirds, of all conceptions end in miscarriage, many of them before the woman is even aware she is pregnant. So, if there is some soul that enters at the moment of conception, then more than half of all souls ever created die before birth, unless you think they just migrate to another embryo until they land on one that actually makes it to birth. Again, not a very Christian idea.

"So, for sake of argument, let's toss this idea of a soul at conception out and ask what is it that makes someone a human being, and when does it happen. Some would argue that human beings are just smart animals not much different from bonobos or dolphins, so the same rules we apply to them should apply to us. Others maintain that there is something different, some level of consciousness, some self-awareness, some spiritual essence that makes us different from all other animals. That our superior brains allow us to think and feel and recognize the mysteries beyond ourselves. So they look at the development of the fetus and ask when is the brain or nervous system developed enough to feel pain or respond to external stimuli or be self-aware.

"Throughout history, the answers have been different, from the Jews and others looking at breathing, to the medieval church and even into the Puritans looking at the 'quickening' when the fetus starts to move in the womb enough for the mother to feel it, to the Supreme Court trying to determine when the fetus is 'viable' in the sense of being able to live outside the womb.

"And if you are looking to me to provide the definitive answer, I don't have it. I don't know what it is that makes us different from bonobos except that we are smart enough to ask what makes us different from bonobos. And I don't know when in the development process we become whatever it is that makes us human beings. Some people, I am tempted to think at times, never make it that far."

Angie interrupted. "That was a joke. He's saying some people seem to remain at a primitive level of thought even when fully matured." That got a smile from Golda and at least an expression of understanding from Strom.

"So, with no hard answer, I turn to the question of who decides and what are the limits of their power. To me, every abortion is a tragedy, but some may be avoiding worse tragedies. All of you should be familiar with the idea of a necessary evil to avoid a greater evil. That's the sermon we got from the Dragon Lady. Certainly saving the life of the mother could justify an abortion. Every situation is different. Do birth defects that would result in a longer, perhaps painful death after birth justify an abortion? It probably depends on the birth defect and the health of the mother. Is it really holy to force a child to bear a child of rape or incest? Somehow that seems very cruel to me, though it's admittedly not the fault of the unborn child. There are no easy answers here, even when it comes to bearing children into poverty in a situation that makes life worse for other children.

"So, who decides? Personally, I don't think any legal scholar or religious ethicists could come up with any law or tenet that would cover all the possible situations without creating more cruelty and evil than it solved. I know many have tried, but my opinion is that they have all failed. So, I am forced to the position that the mother must decide. She is the one who must live most with the consequences, just like we have to live with the consequences of our recent decisions. They are all bad decisions, bad choices. There is not a good choice here, and what is less bad in one situation is more bad in another. But there are no absolutes. So, our dear rioters who are out trying to save the unborn are just making things worse, creating more evil, destroying more lives. If they were also out rioting for birth control and more adoptions, I might be more sympathetic, but as it is I cannot consider them other than power-hungry fanatics so focused on one point of view that they ignore every other consideration, thereby causing more trouble than their cause is worth, no matter how noble. But again, that's just my two cents' worth.

"As for the practical question of how to handle them, well, there aren't any good answers there either. They are responding emotionally, so reason and logic aren't going to do you any good. Forcibly suppressing them might stop the riots, but might make them turn to rebellion, assassination, or terrorism, which would be harder to deal with. Long term the answer would be education of the general population and diversity of theology within the various sects involved. But short term the only thing I can think of is to convince the religious leaders that riots are just going to get a lot of people hurt and not change many minds or laws. Otherwise, you let them take just enough power to expose the danger of their becoming dominant, which would mobilize the opposition. Then maybe you get a political standoff or possibly a war. There are no good answers to religious fanatics who cannot even recognize the possibility that they might be wrong. Questions?"

This time it was Golda who responded. "There have been some Aliens that speculated you would suggest that the rioters be Disappeared."

"I didn't think you could Disappear people based on their religion or politics. And even if you could, where do you stop?"

"Another good question."

"Listen, you asked for my opinion. You have it. If you don't like the answers, tough. I don't like telling people what to do because I realized long ago that I don't think like other people, so what works for me usually doesn't work for other people. If that makes me a lousy king of the planet, so be it. You are more than welcome to replace me at any time."

"No, this is helpful. We were not expecting a list of specific steps to take," said Golda.

"Fine, glad to help, whatever. Now go do whatever else it is you do."

"Yes, sir."

And so Golda, Strom, Milton, and Dale rose, made slight bows, and left the conference room. Only Angie remained. Hal turned back to the window, dreading the coming cold of winter.

"Is there something else?"

"You're in a lousy mood."

"This is not my idea of fun."

"Yes, we know, you hate being king."

"You really have no idea."

"Well, as king, you get wealth, power, and women. You have dealt with the first two today. Don't you want to tackle the third?"

It had started to snow. Hal watched the flakes fall on the ground, which was still too warm for the snow to stick. He hated snow. Yes, it was beautiful, and as a child he had loved eating bowls of snow cream made from fresh snow by adding whole milk mixed with vanilla. But now there was so much pollution in the air it was hard to find snow clean enough to eat. Maybe Disappearing four billion people would bring back snow cream. Now snow just made him think of being cold, of slick roads and epic traffic jams, of tree limbs falling on power lines, of once huddling in bed in a dark house with the covers piled on and his baby daughter crowded between him and his wife to keep her warm as the cold crept into the house while the power was off. That had been so long ago; another era, before everything changed.

"Eight o'clock tonight. I'll go over there. The housemother can pick one."

"I'll let them know."

Hal walked out and went up to his room to look for winter coats and warmer shoes. He ate lunch alone, just a pimento cheese sandwich and lemonade. Angie forwarded a text from Arby the cook suggesting oysters for supper, but Hal declined and opted for a small ham steak, macaroni and cheese, and crowder peas, no dessert.

• • •

At 7:45, he came down the stairs wearing a long, wool, double-breasted overcoat he had found in the closet, over jeans and a plaid wool shirt. His shoes weren't fully boots, but seemed to be lined with something warm and came up to his anklebone, so maybe the snow wouldn't get in. He had half expected Angie or somebody to be there to walk him over, but the hallway was deserted.

So, he plunged out into the dark, treading carefully through the half inch of snow on the ground. The snow had stopped and the stars were out, but he paid more attention to the moisture in his breath condensing in the cold air than the scenery. He arrived at the seraglio a couple of minutes early, but Donna Reed was waiting to hang his coat on the coatrack by the door and escort him on the elevator to the second floor and down the hall. She knocked twice on one of the doors, then opened it. He stepped through, and the door was closed behind him.

In front of him, standing at the foot of her bed, was a small Asian woman wearing a very short, silk robe. He stood there for a moment trying to narrow down the geographic origin of the woman, but without a name or the sound of a language, Asian was about the best he could do.

There was one of those awkward pauses where neither one of them seemed to be able to figure out anything to say. Then the robe slid off, giving him a moment to stare at her small, upturned breasts and scant pubic hair. He realized it had been more than two years since he had seen a nude woman for real, long ago, when the world was different. Still, he stood silently, not prepared to make the first move. She crossed to him, the top of her head not even reaching his chin, and began unbuttoning his shirt. Somehow, this felt right, her doing the work, taking the responsibility. She removed his shirt, then guided him to the foot of the bed and had him sit as she removed his shoes and socks, then lifted his undershirt over his head. She had him stand again so she could undo his belt and pull down his jeans and jockey shorts, then sit again so she could pull them over his feet.

She then had him slide back so he was fully on the bed. Not much more needed to be done to excite him, so she straddled him and slid his penis into her. She was very light and moved slowly, so by staring up at the ceiling occasionally instead of at her breasts he was able to hold off until she had time to at least fake an orgasm when he came. Then she slowly lay down on top of him, her head on his chest, her breasts gently pressing into his ribs.

He was enjoying the warmth of her body on his when he realized that his hands, which had been on her hips to guide the rhythm of her movements, had slid around to her buttocks. He was just wondering if that was good or bad when he realized that his penis, which had detumesced after his ejaculation and slid out of her vagina, was stirring back to life and erection. It had been a long time since his last orgasm, but he was an old man. Such rapid recovery was a long-lost memory of his youth. Had that Alien doctor done more than cure his aching knees? Whatever the cause, he decided this was not the time to look a gift horse in the mouth.

Carefully, he rolled her over and, noting no objection, entered her again, taking his time, trying to respond to her movements under him, giving and taking without urgency until he was reasonably sure there was no falseness in either of their reactions.

Somewhat later, he awoke in her bed, her naked body curled beside him. Her presence was a reassurance that the evening had not been a dream, which left him both pleased and puzzled. As carefully as possible, he eased out of the bed, found his clothes in the near dark, dressed, and left as quietly as he could, not sure if she was really still asleep or just being very polite and letting him leave with no awkward words being said.

Down in the lobby he checked his watch to discover it was nearly midnight, reclaimed his heavy coat, and walked back through the cold, finding no clarity of thought even in the bracing air. He had not seen anybody observe his exit, but somebody must have passed the word because Angie was sitting on the steps, wrapped in a parka, as he came back to his castle.

"So, how did it go?"

"It went."

"Shall I schedule another for tomorrow?"

"No. Give me a day off. The next day."

"That can be arranged. I've been talking to Golda and Strom."

"Yes?"

"Some of the stuff you came up with this morning wasn't in the briefing books."

"I read a lot."

"You've had quite a day, haven't you?"

"Do we have to rehash it out here in the cold?"

"No. I just wanted to make sure you were OK."

"I hate the cold."

"You hate being king."

"Yeah."

"What do you like, Hal?"

"What?"

"What do you like? Anything?"

"Good books. Warm days. Understanding how things work. I don't get much of that last one. I also like warm beds on cold nights."

"Go to bed, Hal. There will be time for other things. Go."

So he walked up the steps past her and into the house, leaving her clutching her parka around her and staring at the stars as if searching for home.

9.

THE DAY AFTER

He slept late the next morning, well past the usual hour. During his shower, standing amid all the nozzles spraying hot water, he slowly and carefully did all his usual range-of-motion exercises. He experimented with each joint, noting that none of them caused him any pain. Moreover, the ankle that used to crack like a knuckle when he rotated it was now silent and smooth, and the stiffness that had been creeping into the fingers on his left hand was barely a memory.

He picked out some pants with a lining that looked warm and another plaid, wool shirt. The shoes from the night before had worked well in the snow, and even though the snow seemed to have melted away, he slid them on over wool socks. As usual, Jack was in the dining room pulling out the chair for him, but he waved him to follow into the kitchen where Moe and Beverly were going about their business now that Hal was up.

"OK, instant holiday. Day off for everybody."

"Sir?"

"Day off. Nobody works today. Grab your coats and go home or wherever you go when you're not here. Have some fun, go shopping, tour New York, whatever. Just don't be here."

"Uh," mumbled Jack, "I'm not sure we can—"

"I'm the king, right? I'm trying to be a good boss and give you some time off. Paid holiday. You're great, you're wonderful, now get out of here. I can take care of myself for one day. Go, go."

There was an exchange of glances among them as they waited for somebody to make a decision. Finally Jack give a little nod, Moe turned off the stove and slid some food back into the refrigerator, Beverly got their coats from their break room, and they headed out the back.

"If you need something, you know how to reach us."

"Yes, Jack. But I'll be fine. Enjoy yourselves."

He watched them trudge past the kitchen window, very slowly, as if waiting to be called back. Hal opened the refrigerator, found a stack of yogurts of various flavors, selected two, closed the refrigerator, found a spoon in one of the drawers, and sat down at the kitchen table to eat. As expected, Angie appeared within minutes.

"What's going on?"

"Want some yogurt?"

"You made everybody leave."

"I'm a compassionate boss; I gave them the day off with pay."

"You kicked them out."

"I'm an insane megalomaniac of a king. I wanted to be alone for a while."

"Well, for the record, I live here too. I have my own room upstairs. And you can't just send me to my room."

"Well, I guess there are limits on the king's power after all."

"And limits to my patience."

"What did that royal doctor do to me?"

"What? Don't change the subject."

"But that is the subject. That is what we are alone to talk about. What did that Alien doctor do to me?"

There was a pause.

"There was that thing to the neck, then two pills. And don't tell me you don't know. You know everything there is to know about me. That's your job, and you work very hard at it."

"One pill was for your knees; he told you that."

"My knees and every other joint I ever had a problem with."

"So are you complaining about your arthritis being cured? My God, you complain about having money, you complain about being able to order people around, you complain about having to have sex with beautiful women, now you're going to complain about being healthy?"

"I am going to complain about being manipulated, about being used, about being lied to, about being experimented on like a lab rat."

"You were never lied to."

"Withholding information is a form of lying."

"We can't tell you everything. You wouldn't understand everything."

"Then tell me what you can, dammit."

There was a long pause, like the CIA redacting a top secret document for a Senate committee.

"There were no experiments on you. We knew what we were doing. We were very sure."

"So what did you do?"

"We cured your arthritis."

"And?"

"And a couple of other things."

"Such as?"

"Such as you don't need to worry about anymore."

"So maybe now you can share these great treatments with others?"

"Actually, no."

"No?"

"It's not that we aren't capable. It's that we need people to keep dying. The four billion was the absolute minimum to Disappear to save the planet. We need to stabilize the population and slowly let the birthrate reduce naturally as the economy improves. Then we can gradually share the medical advancements; let people live healthier lives. Otherwise we end up with the same problem we had before, too many people for the planet to carry."

"But I am the exception. I get the miracle medicine now."

"You are the exception."

"And if I don't think that's fair?"

"It wasn't your choice."

"You know, for a king, I seem to have damn few choices."

"I'll make a note of that in the official record."

"You know, I was just starting to like you."

"I'm sorry if you are taking this personally."

"Go to your room for a while."

"Yes sir."

And she took some yogurts from the refrigerator and went up the stairs. Off in the distance he saw three figures still waiting for the signal for them to return. He ignored them and decided to grill himself a cheese sandwich for lunch.

10.

AFTERMATH

After lunch he fetched his heavy wool coat and went walking along the rocks lining the shore of the island. He wondered how much longer the weather would allow such walks, even with winter clothes, and what he would do for exercise in place of them. He soon saw Angie striding across the lawn to catch up with him. He paused to wait for her, then resumed his stroll once she was alongside.

"I think we may be experiencing one of our cultural communications gaps," she said.

"No kidding."

"So, enlighten me."

"Just how did you think I would feel finding out you had done things to my body I didn't know about, that my arthritis was cured, plus heaven knows what else, but I was the only one?"

"Feel? Lucky. Relieved. Honored."

"It never occurred to you that I would be worried about what else you might have done, that maybe I was not fully myself anymore? You never thought I might be offended by the unfairness of being the only one? That somehow I wouldn't think I was being used again for something I had no idea about?"

"We thought you would be glad to be out of pain. We told you we need to keep you alive to prove we reward those who help us. We told you that."

"So I had something else that would be killing me by now if not for the good doctor."

"Not this quickly, but down the road. A couple of things actually. Not a concern anymore."

"Oh."

"You can thank us later."

"I'll add it to my list of pros and cons."

"I'll bet you actually keep such a list."

"In my head."

"OK."

"I still want some changes around here."

"I'm listening."

"The maids come in once a week to clean and do laundry. I'll provide a list once a week of groceries and other things I want. Mostly I'll cook for myself. If there's something I want that I can't cook, I request it on the list and Moe or Arby can come over and fix it. Jack needs to find another job."

"You know they've been cooking for me too."

"OK, so you eat my cooking. I'll even put marshmallows on everything for you."

"Can you really cook?"

"I'm passable. There have been several periods in my life when I had to cook if I wanted to eat. Not gourmet, of course, plain food. Southern mostly, with occasional Southwest dishes. Not much of this Yankee stuff. I like my green beans soft and have no use for cream of wheat. But these days you can get just about anything canned or microwaveable. But if you don't like my cooking, I'm sure Moe or Arby can send something over or you can go eat wherever all the rest of you eat. I just don't want them in the house with me all the time."

"I see. And me? You want me out too?"

"I didn't think I had a choice."

"You don't. But if you did?"

"You I can tolerate. You're either gone or locked in your room half the time. I think we can develop a routine, give each other space."

"You really are a charming man, Hal. So full of compliments. How do women resist you?"

"Do I detect a hint of irony?"

"I'm still working on that sense of humor."

"You'll be doing stand-up routines in no time."

"Somehow I don't think you mean that literally."

"English is a very subtle language, isn't it?"

"OK, so say I get the house staff out from under your feet at least part of the time; what do you do for me?"

"What do you want?"

"A little more advice for Strom and Golda, a little more attention to what Milt and Dale bring you, a little more attention to the harem, maybe a little more courtesy in dealing with others."

"Tell you what. House staff out, anything Strom and Golda want me to spout opinions about; Milt no more than once a week; keep Dale out of my face; I hit the harem maybe every other night, if I'm as healthy as I seem to be; and I promise to observe the niceties with everybody except you. Deal?"

"Let me run it by the Dragon Lady."

"OK. Now could we please go back inside? It's cold out here."

"You go. I need to get on the Dragon Lady's calendar."

"I guess I need to figure out what's for supper."

And so they took off in opposite directions as the clouds began to blow back over the harbor.

11.

ROUTINES

At least as far as Hal was concerned, the new routine worked well, at least at first. He went through the pantry, cabinets, and refrigerator (finding the canned peas stored separately from the canned beans in the highly organized storage system) and came up with a grocery list, which was filled the next day. At first Angie ate what he ate, only in larger portions than he anticipated, but she quickly tired of the Cheerios and whole milk every morning, even if he did alternate between strawberry and blueberry yogurt as the second dish, along with a glass of orange juice. She evidently sent out her own grocery list and was soon chowing down some days on Eggo toaster waffles with mini marshmallows in between and boysenberry syrup on top, assorted Dunkin' Donuts on other days, with occasional deliveries from Moe or Arby of hot biscuits with ham and cheese.

The same kind of problem came up with the lunches. Hal alternated between pimento cheese sandwiches and egg salad sandwiches day to day, with a couple of Oreos for dessert, chased with a large glass of iced tea with just a hint of sugar. Angie was getting deliveries of tuna subs from Subway, Big Macs from McDonald's, and other types of sandwiches Hal had never heard of from delis all over New York, always accompanied by a very large Coca Cola and a variety of fries, chips, pickles, and sauces. Hal did try to have a little variety with the evening meals, but he tended to do things like toss cans of green beans, pinto beans, and crowder peas into a Crock-Pot and cook them until they were soft, then use that as the side dish for three or four days. He would fry up a big ham steak and save whatever was left over for the next supper. He was perfectly content with mashed potatoes from a box and biscuits from a can. He did open a few cans of sweet potatoes, drain the liquid, mash them in a baking dish, and bake them in the oven, adding a layer of marshmallows right at the end so they would melt a little and turn brown. Angie did seem to like that dish, at least the first and second days.

Before long they were not even eating at the same time of day, which Hal didn't mind because it saved time. He assumed Angie was taking her suppers in whatever dining hall, cafeteria, restaurant, or refectory the Aliens took their meals, or rotating as a guest among whatever passed for families or groups among them. He was sure she could take care of herself, and he had other things to deal with.

As it was, he was busy going through the fine print of all the legal documents and charters for the foundations Milt was setting up. Hal would email comments and questions to Milt, and then respond to the response as they slowly worked through a long list of documents required for all the various charitable foundations and financial organizations needed to do good work all over the world.

Hal did take a little time in the afternoons, at least on sunny days, to bundle up in his wool coat, a red scarf he had found in his closet, and a black wool cap that had flaps to cover his ears. He would then take a power walk, followed by a leisurely stroll around the section of the island that had been converted to a park after the island was donated by the military to the City of New York. On rainy days he just walked up and down the stairs of his castle and hoped he was doing enough to keep his heart healthy and his joints moving, not fully trusting to whatever the Alien doctor had done for him.

As for the harem, the second woman was a Nordic-looking woman who soon proved she was a natural blonde. She was taller and curvier than the first woman, which Hal enjoyed. The pattern was the same except this time he took off his own clothes, carefully placing them where he could find them easily in the dark for a quick getaway. The blonde was also a little more aggressive than the Asian, quickly showing a decided interest in multiple positions and multiple orgasms. With a couple of short rest periods he found that he could accommodate her until he felt an arching of her body, a long shudder, and a collapse into an almost fetal position that indicated she was done for the moment. Since they had never turned out the lights, Hal was able to dress and depart quickly, before there was any request for conversation or discussion.

Two days later he went to the seraglio the third time. Woman number three was black, with tiny scars on her cheek. This provided some visual novelty for Hal, but otherwise there was little variation. This woman did try to start a conversation during the early part of the evening, but Hal touched a finger to her lips and she took the hint. She was not quite as active as the Nordic woman had been, but the evening seemed to proceed satisfactorily for both parties, though Hal started to notice the cold even more on his trek back to his castle.

After that, he began to lose track. He knew there had been a Hispanic and a Polynesian, but he forgot in which order. Without letting them talk, he had no languages or accents to go by, so they could have easily been from either the Georgia Hal used to live in or the Georgia that was unpleasantly close to Russia, or just about anywhere else for that matter. And so, several weeks passed in a quiet routine that he would remember with longing.

12.

WINTER

Christmas came and went with barely a whisper. He worked with Milt to send his daughter an envelope with 500 dollars in old, untraceable twenties and a card that said "Happy Christmas, Love you" with no signature. She had not touched the half billion fund, so he was afraid if he sent more cash, she would not accept it. He got back a file of pictures of her and her new fiancé and a long, rambling e-mail about how she loved him but that the wedding was going to be a very quiet, very private event at which no one would walk her down the aisle and to which he probably should not expect an invitation. He remembered her talking when younger about wanting a church wedding, not giant, but with family and friends, a wedding dress, and a meal afterwards, and he was sorry she was paying the price for his choices.

He had also asked Angie about gifts for the staff or throwing them a Christmas dinner, and she had replied that Christmas was not like any Alien holiday, they really didn't think they understood it, and it would probably be best if he just left them out of it. He settled for adding a turkey breast with gravy, dressing, and some cranberry sauce from the Honey Baked Ham store (wherever the nearest one was) to his shopping list, which he combined with some canned green beans and canned biscuits to create a big meal and leftovers for several days.

He did find a star-shaped cookie cutter among all the cooking implements left behind by Moe and Arby, added some green and red food coloring to his shopping list, and made two pans of Rice Krispy candy, one red and one green, which he cut into stars and left in the kitchen in a plain box with Angie's name on it. The box disappeared, but was never mentioned by either of them.

Donna Reed, the harem housemother, did ask if perhaps he would like two women for a threesome on Christmas Eve or New Year's Eve as a little celebration, since those would both be his regular nights at the seraglio, but he decide to take both those nights off from his routine and stayed in his castle, eating and watching football on TV.

There wasn't even any snow on the ground at Christmas, though three days later a major storm hit, making even New York Harbor beautiful and white for a few hours, before the snow turned grey and was piled up to get the traffic and the harbor going again.

So, he spent his days working by e-mail with Milt, slowly building a structure of organizations to try to get most kids through childhood with at least a fighting chance of succeeding. He would see Angie around the house occasionally, perhaps sharing a table to eat their separate meals, passing her his requests for books or food. As the winter closed in, he went out less and less, exercising on the stairs. Every other evening he ventured out to the seraglio for a couple of hours, braving even heavy snow to avoid their offer to come to his castle.

Strom and Golda did interrupt his routine a couple of times to ask about wearing white after Labor Day and why American football was becoming more popular even though it was such a brutal sport.

(Nobody cared anymore, and it was such a brutal sport that it allowed young males to prove their masculinity and fitness to breed without actually engaging in real trials by combat.) Otherwise, he was left to his unlimited supply of books and a television that could get any channel in the known world. And the weather just got colder and colder.

· · ·

So it was that he came down to the kitchen one frozen morning in February to find Angie and the Dragon Lady sitting at the table chowing down on stacks of pancakes with lots of maple syrup and what looked like butter oozing out between each pancake. Angie was in her usual winter attire of jeans and a sweater over some kind of shirt. The Dragon Lady still had hair going every which way, but had traded the skirt and blouse for a business-dress pantsuit only notable for being lime green. He just muttered, "Excuse me," and turned to leave, but was not quick enough. The Dragon Lady was able to gulp down enough of what was in her mouth to stop him.

"No, no, come in, come in."

"I don't want to interrupt anything."

"No, not a thing. Would you like some breakfast? Angie could fix you some pancakes."

"No, thank you. I usually try to eat a little lighter at breakfast. But go ahead with yours."

"Well, get whatever you usually have and join us."

He hesitated a moment, then grabbed a yogurt out of the refrigerator without even looking to see if it was blueberry or strawberry and got a spoon from the drawer while Angie and the Dragon Lady took a few more bites of their breakfast. The easiest chair to get to was the one on the end of the table, between the two Aliens, so he sat there, peeled the top off the yogurt, and began to eat. After a moment of silent chewing and swallowing, the Dragon Lady began again.

"Angie tells me you haven't been happy here."

He began to stir the yogurt even though it didn't need it. "There were some rough spots that had to be worked through."

"And now?"

"I understand there are certain limitations on my options."

"Are there things within those limitations that could be improved? You seem to be very alone here."

"I like it quiet. I have a routine to my life. It's comfortable. The weather's no fun right now, but I guess even Aliens can't do anything about the weather."

"Well, there are some things we could do, but we choose not to. It doesn't pay off in the long run. What helps one place usually causes more problems in another."

"Sure. Of course."

"But you are content with the food and the service?"

"Almost always, now. If I'm not, I just tell Angie and it gets fixed fast."

"And the harem?"

"That took some getting used to. There are still some things about that that make me uneasy, but that's me, not something they do. Some visits are better than others, but that's no big deal."

"And your council of advisors? Are they too bothersome?"

"I think we have worked through most of that."

"I understand you and Milton have been working on either setting up or funding certain foundations to improve the situations of children and their education."

"Yes. It was slow going at first, but Milt has gotten the hang of it. I rarely have to change any of the foundation charters now."

"And Angie? How is she treating you?"

He looked over at Angie just as she lowered her eyes to cut another forkful of pancake.

"There were some miscommunications at first, as should have been expected. But I think we have reached perhaps not an understanding but an accommodation. I don't think I would like to have to break in a replacement."

"As I mentioned, she is concerned about you. You have not reacted as we expected."

"I have no idea what you expected."

"We heal your body and relieve your pain, and you get angry. We provide you beautiful, eager young women, and you turn it into a chore, a reluctant duty. We provide wealth and you complain about having to take weeks to figure out how to give it away."

"I'm like a cat; I hate being made to do anything."

"I'm not that familiar with Earth cats, but I think I get the idea. Perhaps we could renegotiate our deal."

He ate a spoonful of yogurt and set the spoon on the table, using the pause to think.

"Uh, forgive me, but I can't help being a little suspicious of that. Our existing deal was not exactly a fair negotiation."

"You think the Dragon Lady, as you call me, is going to railroad you again? Angie, did I get that idiom right?"

"Yes, ma'am."

"So, Hal, let's stop being polite and put our cards on the table, to use another idiom."

"OK. You first."

The Dragon Lady stopped eating and put her fork on the plate. She looked at Angie, then out the kitchen window for a second, then right into Hal's eyes.

"We, the Aliens, have a big decision to make. It will affect how we relate to you humans, probably forever. So we don't want to make the decision blindly, just based on what we think would happen. You, among other humans, have shown us we don't always guess correctly what humans will do."

"Keep going."

"So, we want to set up a little experiment. And we want you to help us."

"To be a guinea pig again?"

"You have never been a test subject, just a part of a naturally occurring experiment."

"Whatever."

"Of course, there would be certain rewards for participating."

"I think I have had about enough of your rewards."

"Perhaps those could be more open to negotiation. But I think you need to know about the experiment first."

"OK."

"The question is how Aliens and humans should relate, at least on a geographical basis. Do we live separately or in the same areas? Right now we Aliens have taken over certain areas, like this island. In most of these areas, only Aliens are there. The humans are kept out. You and your harem are one of the few exceptions. But is this the best way to proceed? On a long-term basis, to keep things separate, we would need several larger areas to replace the more numerous but small areas we currently control. Borders would have to be established, transit corridors set up, commercial exchange locales developed. Those all inherently create conflict."

The Dragon Lady pushed her chair back a little and turned so she was facing Hal directly.

"Would it be better, on the other hand, to gradually phase out the separations? Should we Aliens become, shall we say, an elite group living among you humans, strategically placed in your societies, an oligarchy interspersed and imbedded into communities to create a hopefully symbiotic relationship that benefits both groups, to put it technically?"

"Well, I can tell you right now that humans have a very bad history of getting along with 'the other.'"

"Yes. We are aware of that. Which brings us to the experiment. We want to set up a test community. Mostly humans, a few Aliens, a new set of rules and norms, try things out; see what works and what doesn't."

Now he pushed back his own chair to squarely face her.

"I see. And where do I fit into this?"

"You have dealt directly with us more than any other single human. Admittedly, this isn't a normal community here, but you have lived with us, especially with Angie, more than anybody else has. Normally, we would not try to renege on a deal. We find sticking to agreements works best in the long run, even if it causes problems in the short run. But Angie has been reporting that you have complained about your situation here, gradually isolating yourself more and more."

They both glanced at Angie, who was cutting a bite of pancake even more carefully than usual, before the Dragon Lady looked back at him and continued.

"That brought up the idea that maybe you would welcome a new deal, something that would get you back into a human society. It also suggested that you would be a good indicator of when this new, integrated society was working, and when it wasn't. So, the proposal is to include you in the experiment."

Warning alarms went off in his head.

"What exactly does that mean?"

"We want to take over a small, isolated town, probably out in the Western United States, a few thousand people at most, add a few Aliens, and install you as the liaison, the go-between, you and Angie."

"Rich, powerful outsiders coming in to take over the town. Yeah, that will go over like a lead balloon."

The Dragon Lady turned to Angie with a question in her eyes.

"A lead balloon would be heavy and would fall rapidly, not rise or float in the air as balloons are intended to do. He means the experiment would fail quickly, not because we are Aliens, but because we would be perceived as disrupting an existing power structure and culture that we did not understand and did not care about. Any outsiders, human or Alien, would be resented and opposed, actively or passively, under those circumstances."

"Ah. Good point. There were some who recommended a totally new town with a diverse population, but that was opposed as not representing the reality of what we would be dealing with if we actually tried to integrate into existing communities."

Hal interjected himself back into the conversation.

"It's a lost cause anyway. What works in a little town out West is not what's going to work in South Asia or Equatorial Africa. The cultures are too different. Africa has the whole history of imperialism you would have to deal with. Asia has the problems between the Han Chinese and the various minority cultures, who already feel like they have been taken over or soon will be. And don't even get me started on the way this might translate into racial conflicts in the American South."

"We are aware of the cultural differences. Believe me, we are well aware. Even in your own harem there have been conflicts we have kept you out of. I believe the term is 'catfights.'"

"Well, I guess I owe you one for that."

"What we are interested in is the process. Is it even possible? Say we have an optimum situation, whatever that would be, would it be possible to work out a way to develop a bicultural society? And what would that take? We need to know if it can even be done once. Think about it. Talk to Angie. She can answer any questions as much as they can be answered. We don't want Aliens and humans to end up being enemies a century or two from now."

And with that the Dragon Lady got up, took her matching lime-green parka off the back of her chair, and went out the back door, leaving a few bites of pancake on her plate. Hal and Angie sat in silence for a few seconds, then finished their breakfasts.

"Just who the hell is she?"

"Actually, in English, she goes by 'Dragon Lady' now. Once we picked up on the allusion to a Chinese empress or other strong female ruler, it sort of spread like wildfire among those of us who speak English. I'm not sure whether she likes it or not, but sometimes she refers to herself as the Dragon Lady when talking to us. Her title in our language doesn't even come close to being translatable: 'the person who holds the box of secret fires' or something like that. Actually, in an interesting twist, it's sort of gone the other way. 'Dragon Lady' translates in our language into a sort of delicate growl sound, if that makes any sense, and sometimes I hear other Aliens using that to refer to her in our language. You're rubbing off on us, Hal."

"Then heaven help you."

"You want another yogurt or something?"

"No, thank you. Not today."

Angie got up and started to clear the table and rinse the dishes. Hal watched the Dragon Lady through the window, walking off to the buildings where the Aliens lived.

"This experiment thing, is she serious?"

"Very. She really is thinking centuries down the timeline. That's part of what makes her good at her job. This experiment wouldn't be a make-or-break test, but it would be an important indicator of what is possible and what isn't. It's a big deal for both humans and Aliens. You could be a big help, and it would get you out of being cooped up in here."

"Don't push me. Go read about cat behavior. And maybe I like being cooped up in here."

"I don't believe that."

"I just don't like winter. A hangover from having arthritis. Otherwise, I'm enjoying the quiet."

"Sure."

"I think I need to go figure out what I don't know I don't know."

And he went up to his library, leaving Angie to recycle the empty yogurt cup and put the dishes in the dishwasher.

13.

AND THEN

He spent the rest of that day doing research on the internet, occasionally referring to real books in his library, and staring out the window without actually looking at anything, taking breaks only when necessary. Lunch was a pimento cheese sandwich and dinner was an egg salad sandwich, both eaten at odd hours so that he missed running into Angie.

The next morning he was up earlier than usual, eating a bowl of Cheerios in the kitchen, when Arby entered through the back door carrying a bag with a McDonald's logo on it.

"Oh, sorry, Your Highness. I was just bringing something for Angie."

"No problem, Arby. Go ahead and do what you need to do."

"Uh, I'm sure Angie wouldn't mind sharing, if you—"

"I'm set, thank you."

Just then Angie entered.

"Uh, your breakfast, Miss Angie."

"Thank you, Arby."

"If there's anything else?"

"No, this looks good. Thanks."

And Arby left as quickly and quietly as he could. Angie poured herself a large glass of grape juice from a carafe in the refrigerator, sat at the table, and began taking out a half dozen assorted breakfast biscuits from McDonald's: ham, sausage, bacon, all with cheese, eggs, and butter.

"How do you eat all that and not weigh three hundred pounds?"

"We can adjust our metabolism a little up or down. Burn calories off when we want to or dial back and get by on very little when we need to."

"That's a trick every woman in the world wishes she could do."

"It's not unique to Aliens. You could learn, though it might take a few months, maybe a year. It's sort of like yoga taken up a notch."

"Let me think about that. In the meantime, I have been thinking about your Dragon Lady's little experiment."

"Yes?"

"What I would recommend is that she find a little town that has been losing population, both before and after the Disappearances. Some farming town where the farms are being consolidated or a one-factory town where the factory has closed—someplace that's really going downhill, has only a few hundred people left, and everybody realizes there is no future there for the young people."

"OK."

"Then bring in a high-tech business, software development or a lab of some kind, something where the Aliens have an obvious edge so it's natural they would be the experts and the bosses. It doesn't have to be your cutting-edge secrets, just something a step or two ahead of us. Something where it's obvious the locals couldn't be the employees for most of the lead jobs."

"I think I'm with you so far."

"Then hire human employees from all over, educated people

who know the world doesn't stop at the state line, who are used to working with all kinds of people. Hire enough of them to outnumber the locals, but provide some funding to help the locals open the restaurants, shops, and other businesses needed by the new outsiders."

"So the locals see the outsiders moving in as a good thing."

"And the Aliens aren't the only outsiders moving in."

"That seems to make sense."

"If I come up with a better idea, I'll let you know. One other thing."

"Yes?"

"Leave me out of it."

"Hal, please."

"One, with that many people there are bound to be some who would feel justified putting a knife in my back. Two, I am absolutely terrible at handling conflict, as proved by my performance as king. Three, I am touched by your concern for me, but I've gotten used to living here. Sure, I'll be very glad when spring comes, and I wish I could visit my daughter, but living this way doesn't bother me as much as you think it does. I like living this way."

"We would screen the humans carefully, not hire anybody that might blame you too much. We would also change your identity, you could grow a beard, let us change your appearance just a little, become a different person. You and I would be the only ones there who knew; not even the other Aliens would know. As for your dealing with us, well, I know what we were expecting and I know that wasn't what we got, but that's the point. You and I know not to trust our expectations of each other. We would be able to see when the Aliens and humans were falling into some Grand Canyon of miscommunication. We know where some of the cultural gaps are. I need you there with me."

"So you're going whether I go or not?"

"Yes. I'm not doing anybody a lot of good sitting around here watching you be miserable."

"I'm not miserable."

"Grumpy, rude, antisocial."

"OK, that I buy. But maybe I like being grumpy, rude, and antisocial."

"You have to be the only human in history who complained about eating well and getting laid a lot."

"Yes, the prison has good food and hot women, but it's still a prison."

"So come with me. It may still be a prison, but at least it will be a much bigger cell."

There was one of those long pauses where two people stared at each other waiting for somebody to say something.

"I need to think about it. Maybe draw up a list of conditions."

"The Dragon Lady said she was open to negotiation."

"Are you?"

"The Dragon Lady decides things."

"I might want some things about us, about how we work together. This would not be king and keeper anymore, not if you want this to work."

"I'm not sure what you're driving at."

"Neither am I. I'm just saying be careful what you ask for; you may get it."

"I think we could work something out. An accommodation, if not an understanding."

"How long do we have to work this out?"

"Maybe a week, if they buy your recommendation. We wouldn't actually leave then, but the planning would have to start."

Hal finished his cereal and went to the sink to rinse his bowl.

"Eat your sausage and egg biscuit, Angie. I've got to go stare out a window for a while."

And he left her there alone with her calories and grease.

14.

CONDITIONS
CONDITIONS
CONDITIONS

Actually, it was nearly a week before the topic came up again. He avoided Angie as much as he could, reviewing a couple more foundation charters from Milton, reading everything he could find about culture clashes throughout history, and composing an email reply to Strom and Golda explaining why puns were both funny and not funny (the element of surprise tending to be funny, but the lack of an element of truth tending toward not funny). The weather did not help, cold rain and sleet keeping him inside and not even improving the scenery. His expeditions to the seraglio became exercises in walking in slush or sliding on ice, sorely tempting him to call them off or have the women come to him. However, the options of either kicking the woman out into the cold night or letting her stay with him all night were both so unattractive that he persevered with his every-other-night trek.

He was actually in his library, poring through one of his history books from college about the Peloponnesian War between Athens and Sparta, when Angie knocked on the open door. Usually she left him alone on the second floor, except for occasionally passing in the hall, so he was a little surprised she would enter one of his private spaces, though he knew she probably came in occasionally when he was not there to check on the maids' cleaning or something.

"The Dragon Lady has given tentative approval to a plan very similar to what you proposed."

"Really."

"But it includes you as part of the plan."

"Really."

"We need your conditions."

"I see."

"So?"

Angie crossed from the door and sat in one of the chairs, turning it to face him.

"Has she proposed a modification of my 'deal'?"

"You finish out the year here so all the women in the seraglio get at least one crack at you. It would take us that long to set things up anyway. We put another half billion in your daughter's trust fund and start feeding her some of the interest earned, just a few thousand a month disguised as lottery winnings. We think we get the idea of funding educational programs as the long-range solution to a lot of problems, so Milt would take that on without bothering you further. We put a couple of billion in an investment fund for you, give the rest to the foundations Milt is putting together, then pay you a very generous salary that's really part of the interest on your investment fund. At the end of the year the harem and the rest of the staff here move on to other things, this building is converted into a museum honoring the recently deceased king of the planet, and you metamorphose into somebody else, new name, new face, new town, new job, new life."

"And my daughter is told that I am dead and we never see each other again."

"Wouldn't that be better for her, in the long run?"

"Your deals have a nasty habit of breaking my heart."

"We could tell her it was all some sort of 'witness protection' plan, if that would make you feel better. If you think she could keep it secret. Arrange an email now and then. She could post pictures and things on the internet, knowing you could see them like anybody else. But one slip from her and the whole plan is in the toilet."

"Let me think about that. Now tell me about this little plan the Dragon Lady has come up with."

"Sharon Springs, Kansas, out on the west end of the state, not far from Colorado. Less than a thousand inhabitants, population declining steadily since the 1970s. Two hotels on Highway 40, which is pretty much ignored since Interstate 70 was built a ways north; one hotel, three restaurants; one movie theater. It's the county seat, so it has the high school and the post office as well as the courthouse. Cattle and wheat-farming country. High Plains, not far from the highest point in Kansas, which isn't saying much. Pretty much a long way from anywhere. Definitely not used to outsiders."

"Kansas. Flat as a pancake, frigid in winter, blazing in summer."

"Pretty much."

"Windy too."

"Maybe not as windy as Oklahoma."

"Tornados."

"Occasionally."

"Great."

"It's what you recommended."

"I should have recommended Las Vegas, Tucson, even Yuma. At least I'd be warm there."

"So you're going."

"Do I have a choice? A real choice?"

There was a long pause. Angie got up and seemed to be examining the contents of the murder mystery shelf on the bookcase.

"No. Not really."

"Have I ever?"

"No, not since you made your list."

"Thank you for at least being honest."

"But you can ask for things. 'Conditions' as you call them. Your new life can be better. We are going to have to pretty much make over the entire town, build offices, houses, schools, businesses for the locals to run. Ask for what you want; I'll try to get them."

"So I can have a Corvette that will stop dead at the city limits. A superfast hookup to the internet that won't send emails outside the company network. A new identity, but no old friends."

"Actually, we were thinking any car should stop at the county line. The city's not even a square mile in area. You'd have trouble even getting up to sixty inside the city limits."

"So scratch the idea of a Corvette."

"What do you want, Hal? Really?"

"Really?"

"Your ideal life."

He got up and walked to the window, watching the cold river run to the sea, noticing the eddies and swirls of the current near the island. What did he want?

"I want to walk my daughter down the aisle when she marries a wonderful man. I want to play with my grandchildren. I want to know they will be healthy and raised by a loving, happy mother and father. I don't want anybody telling me what to do, and I don't want to tell anybody else what to do."

"You know I can't give you those things. Nobody can."

"I want to live alone in a quiet, orderly house with an endless supply of books to read and interesting places to walk all around. I want just enough money that I don't have to worry about money. I like my own cooking, but I wouldn't mind eating out in restaurants now and then, places that have lots of foods to choose from."

"People?"

"Maybe a few friends, but just a few—intelligent, well read, both in the sciences and history, maybe some arts background too. People who don't agree with me about things, who challenge me to think, but are not concerned about converting me, are happy to agree to disagree."

"Women?"

"Well, since your Alien doctor pepped me up, so to speak, I wouldn't mind dating and having sex with two or three women, if you could find some that wouldn't be jealous, which you couldn't, so scratch that idea too, but women who are old enough to talk to, to understand my references, who would know that Paul Simon and Leonard Cohen were not politicians. But I don't want to live with a woman again. I did that once and it was wonderful while it lasted, but she's dead now and I don't think I want to make all those accommodations again."

"I see."

"No, I doubt you do. Nobody ever has."

"Well, I think I can arrange the endless supply of books, and set it up so you don't have to worry about too little or too much money, but I'm going to have to think about the rest."

"I also hate being cold. Even if the joints don't ache anymore."

"Duly noted."

There was a pause that felt awkward to him, then Angie stood up.

"I'll send you some briefing books on the plan."

"Thanks."

Just as she reached the door, he had one more comment.

"And thank you for being honest with me."

And she smiled, then left him alone for a while.

15.

GOODBYES

Over the next couple of weeks he wrote, rewrote, revised, edited, and repeatedly proofread a long email to his daughter. In it he congratulated her on her engagement and wished her every happiness in her marriage. He apologized for the "unusual circumstances" that made it impossible for him to attend the wedding or to otherwise participate in her life.

He wrote how much he missed their occasional Skype calls and emails. He told her how much he had enjoyed being her father, recalling singing her to sleep as a baby ("Yesterday" by Paul McCartney was her favorite lullaby), the time she won a Halloween costume contest for little kids at a grocery store and was awarded a pumpkin so big they couldn't even get it in the car and had to give it to her school, with the janitor coming to get it in his pickup; going to all her basketball and volleyball games when she played in high school, and the three of them eating out afterwards on the way home from the games; the vacations at beaches and national parks (including an expedition to most of the Civil War battlefields in the east); the spring break spent touring the colleges she was considering; how proud he was of her college and graduate school achievements and her advancement on the job at the state health department.

He wrote how much he loved her and how he thought she had become a wonderful woman, fully equal to the task of living life without him and handling any challenges she might have to face. He added that he hoped if she had any children that she would tell them about what he had been before the Aliens came and that she would remember him the same way, as the father he had been before her mother died and before life on Earth had changed forever.

It was a long e-mail, agonized over, trying to keep in mind that it would be read soon after he sent it and, he hoped, many times later, after he was "gone." He did not mention anything about money or what might happen to him. Before he sent it, he printed it out in hard copy and read it carefully, caught one typo even after all these revisions, corrected it in the electronic version, put the paper copy in his desk in the library, and sent the electronic version. Of course, there was an hour-long gap before he got the notice that the email had been sent while Angie or somebody reviewed it to make sure he was not tipping his daughter off about anything. Eventually he got the electronic notice that the email had been received and opened at the other end, but the only response from his daughter was a simple "Thank you. Love you" the next day. But that was enough for him.

• • •

Time passed quietly after that. Gradually hints of spring began to appear, daffodils raising their heads in the park section of the island. Angie sent him summaries of the plans for Sharon Springs: a new office building, very high-speed Wi-Fi for the whole town, people imported to run authentic Chinese, Mexican, and Italian restaurants. There would be both new townhouses and apartments.

The schools would be expanded and a small community college developed later. They would produce software for various uses, but only a generation or two in advance of what Silicon Valley was already spitting out. What the Aliens actually had was far too big a jump for even the MIT AI researchers to understand, and depended on drastic changes on the hardware side for processing the data, but what the Aliens would give the humans in Sharon Springs Software would be more than enough to put them in front of the cutting edge, make plenty of money, and lay a foundation for future development.

Hal read all this, understood part of the technical stuff, at least enough to get the general idea, and generally didn't care. He wasn't worried about getting good Moo Shu Pork in Kansas or how many plus signs could come after a C in computer languages. Other things were starting to worry him, and as the days warmed, he started compiling a list of questions he needed answers to.

16.

QUESTIONS

By April the cold was gone, the air over New Jersey across the harbor seemed clearer than he remembered it from last summer, and he had narrowed down his list of questions. An email to Angie brought her to his library one bright morning not long after breakfast. He had moved a chair in front of the window where the light was strongest and was sitting there enjoying the sunshine. When she came in he turned the chair around and gestured for her to sit opposite him.

"What's up?"

"It has occurred to me that when we get to Sharon Springs, if I am presented as the liaison with the Aliens, I am going to be asked, either directly or indirectly, some questions that I'm not sure I have the answer to."

"Ah. Such as?"

"Such as what makes us think we can trust the Aliens when all they've done so far is kill four billion people, take over all the governments, and steal several big pieces of land for themselves?"

"You know that's not the way it is."

"Doesn't matter what I know, or think I know. That's the kind of thing I, or we, are going to have to deal with. Angie, I may like you as a person, but the bottom line is that whether you say 'killed' or 'Disappeared,' four billion people are gone, and that caused a lot of emotional hurt to those still here. The Aliens redrew the borders of countries, destroyed militaries, and kicked the humans off several significant pieces of land, including this island. This makes a lot of people feel like defeated losers, like inhabitants of countries occupied by enemies. Even if you screen the people you import to Sharon Springs to weed out the real troublemakers, you still have to face the doubts people are going to have if you want to live with them."

"We expect that."

"So what are the answers? What do I say?"

"The four billion was a necessity. We gave your scientists the data about the phytoplankton afterwards, and they agreed."

"You gave them your data. Alien data. How do we know it was right?"

"They checked it against their own data. We had a little more data than they did, but where they overlapped, it agreed. They just hadn't put two and two together yet. It was the analysis that was lacking, not the data. Once we walked a few of them through the analysis, they agreed with us and passed the analysis on. I can send you the articles they wrote."

"I've read them."

"Then why . . . ?"

"This is a potential cultural miscommunication thing. If I get asked these kinds of things and I say exactly what you say, that makes me look like your puppet. But if I say something too different, that makes one of us into a liar or a fool, and I'm not sure which one would be worse."

"The military shutdown, that was just basic self-defense. Surely they can understand that."

"I think we do. But it still makes us feel helpless."

"Even you?"

"I am the most helpless of all."

Angie stared at Hal for a long time. He couldn't read the expressions running behind her eyes, but her shoulders seemed to slump, and she turned away slightly.

"We only took the places we had to have. You never saw us lying down and embracing the ground, stripping off our clothes to feel a real sun on our skin, standing in the storms to feel the wind and the rain. We didn't let you see that. Maybe we should have."

Now it was his turn to hesitate. But he decided this was not the time for sympathy.

"You're missing the point."

"Which is?"

"All of the people in Sharon Springs, new and old, are going to be at least a little bit afraid of Aliens, of you. People tend to hate things that scare them."

"We are not the bad guys here."

"No?"

"We're just doing what we have to."

"So you lock me away on an island, monitor my every move, and force me to advise you about how to manage other humans. This is what you had to do?"

"We were rewarding you, protecting you."

"The way we protect our pets?"

"Hal, please. You don't really feel that way. Not after all this—"

"You're not listening. When the occupying army stays on their bases, life can go on almost normally; hate and fear can be kept at bay because the enemy is not there and doesn't interfere in the little things. When the enemy moves in next door, decides what gets taught in schools, and controls your paycheck, hate and fear become very present."

She stood up.

"We are not the enemy!"

"Aren't you?"

"No!"

He stood to face her.

"Where's the upside for humans? Where's the cure for cancer? Where's the pollution-free flying car? Where's the twenty-hour work week? If we're not your slaves or your pets, when do we get to live like you do?"

"Believe me, we work more than twenty hours a week."

"That's not the point!"

She sat back down and waited for him to also sit down before continuing.

"OK, OK. I know those were just examples. It takes time. There are gaps in knowledge that have to be filled."

"There are people in Borneo whose parents never met a white man, never saw an electric light, whose children grew up to be airline pilots. We can learn pretty damn fast when we get a chance."

"I know. I know. But not some of . . . there are just differences that—"

"What damn differences?"

Once again, Angie took a long pause. She got up again and crossed to the window, looking out across the harbor at the sunshine. He had to wait a long time before she spoke again, by which time her whole demeanor had changed.

"Thank you, Hal. You have raised some interesting factors that need further consideration. I believe we have anticipated most of them, but perhaps not to the level of severity you are pointing out. I will try to communicate them, as best as I understand them, to the proper channels. I think we are in one of those areas of cultural misunderstanding, you and I. I am going to interpret some of this as being dramatic in order to make a point, and not as something you truly feel yourself. At least not about me. I personally am going to believe you are so emphatic because you care, about the success of our peoples finding a way to coexist, and maybe about me and my own ability to handle the challenges ahead. I will proceed on that assumption and discuss these issues again only if necessary."

And she turned and left the library, leaving Hal sitting in the sunshine for a long time.

17.

AND SO IT GOES

Angie seemed to be in and out a lot for the next few months. They communicated regularly by e-mail, but it was over things like whether the offices in the new office building should have cubicles or hard walls, how many conference rooms were needed, should the snack bar in the building serve hot food or just have snack machines, should the paint in the ladies' restroom be pink. Even when she was in the castle, they often ate separately or only talked about the flowers blooming in the park or the latest Alien fad of putting marshmallows on top of banana pudding and somehow freeze-drying that and making it into a breakfast bar. Hal tried one, just to see what it was like, and decided it was a little like a Twinkie or a Moon Pie, but was a little too sweet for regular consumption.

So, the days passed quietly, with lots of reading and walks around the areas of the island he was permitted to visit. His every-other-night visits to the seraglio continued until one night walking back it occurred to him that the woman might have been someone he had had sex with before. But he wasn't sure. It wasn't the first woman, or even the second or third, but it might have been the seventh or eighth. Had he really had sex with 100 women and started over again? How did you lose count of how many women you had sex with? They weren't like potato chips where you just ate a few and then were surprised to find the bag was empty. He tried to create a calendar in his head. Had it been 200 days? But he had skipped Christmas Eve and New Year's Eve, so it had to have been 204 days. And what was the date he started? He could remember the event, but not the date. Even consulting a calendar when he got home, he still was not sure.

Two nights later he got his answer. It was definitely the second time through; this woman had breasts that were unforgettable, even compared to all the others. But this woman had been much later, somewhere between twentieth and thirtieth. Why was the order so different? Did it have to do with where they were in—or more likely out of—their fertility cycle? Had the Aliens let some of them take their scholarship and go home early since he would be leaving eventually? Had some of them gotten pregnant? Had the royal physician souped up his fertility as well as his virility? If that was it, were these two really the only ones out of the first twenty or thirty that didn't get impregnated? Did he have little babies and knocked-up women scattered all over the world?

He was still trying to figure out if he wanted an answer to that question two nights later, after a particularly vigorous evening with a woman who he thought came even later in the series, past the midpoint. He went back to his bedroom, stripped off his clothes, rinsed off in the shower, climbed into bed, and fell quickly asleep.

When he woke up, something was different. He realized he was in a bed with railings. Hospital room? Then he saw Angie sitting by the bed. She was wearing her jeans and "Alien Power" T-shirt. She looked like she was playing Candy Crush on her cell phone, but it was a cell phone he knew you couldn't buy at any Apple Store, and the game was more likely to be the real manipulation of lumber or steel for buildings at Sharon Springs.

"Well, look who's waking up."

"Uh, where am I?

"Wrong question."

"What happened?"

"Nope, still not relevant."

"So what is?"

"Let me give you a hint. The king is dead. Long live Jim King."

"Who?"

"You. James Edward King. Goes by Jim. From Atlanta. Born fifty years ago. Widower with no children."

At that point the royal physician entered, accompanied by a woman who was the one who actually waved the Star Trek instruments over him.

"I'm sure you remember Dr. Harvard. This is his associate, Dr. Vassar. She's a cosmetic surgeon."

"Nice to see you awake, Mr. King."

"What have you done to me?"

"Well, have a look."

She pulled a large hand mirror out from a drawer in the nightstand beside the bed and handed it to him. He held it up to his face. There was some faint bruising over his eyes and on his nose, but what surprised him was that his hair was three shades lighter, thicker, not receding at all, no grey, and curly as all get-out. He had had curly hair as a little boy, but that had straightened itself out during elementary school. He also had a two or three-day growth of beard that matched the color of his head hair but otherwise seemed unaltered from what would have grown naturally.

Moving the mirror closer and examining the area around the bruises, he thought his nose was a little smaller but a hair rounder, not quite the hawk nose he remembered. The eyebrows not only were the lighter shade of the rest of his hair, but they seemed to be a little bushier and a little more arched. He noticed a little bruising under his chin, which led him to notice that his chin was a little more pronounced, a little stronger. All in all, not big changes, except for the hair, but enough in combination to make him not sure if the mirror was creating an illusion.

"We also did a little work on the teeth, making them line up a little better, whitened them, replaced some of those caps and fillings with real teeth."

"Real teeth?"

"Custom grown, just for you. In a couple more days all those little bruises will disappear and no one will ever be able to tell anything was done. It's just enough that even facial recognition systems wouldn't be able to make a connection. Plus, I think it makes you a little more handsome. The ladies will love it."

"No doubt." He turned to look at Dr. Harvard. "Any other 'improvements' I would want to know about?"

"Nothing significant."

"According to who?"

Dr. Harvard looked at Angie, who gave a little nod.

"We gave you a little higher tolerance for alcohol, just in case you need to be more social in your new position."

"I'm not a drinker."

"Well, if you do need to indulge, your body will process the alcohol faster than a normal metabolism. Same for marijuana."

"I don't do drugs."

"Nonetheless, merely a precaution on our part."

"Anything else?"

"You will look and feel like a very healthy fifty-year-old. Your mind and your memories are unchanged, which could cause problems if you start talking about remembering things that happened before your new birthdate. Barring accidents, you will live a long, healthy life, especially if you keep up your exercises, but you will still age, you can be injured, and nobody lives forever, not even Aliens."

"Something else we have in common."

"Yes."

Angie spoke up. "Thank you, doctors."

Dr. Vassar replied, "He needs to stay out of the sun for two more days. He can take a sponge bath, but no shaving or washing or massaging the face either. As little touching the face as possible. Soft foods today, solid foods tomorrow. Then he will be ready for anything."

"I will see he behaves. Thank you."

And the doctors took their leave.

"So, Jim, how are you feeling?"

"Are you still Angie?"

"Yes, I am Angie Winston and you are Jim King, and we are the co-managers of Sharon Springs Software. How do you do? I hope we will be friends."

"You could have given me some warning. I'm not sure my underwear made it into the laundry basket."

"I took care of that, though we did leave your shirt and pants on the chair so the museum would look exactly like you left it. After all, you died in your sleep after a night of hot sex."

"Oh really."

"Really."

"I still would have liked—"

"You couldn't bring anything with you. No souvenirs somebody could trace back."

"Still . . ."

"What view from the island did you want to see again? Who did you want to say goodbye to?"

"There were some squirrels in the park that were getting used to me. Some seagulls that wouldn't fly off unless I got really close."

"I'll send them your regrets."

"I'm going to miss some of those books."

"I have already arranged for you to have electronic access at the new place to every human book ever printed. Suck it up, Jim. It's a new day."

"The king is dead."

"Long live Jim King."

"So, I just lie here for two days trying not to touch my face?"

"There's a really hopped-up tablet computer on the nightstand for you with lots of special features, including your complete biography and stills and video of major events in your life. That should occupy most of your time. You can get out of bed, bathroom behind that door. But otherwise stay in the room. We will sneak you out when the time comes."

"And if I need a nurse?"

"You got me, Jim. Fewest people possible involved in this. Harvard and Vassar did all the medical stuff. Nobody else involved, and those two know what patient confidentiality means, and they are already leaving for somewhere else. It's you and me, kid."

"Dragon Lady?"

"Oh, she knows, a few others have a general outline of the plan. Everybody else on both sides will think you're some hotshot software development manager we hired because you get along well with Aliens."

"Well, that's probably an exaggeration on both counts."

"Yeah, well, we got two days to straighten that out, OK?"

"You mean I actually have to like you?"

"Whether you like it or not. Now start looking yourself up on the tablet and I'll go get us some Jell-O and juices."

"I like the green kind."

"Green Jell-O for Jim. I'll see what I can do."

She went out the door. Jim looked around the room. No windows, door to bathroom, another one probably to a closet. The bed he was in, one chair, nightstand, a hospital table that could be swung over the bed to put food trays on. Nothing else. He pulled the hospital table in front of him, picked up the tablet computer from the nightstand, put it on the table, and touched the power button.

. . .

The rest of the day was occupied eating Jell-O, then soup and yogurt, and reading about his new past life in the form of resumes, job applications, old letters, and various other documents. Suddenly he had graduated from Boys High in Atlanta, then Emory University in physics, followed by a master's at Georgia Tech in computer science and management. He had had a steady girlfriend while in college, but ended up marrying one of the few female Ramblin' Wrecks from Georgia Tech back in the day, who had died of breast cancer ten years ago.

He spent hours looking at pictures of himself when he was a kid, with parents he did not remember, and videos of Christmas and graduations. His father had died of a heart attack five years ago, his mother of a stroke just over a year ago, right before the Disappearances. He had no siblings, his parents had both been only children, so there was no family left. He had taken early retirement after twenty-five years at the Southern Company, and signed on with Sharon Springs Software as a late-in-life adventure, getting out of his rut in Georgia. He had had coworkers who Disappeared, but no relatives, so he had a little less of an axe to grind against the Aliens, and a nagging concern with conservation and climate change aroused by brochures he got from an organization concerned with saving the sea turtles who nested on the Georgia barrier islands, which made him more accepting of the Aliens' claim that the Disappearances were necessary.

All in all, not a bad cover story. He had at least driven by all the places noted in the biography and been inside many of them. He wondered what they had done about his fingerprints on file with both the federal government (as an ex-federal employee) and the state of Georgia (for his driver's license). Would anything happen when he applied for a Kansas driver's license? Then he happened to notice a wallet in the drawer of the nightstand, took it out, and found a complete set of IDs (Kansas driver's license, First National Bank debit card with picture, VISA and American Express credit cards with his picture, even a Wallace County library card for James King), and decided he would stop worrying for the time being.

• • •

The morning of the second day, Angie brought him some bacon with his eggs and grits (he wondered if they had grits in Kansas) so he could test out his new teeth and jaw, as well as his stomach. All seemed to go well, so he sipped his orange juice while Angie sat in the chair chowing down on Egg McMuffins.

"OK, I've read all about me. What's your story?"

"What?"

"Your story. As such close, if newfound, friends and coworkers, I have to know something about your background, don't I? Do I tell people you were the liaison with the king of the world until you got reassigned after his unfortunate death during a wild orgy?"

"It wasn't an orgy and it wasn't during."

"Sorry, just trying to improve the legend."

"No, the less said about that period of our lives, the better."

"So, how did we meet? The biography ends with my employment as co-manager of Sharon Springs Software three months ago."

"We met after you were hired. We've been meeting privately every couple of weeks since then at an office we rented in the King and Queen office complex in Sandy Springs, outside Atlanta. The Queen building if anybody asks. Mostly we worked by e-mail between meetings, planning office spaces and reviewing resumes."

"Funny, I remember lots of e-mails about offices, but none about staff."

"We've been running background checks, trying to determine pro- and anti-Alien leanings, personality types, that kind of thing.

Weeding out the troublemakers, as you call it. The job ads we placed didn't say anything about Aliens running the company. Just the need for top-level software developers of all kinds for a radical new software development startup, English proficiency required, well-above-average pay. We used a Kansas City return address to let people know we weren't in Silicon Valley, but didn't specify a location. Ads went up on developer jobsites all over. You'll get to put your two cents' worth in about which humans to hire once we get to Sharon Springs."

"OK. So what had you been doing before?"

"I was a mid-level manager at the main office in Ecuador. I've been in an intense course in English and human customs for the six months prior to starting on the Sharon Springs project."

"Ah. Very good. Married, single, boyfriend? Parents, brothers or sisters?"

"Those words don't have equivalents with us. Marriage is one of the hardest of your cultural concepts for us to understand. There are other Aliens with whom we develop strong emotional bonds and members of our kind with whom we have sex, but it's not always the same ones. Some of the ones we have sex with we reproduce with, but not often. You think population control is important now, think about us all jammed into that little sphere counting every molecule of oxygen we could produce or recycle. And we know who our DNA comes from and who we share strands with, but care is provided by many, and some fathers and mothers are not the ones who do most of the 'parenting.' There is a lot more variation in our culture in order to provide the best situation for each of us. Some of it English doesn't have the words to describe."

"I guess I see that I don't see."

"Yes."

"Did you leave any of those with whom you shared emotional or DNA bonds behind on whatever planet you came from?"

There was a pause.

"Do you really need to know that?"

"No. I'm sure that is one of the questions I will be asked about you and that will be asked of you and the other Aliens, along with which star did you come from, and how long it took to get here, etc., etc., etc., but it is not a question you have to answer. Or should I say you and your friends need to have stock answers prepared that basically say nothing if those are secrets you want to keep."

"Hang on a second."

Angie took out her cell phone and tap-tap-tapped. Then she waited, staring at the screen. Then she held a finger to her ear as if listening to an earwig. Then a single tap to the cell phone.

"I can tell you the facts, or at least some of them, if you want."

"Please."

"I was born in the sphere, as was the generation before me and the generation before them. None of us alive now ever knew anyone born on our planet. So it took a long time to get here, even for us. Our star is in this galaxy, of course, in the same spiral arm, but nothing you could see without a moderate-sized telescope, just a dot among billions of other dots. We know your number for it, but what is the point of knowing a number? You and I, we look at the night sky and see different things; you see possibilities, I see regrets. To put a number on blue oceans and green fields none of us will ever see seems wrong. You call your planet Earth, Terra Firma; it means the firm land, the soil, a solid place to stand. Our name had almost the same meaning; we called it the place to grow. It meant not just a place to grow plants, but a place for us to grow, to live. A place to become something more.

"And we did. And then we didn't. Don't ask why we left. I'm not even sure I know, not the complete story anyway. It just became necessary. For ages we have been doing what was necessary. We are very good at finding out what is necessary and doing it. And don't ask what was left behind because none of us know for sure. There is another human word we had trouble with for a long time, 'orphans.'

That somebody would be left alone was inconceivable to us. But now we understand that we are the orphans here, alone and far, far from the past. We are the fosterlings looking for another home. Now orphan is a word we understand."

And neither Jim King nor Hal Southerland knew what to say and so said nothing. After a moment Angie gathered up the breakfast dishes and carried them out of the room.

18.

NIGHT FLIGHT

That night, in the wee hours, Angie stuck her head in the door and told him to get dressed before she ducked out again. He availed himself of the bathroom facilities as a precautionary measure, then opened the closet to a complete set of clothes, including Under Armour underwear, black jeans, black T-shirt and a black sweatshirt, even black socks and black New Balance running shoes. He wondered if Jim King was some kind of ninja. He dressed, pocketed the wallet with the IDs from the nightstand, along with a handkerchief and a plastic comb. He grabbed the tablet computer and what seemed to be its case, but the case was way too small. A moment's experimentation and fiddling around surprisingly revealed that the tablet folded repeatedly into something slightly smaller than a cell phone, then slipped into its case easily. He was even able to stick it into a jeans pocket. He glanced around and saw nothing that would reveal he was ever here unless they could get DNA off the hospital gown or the bedsheets. Suddenly, Angie reappeared, also all in black.

"Ready?"

"I guess."

"Quietly then."

He followed her down the hall, out a side door into an empty parking lot, where another one of those small spheres sat waiting, ramp down, making no sound. This time she did not wait for him to enter, but went first and took one of the seats. He followed her, sat in the other seat, and was not surprised when the ramp closed, dim lights came on, and everything seemed to be still.

"This will take almost an hour, so you can sit back and relax. We're taking a diversionary route, and that takes longer."

"Who are we trying to fool?"

"Everybody. That's why it takes so long."

He looked around as best he could, but all the light, such as it was, was directed down at him and Angie. Whatever controls or instruments there might have been in the "cabin" were deep in shadow. He wasn't even sure where the wall was. He tried to reach out to touch something and found his arms could move freely, but that his body could not get out of the seat.

"I believe the term is that the seatbelt light is on."

"No wonder the stewardess didn't give that speech about seat belts and exit doors. I bet there's not even an oxygen mask that drops from the ceiling."

"There are some peanuts and a drink in the seat pocket beside you, if you're interested."

He leaned over and saw a small flap, pulled it up and stuck his hand in the opening, pulled out a small bag of Planter's Peanuts, then a small can of Coke, which was actually cold. He put the Coke can back in the seat pocket and the peanuts in the pocket of his sweatshirt.

"I think I'll save these for later."

"Suit yourself."

"Why the all-black outfits? Are we sneaking into somewhere?"

"Our new houses. We are new next-door neighbors. We'll land in your backyard; I'll go through the gate in our backyard fence into my backyard. We go in our own back doors, use these red-light flashlights to find our bedrooms, undress, set the alarm for 7:00 a.m., and get as much sleep as we can with the time change. We get up in the morning, get dressed in the clothes we find in our closets, eat the food in our kitchen, and meet at the office at 9."

She handed him a flashlight barely as long as his hand. Then she gave him a key ring with three keys.

"One key is to your house, all the doors. It's a new, ranch-style house, brick, living room, dining room, kitchen, den, three bedrooms, only one bedroom is converted to a home office and library for you. It does have a basement with a recreation room, laundry room, and a well-stocked tornado shelter. What nobody else knows is that the middle set of shelves in the shelter will swing out and there is a door behind them. That opens to a tunnel that goes to my tornado shelter. This is one of those 'just in case' features that we don't want showing up on any real estate listing, OK?

"The car key is for the Lexus Hybrid in your garage. We considered getting you a Corvette or a Ferrari, but decided the Lexus fit better with your social position and your environmental consciousness. It is kind of a racy blue though. The third is a master key to the office building. Don't worry if you lose them; they won't work for anybody else anyway, and you can just look straight at the lock and say your name while holding the knob to get it open. Just let us know and we'll get you new ones, if necessary. You already have your bank card and some cash in your wallet. Your tablet computer has a list of your passwords, and it only works for your touch and voice, but don't lose it—that model is expensive."

"I guess I should say thank you."

"There is a small safe in your bedroom behind the Picasso painting of a woman, the one that's just a curve and a dot. Don't worry; it's not the original, but it is a good copy in oil."

"Well, I should hope so."

"Inside the safe are several thousand dollars in old twenty-dollar bills with random serial numbers, plus your passport, birth certificate, marriage certificate, death certificates for your wife and parents, and some other documents you would keep in a safe. You already have three months' salary in your bank account, plus your savings, IRAs, and other retirement investments from your old job, plus you get retirement payments every month from your old job's retirement. Some of the retirement investments are stocks, bonds, and mutual funds with the investment management company that has an association with the bank. They tend to pay very well. You are not poor, Jim King. You can get all the cash you need from any ATM; the cash in the safe is for any emergency that might come up."

"So I can pocket the passport, hop in the Lexus, and drive down to Mexico for a little vacation come the next long weekend."

"Actually, the car tends to break down across county lines."

"Funny thing, that."

"The passport is very real, but like so many things, it tends to set off alarms at border crossings."

"Ah well, I can dream."

"This is going to be good, Jim. Really. And it's important work. There's a lot riding on this."

"Yes, it's what's necessary."

Angie was quiet after that, until they were about to land.

• • •

"We're here."

The ramp slid down and open. Angie was out almost instantly. Jim followed quickly, but as soon as he felt dirt under his feet, he turned to look at the sphere. It was already rising silently, punching a black hole in the stars overhead. It faded quickly and was gone. Jim turned back toward the house, but could barely make out the outline of the house and a fence. It occurred to him that he wasn't in a city, or even a suburb with streetlights that stayed on all night, anymore. As his eyes adjusted, he was able to see Angie wave to him just before she opened a gate in the fence, stepped through, and closed it behind her.

He stood very still for a few seconds, listening, looking around. He thought the dark would be silent, but air conditioners pumped away in the distance, keeping even the night cool. The sky was full of stars. The one streak of bright was definitely the Milky Way, but there were so many of the stars he usually couldn't see that he had trouble picking out the ones he knew. There seemed to be at least three Orion's Belts, four or five Ursa Majors and Minors, with an equal number of North Stars. But at least the outline of the roof was silhouetted against the stars, so he started moving toward his house.

The back steps were easy to find, as was the door, but the keyhole was not so obvious. Below the knob, in the knob, in the door above the knob? Rather than feel around or use the flashlight, he grabbed the knob, looked in the general direction of the knob, and whispered, "Jim King." The lock clicked, the door opened, and he entered his new life.

Once inside, he turned on the flashlight, which emitted only a dim, red glow, but it was enough. He was in the kitchen. He navigated past the kitchen table and into a hallway. The first door on the right turned out to be a half bath, but the second opened into what was obviously the master bedroom. There were doors that appeared to be to the master bath and a walk-in closet, but he settled for following the glow of the LED alarm clock numerals to the side of the king-sized bed, turned down the cotton sheets, laid his clothes on the chair near the bed, figured out how to set the alarm clock for seven in the morning, crawled into bed, and stared into the dark room thinking he would not get any sleep.

At which point the alarm rang, waking him from a sound slumber. Light was streaming in through the windows, and he looked around at his new existence. The bed backed into the wall that had the hall on the other side, so he faced a long picture window that looked over the backyard. The curtains were open, but one glance convinced him no one was looking in. The backyard was totally empty and was enormous, at least two acres. A fence about eight feet high ran around the entire yard, and beyond the back fence was nothing, no buildings he could see, just fields of grain or grass, an occasional low tree of some kind he didn't recognize. The brown fields were wheat fields, he assumed, never actually having seen one before. The green ones he assumed were pastures, though he didn't see any cows. Maybe they were fields left fallow or planted with alfalfa or something to fix nitrogen for next year. He really needed to read up on High Plains farming.

He shifted his gaze back to the yard. It wasn't quite totally flat, but not even a shrub bush broke up the emptiness, hardly even any grass. No buffalo roaming around here, he thought. Maybe he could hang a couple of bird feeders and at least attract a few squirrels. They did have squirrels in Kansas, didn't they? Or were they another creature of civilization, only living where both the trees and the population produced nuts. Or did farmers hate squirrels? Maybe attracting rodents wasn't the best idea. Maybe he could hire some teenager and have them put in a garden in the backyard. Or was that something you had to do yourself? Would the farmers around here look down on anybody who didn't take care of their own garden? Oh well; it was probably too late in the season to do it this year anyway. By next spring he should have the local garden etiquette figured out.

Getting out of bed, he crossed to the window at the end of the house. He saw where the backyard fence T-boned into another fence that ran between his house and Angie's, which didn't seem very far away. She also had a window overlooking the fence connection, but her curtains were closed, so he closed his curtains on the end of the house and turned to look at the room.

It was very basic house décor. All the walls were white. The only decoration was the minimalist Picasso hanging on the wall at the other end of the room, between the doors to the bathroom and walk-in closet. The king-sized bed had a nightstand on either side, white cotton sheets, and a white bedspread. There were actually two wooden chairs, one beside each nightstand, with squared-off backs to make it easy to hang shirts and pants on the chair.

He crossed the room and picked the door that looked like it led to the bathroom. He was correct, so he relieved himself and tested the plumbing, which seemed to work fine. There was a separate shower and tub, so he stepped into the shower. This one only had three showerheads, though one could be handheld. The shower stall was a little bigger than standard, though, and he found he could do all his range-of-motion stretches without banging into the walls, if he was careful. Drying off using the towel on the rack, he realized there were two sinks in the vanity. He decided the one closer to the door would be most convenient. Checking the medicine cabinet, he found the necessary accoutrements: toothbrush and toothpaste, hand soap, electric beard trimmer, cologne, deodorant, comb, etc.

Finishing up his morning preparations, he moved on to the walk-in closet. Several suits hung on the racks, along with some much less formal shirts and pants. Drawers opened revealed the usual underwear and socks, along with a drawer of sweat suits, several decorated T-shirts (the one on top said "Aliens Are Beautiful"), and various other clothing that did not require hanging up. Shoes were along a rack under the suits. Even when he was a fed, in another life as it were, or maybe this life when he was a techie at the Southern Company, he had exercised the techie prerogative of not dressing in a suit, so he selected some Fruit of the Loom underwear, tan Dockers pants and matching socks, a dark-blue shirt, and New Balance cross-trainers.

After dressing, he moved back to the chair by the bed, took the stuff out of the pockets of yesterday's clothing and moved it to the pockets of today's. He checked the drawer of the nightstand, which turned out to be empty except for a box of Kleenex. He moved the flashlight from last night, which he had left on top of the nightstand, into the drawer, checked the clock to see that it was now 7:30 a.m., and moved into the hallway.

There were two doors on the left side. He went to the farthest, opened it and saw his home office. Again, white walls, a dark-wood roll-top desk, desk chair on wheels, two walls of empty shelves, one window facing Angie's house, another overlooking his front yard. They seemed to be giving him a pretty much blank canvas to decorate in his own style and time.

He moved back up the hall to the next door. A bedroom. Double bed, nightstands, white covers, bathroom and walk-in closet, no decoration. He wondered what he would do with a second bedroom since he obviously was not expecting any family or friends to drop in for a visit, but he guessed it would look strange not to have one. He closed the door and decided that room was low priority.

Back up the hall he came to a junction. On the right was the living room, which had the front door to the house. Directly in front of him was a door. To the left, the kitchen. He turned to the living room. Again, basic furniture, sand-colored couch and two matching armchairs, oval coffee table, white walls and matching curtains covering another picture window that he presumed would reveal his front yard. He peeked around the edge of the curtain and saw across the street a light-colored house with a double-door garage sticking out and tall walkway lights leading to the house.

Returning to the junction, he opened the door to see steps leading downward to a basement. The rec room and tornado shelter, he guessed. That could be explored later. Walking into the kitchen, he saw the basic wood table and chairs for eating, a country-style kitchen layout with lots of counter space and cabinets but no center island, but, jarringly, with the most modern of appliances, including built-in double convection ovens, a commercial-sized refrigerator, a microwave, and a stove with four burners and a flat grill. Not exactly what Grandma would have had. The door to the backyard, where he had entered last night, he could now see helped define the separation between the cooking and eating areas.

Directly ahead, at the other end of the kitchen, was a swinging door. He pushed that open and saw a more formal dining room, dark-wood table and chairs for ten people, dish cabinets on one wall, a window to the side yard. Pulling his head back in, he noticed another swinging door, right in the corner of the kitchen, partially hidden by the cabinets and counters. Pushing this open, he saw this was the den—just past the living room, big-screen TV on the back wall, curtained windows facing the front yard, two La-Z-Boy recliners with built-in cup holders, end tables beside each one. He wondered if there was a drink cooler hidden somewhere handy. On the side that would have been the end of the house there was another door. He opened that to see the interior of the garage, complete with bright-blue Lexus Hybrid in one of the two car spaces. The other space was empty. There were tool racks along one wall, complete with tools that he didn't even recognize in some cases, and a narrow workbench. If somebody was expecting him to build or fix something, they had the wrong guy. Anything that didn't come with a typewriter keyboard was out of his league.

He moved back into the den, wondering if this was the most efficient layout of rooms, but decided not to complain to the real estate agent. Back in the kitchen, he examined the contents of the refrigerator and cabinets. There were just the basics: whole milk, OJ, wheat bread, margarine, a few yogurts, pimento cheese, Cheerios and Raisin Bran. He found the silverware drawer and got a spoon, opened a couple of cabinets to find the bowls and glasses, and sat down at the table to a breakfast of Cheerios in milk accompanied by a glass of orange juice. He peered out the window to see if there was any trace of where the sphere had landed, but couldn't see any trace that anything, much less an Alien hot rod, had ever been there. A glance to the side let him know where the gate in the fence was.

When the Cheerios were gone, he put the milk back in the

refrigerator, rinsed out the bowl and spoon before putting them in the dishwasher, and slid the box of cereal back on the shelf. A clock on the wall told him it was a few minutes after 8:00 a.m., so he checked his pockets to make sure the keys, wallet, and tablet computer were there, decided to go back to the bedroom for a jacket to toss in the car, just in case, and headed for the garage. Pushing the button for the garage opener, he closed the den door behind him, made sure it locked, took out his key ring, stuck the key in the door lock, heard the click, got in the car, and started the engine. Backing out into the driveway, he found the garage door remote clipped to the visor and closed the door.

Pushing the icon on the screen in the center console for the GPS, he watched a map of Sharon Springs appear, showing that he was on Carrie Avenue. He had seen the map before on Google Maps, and it wasn't that big a town, so he realized he was pretty much on the west edge of town. Another dot, labeled "Sharon Springs Software," appeared on the screen, showing him that all he had to do was turn north out of the driveway, go a few blocks on Carrie Avenue to Highway 40, which ran east and west along the north edge of town, and his new office would be just across the highway. But his car clock said it wasn't even 8:30 a.m. yet, so he decided to take the long way.

He backed out into the empty street and turned south. Angie's house was next to his, and beyond her house a set of townhomes was under construction. They were unusual in being two stories high, which none of the other buildings he could see dared to do. All the other houses in view also had lots of space between them, but the townhomes were connected by fire walls. He wasn't sure why, but he had a sneaking suspicion that was where the other Aliens were going to live. If so, he would bet two cents there were ways through those fire walls that would not be obvious to any humans lucky enough to be invited inside. In fact, he wondered if Angie had another tunnel on the other side of her house.

Driving south on Carrie, he passed several more houses on the left that looked like they had been there for a decade or two, maybe more, but there were also vacant lots with "For Sale" signs, and houses with yards that would have qualified as subdivision development property back in Atlanta. There were low trees of various types at irregular intervals. He wasn't sure if they had been planted as windbreaks or just left in place when the houses were built prior to the modern tradition of cutting down every tree possible. A few of the small houses looked like they needed a coat of paint, and one or two looked abandoned, complete with more "For Sale" signs. He suspected word had gotten out that lots of people would be moving into town, but doubted anybody knew exactly how "outside" the "outsiders" were going to be.

Just before he got to the railroad tracks that divided the town, he turned east onto Front Street, driving past some of the silos that lined a section of the railroad tracks. Four short blocks brought him to an intersection so major that it actually had a stop sign, unlike the other intersections he had carefully driven through. Here he turned north, onto Main Street, which was also Highway 27. It was a wider street, with diagonal parking on both sides. Here he began to see businesses, but was surprised by how much empty space there was between some buildings. He passed the Strand Theater, which looked like it could hold fifty or sixty people if a Star Wars episode was showing and everything sold out. He drove past a hardware store, the Wallace County Courthouse, Miller's Food Store (which he probably needed to stop by on the way home), the Holy Ghost Catholic Church, the Sharon Springs Elementary School and Wallace County High School (home of the Wildcats), which appeared to need only two buildings for both schools. He did see a couple of trailer classrooms parked out back in anticipation of a population explosion.

Past the school he knew he was back at another major intersection because there was another stop sign. Here Main Street met Highway 40. Across the road were the Shell station, Stephens Restaurant, and the Oak Tree Inn beyond them. There were no cars behind him, so he took a moment to look around, even though Highway 40 was also empty except for a semi pulling away in the distance. Highway 27 took a little jog here, following 40 east for one block before turning back north. Heyl's Traveler Motel was at the corner there. Behind it a Best Western had sprung up recently, and the parking lots for all the motels were full. He realized that the rush hour of traffic getting to work had probably occurred an hour earlier and he was the lazybones.

Farther down the highway, a field had been filled with RVs and house trailers still on wheels, probably homes for the temporary construction workers who had flooded in to build the software company offices, his and Angie's houses, the townhomes he had seen being worked on, and heaven knew what else required by an almost instant doubling of the population. But they would soon depart, as soon as the construction jobs dried up. It was the programmers and other techies that followed who would really test the adaptability of Sharon Springs. Ah yes, he thought, the old America. Where minorities were still minorities, schools were so small one science teacher taught all the science classes, and everybody literally knew everybody and was related to half of them. Boy, were they in for a shock.

Taking the turn to the west, he drove down 40 past a place that serviced semis and a business selling farm-irrigation systems, then turned right into the parking lot by the unpretentious sign announcing Sharon Springs Software. About a dozen trucks and vans of various types were already parked in the lot, ignoring any parking space lines or sense of order. Several labeled themselves as painting companies, while other trucks were being unloaded of office furniture. He pulled around to what appeared to be the front door and saw the parking space to the right of the walk leading to the front door had a sign saying "Reserved for J. King." Beside that space was an area marked as a crosswalk giving access to the walkway, then another reserved parking space, this one for "A. Winston." In that space was, of all things, a Mini Cooper. He pulled into his space, got out, locked the car with the key to avoid the horn beeping, and followed the walkway to the double glass doors of the main entrance.

Inside, the place looked to be finished, but he heard workers down the halls on both sides. Past a small lobby area sat a large reception desk manned by a woman with grey hair and a few extra pounds covered by a flower-print dress. The nameplate on the desk said "Mabel Bentley." Mabel was currently talking on the phone.

"No, Gladys, we can't. The church picnic is that afternoon, you know that. Listen, I'll call you back; somebody just came in. Can I help you?

"Please. My name is Jim King and I'm looking for my office."

"Oh, Mr. King. So nice to meet you. I'm Mabel. Ms. Winston told me to expect you."

"Really. How long has she been here?"

"Oh, just about an hour. She is so pretty. And young! Hard to believe she is going to help you run this company."

"Well, she's an amazing person. And software is a young person's game. I'm the old coot out of his element."

"Oh, you're not that old."

"Nonetheless, it seems I have some catching up to do. If you could direct me to . . ."

"Oh, yes. Let me show you."

And she led him through a set of double doors behind her desk into another hallway and reception area, complete with secretary stations, then yet another set of double doors to an area with two more secretary desks, then side-by-side single doors with "A. Winston, Co-President" and "J. King, Co-President" lettered in gold paint. Mabel went and knocked on Angie's door.

"Ms. Winston, Mr. King is here."

After a beat, Angie opened the door.

"Good. Hi, Jim. Thank you, Mabel."

It took a second before Mabel got the hint, smiled, and went back to her station. Angie was dressed in a blue pantsuit and white blouse, very professional looking. She had also done something to her hair so that it looked like a permanent that was starting to lose its hold. He was again struck by how much she looked like Marilyn Monroe. She gestured to the door closing behind Mabel.

"Local hire. We said we needed somebody to hold down the fort once the phone system went in until the rest of the staff could be hired, but she's actually the local gossip that will tip us off to all the rumors, we hope."

"Does she . . . ?"

"Never even crossed her mind."

"OK. So . . . ?

"I sent you an org chart with the screened applicants for each position linked behind each block. We start with the top position in each division and their deputy, which are each paired with . . . one of us. Then we let them hire from the screened list for the rest of the staff. Look through the resumes and we can get together again at lunch."

"OK."

Angie went back into her office, and Jim turned to his. Inside the door was a round conference table for ten, two sofas facing each other with a coffee table between them, then a large desk and high-backed desk chair. One wall was covered with giant monitors, currently blank; the other had windows looking out onto the fields behind the building. Behind the desk were two doors. Checking one out, he found a small restroom, just a toilet and sink. The other was a small closet and storage area. He hung up the jacket he hadn't put on, and turned back to his desk. The top seemed to be in three sections. Pushing the section on the right slid part of the top back to reveal a lot of buttons, knobs, and other control panel stuff, probably for the monitors. The larger middle section turned out to be nothing but a smooth, polished piece of hardwood. The left segment also slid open revealing a small monitor screen and controls. The drawers on both sides and the one in the middle turned out to be just empty drawers, as best he could tell. He assumed there was something else hidden in there somewhere, but he couldn't find it.

Taking his tablet from his pocket, he unfolded it and navigated to the message from Angie. A couple of taps and the organization chart appeared. There were three main divisions of the company: personal software, business software, and research and development. Each had a double box for the division directors and deputy directors, indicating the pairing of a human with an Alien. He and Angie were also going to get a deputy and an administrative assistant of their own type. The R&D division also had a double box labeled "Chief Researcher." Ten Aliens in total, of course counting Angie. The rest of the boxes in the chart were single boxes.

He touched a finger to the Alien box for business software, but nothing happened. Moving his finger to the other side of the box brought up three tabs. Under each was a detailed vita of an applicant for the job indicated. This, at least, was something he was good at, having reviewed the vitas of all those staff of proposed contractors back in his previous life. He began with the first vita and started going through, looking to see what degrees people had earned at which universities and when they had graduated, estimating how old that would make them, then checking for unexplained gaps in their employment record. He didn't mind if people had been out of work for a while, but he did want to know if they were honest enough to admit it.

He looked for college minors and activities outside computer science, hoping for people who had a broader range of interests. He checked carefully for grammar and spelling errors, trying to gauge English fluency. He looked for what people seemed to think was important about themselves and how much judgement they had about what to include and what to exclude. He remembered a vita he had received once that had looked totally normal until under "Other Activities" someone had noted that they were a chief Wiccan for a coven in New Jersey. That would probably have been easier to deal with in the workplace than some proselytizing deacon from a foot-washing Baptist church, but he had never figured out what prompted that fact to be included in a vita for a computer programmer.

So the morning passed, making notes on vitas and adding summary evaluations. Just before noon his tablet beeped and Angie appeared on the screen.

"How you coming?"

"I'm getting there. I've made one pass through the applicants for the division director jobs and have started on the deputies."

"Can you take time to go out to lunch?"

"What's the deadline on these?"

"It would be nice to set up videoconference-call interviews with the director candidates tomorrow, try to have the interviews within a couple more days, then confirm the recommendations of the top candidates so we could hire next week."

"I can live with that."

"So, ready to try the local cuisine?"

"I'm game if you are."

"We can take my car. Meet you out front in five minutes."

Her image vanished from the screen. He finished making a note about one vita, marked where he was, saved, folded up his tablet, and put it in his pocket. Walking out, he noted that Mabel was gone, replaced by a handmade "Out to Lunch" sign. He hoped she was not aware of the possible alternate interpretation of that. He also noted workmen hunkered down in various places, relaxing and pulling sandwiches and drinks out of enormous lunch pails.

Angie was already in her car. He opened the door on the shotgun side and folded himself into the car, buckling up.

"Mabel says Stephens Restaurant is the place to go for lunch."

"You mean there's a choice?"

"There's Penny's Diner, plus the new Best Western and the old Oak Tree Inn have restaurants. There are going to be others, but they haven't opened yet."

"We can start with Mabel's recommendation."

At this point the car started by itself, backed up, and headed out of the parking lot.

"Neat trick."

"I can put my hands on the steering wheel and my foot on the pedal to make it look real, but that's just for show."

"Why a Mini Cooper?"

"Looks environmentally responsible. Also limits the number of people who can ride with me."

"No kidding."

By then they were pulling into the Stephens Restaurant parking lot, which was almost full, but the car found a space others had avoided because one pickup had edged about a foot over the faded white line, leaving less than a full space.

"It also is very easy to park."

"What do we say if somebody asks where you're from?"

"Well, I moved here from New York City. If they ask where I was born, it was on a spaceship in the middle of nowhere. No point in trying to hide. If there is going to be trouble, let's find out before the others get here."

"OK, your call."

So they unfolded themselves from the car and walked to the restaurant. There was a short line out the door, so they stood and waited. It took about five minutes for the two groups of workmen ahead of them to be seated as other groups of workmen finished eating and checked out. Three more groups of workmen had gotten in line behind them by then. They all seemed to enjoy having someone with Angie's figure in the line, but were polite enough to confine their remarks to facial expressions, which Angie and Jim decided to ignore. Finally a waitress approached.

"Just two?"

"Yes."

"This way, please."

The waitress led them to a booth on the opposite side. The walls were decorated with various plaques and signs promoting God, country, and the Sharon Springs Wildcats in approximately equal measure. They were handed two menus.

"Sorry for the wait. We got construction people from all over the state and half of Colorado here working on all the new buildings."

"No problem."

"Susie will be with you in a minute."

The examined their menus. The main menu seemed to have the full range, from salads and soups through sandwiches and burgers to steaks and seafood, but there was a separate lunch menu focused more on things that could be prepared in a hurry. Jim noted that the coffee and tea came with free refills, but not the sodas. Not quite as good as the South, but he knew the Southern tradition of free refills and a refill to go had not yet fully spread across the nation. They would catch up eventually. Another waitress approached.

"Hi. I'm Susie. Sorry for the wait."

"Not a problem."

"They're building this new manufacturing plant just down the road and a bunch of places for all the new workers to live, so we've got all these construction guys we don't usually have."

"You mean the software company?"

"Yeah, that. So, what can I get you folks?"

Susie looked toward Angie, so she replied first.

"I believe I'll have the double bacon Swiss burger, French fries, and a Coke."

"I'll go with the lunch special fish and chips and some iced tea."

"OK. Coming right up."

Susie moved off, and Angie and Jim began looking around, reading the wall decorations and taking a reading of the construction workers.

Based on the various sayings populating the walls, God was good to those who had the faith and patience to get through those times when God wasn't so good, and America was the greatest nation on earth that needed to be made great again. As for the Wildcats, they were the greatest thing since sliced bread and could probably have beaten the Denver Broncos in football. As for the construction workers, it was obvious none of them were counting Weight Watcher points. There was also not a lot of conversation as they tried to eat and move on so some of their brethren could get a table. It was only a minute before Susie returned with the drinks. Angie's was a medium-sized glass of ice and a can of Coke, while Susie set a huge plastic glass full of finely crushed ice and tea, with a lemon slice on the rim, in front of Jim.

"Here you go."

"Thank you."

Susie addressed Jim. "You folks passing through, or you with one of these construction outfits?"

"Actually, we're with the software company. The advance guard, so to speak."

"Oh, are you the ones Mabel Bentley has been spouting about?"

"I guess word gets around fast."

"Well, it's a really small town when the construction crews aren't here. Least it will be until all of you software people move in, I guess."

"We'll try to be good neighbors."

"We've all been wondering why anybody would put a company way out here anyway. We're right next door to nowhere."

"Have you seen the real estate prices out in Silicon Valley lately? A little house on a quarter-acre lot costs a million dollars. Office space gets rented by the square inch instead of the square foot."

"Even after, you know . . ."

"Even after. There was a little drop in prices for a while; then they went back up."

"Well, I guess all this empty space is worth something after all. Back in a minute."

Angie and Jim exchanged a glance, then she opened her Coke and poured it into her glass. Jim took a sip of his tea and started looking for the sugar container. He was definitely not in Georgia anymore. He found a little cup with all kinds of artificial sweeteners and a few packets of real sugar. He tore one open and poured the sugar into his tea, then stirred it with the straw. Another sip revealed the need for another packet of sugar, so he repeated the process. Then he squeezed the lemon slice, dropped the peel into the glass, and stirred again. Only then did the third sip reveal an acceptable concoction. There was another brief pause for wall reading and contemplation before Susie reappeared with their food.

"Double bacon Swiss burger for you."

"Thank you."

"And fish and chips for you."

"Thank you."

"That fish is right out of the fryer, so it's going to be hot. Tartar sauce is on the plate, catsup bottle on the table."

"Very good."

"I'll check back in a minute."

He picked up a French fry, but Angie subtly signaled him to put it back down. She had a small gadget hidden in her hand that she moved slightly in the direction of her food, then his.

"OK. Just checking."

"Well, you know how to ruin an appetite."

"Mine is just fine, thank you."

He looked at her burger. A Quarter Pounder from McDonalds didn't even come close. At least half a pound of meat, two or three slices of Swiss cheese melted, four strips of bacon forming a grid to hold up the thick slices of tomato and onion, an inch of lettuce, pickle slices peeking out on all sides, all between a bun that was bigger than any bun sold in grocery stores. Angie picked it up and somehow managed to take a bite that encompassed at least a little of each layer. After a bit of chewing and swallowing, she announced,

"Well, I think I'm going to like it here." Jim just sighed and started in again on the fries.

It was a few minutes later that Susie stopped by again.

"You folks doing OK?"

"Just fine."

"Where are you from, if you don't mind my asking?"

"I'm from Atlanta."

"The last place I lived before here was New York City."

"Oh, so you two aren't . . . together?"

"Just coworkers."

"Ah. You know, you don't talk like New York."

"Where do I sound like?"

"More like you're on television or something, no place particular."

"Oh, interesting."

"So where are you from, you know, originally?"

"Well, I was born and raised on a spaceship."

"Oh, you mean you're one of those Aliens?"

"Born and bred."

Jim noticed that with the word Alien entering the air the booths on either side of them suddenly got quiet, an effect that slowly spread by gestures and glances.

"Are you . . . ?"

"No. Georgia born and bred."

"We're just here to write some software."

"Well, Mabel sure didn't say anything about anybody being an Alien."

"I guess you get to have the hot gossip this time."

"No kidding."

And Susie moved off to the kitchen, pulling her cell phone from her apron pocket as she went. There was a short moment when nobody in the restaurant seemed to move or speak; then the whispers started, the glances, the hesitations. Slowly things got back to normal—some people left, others were seated, life resumed. Jim and Angie finished eating and were downing the last of their drinks when Susie came over with the bill.

"Any dessert today? The French silk pie is really good if you've never had one."

Suddenly a big man in a white jumpsuit with "Abram's Painting" printed on it walked in carrying a double barrel shotgun and crossed straight to Angie. Everybody else decided this was a good time to not move a muscle.

"You really one of those Aliens?"

Jim spoke, "Friend, you don't want to do this."

"They killed my father, my sister, and my wife."

For an instant Jim wondered what combination of diseases could have so affected that family and left the son/husband untouched.

"We all lost people, family or friends. But if they hadn't, a lot more of us would have died a lot more slowly."

"So they say."

"It's true."

"Well, you can believe all that environmental crap if you want to. I just think them Aliens need to share some of the pain."

He pointed the shotgun straight at Angie. Jim looked at her and saw she didn't seem very scared and was holding another little gadget hidden in her hand. He looked back at the painter and realized the painter was paralyzed, unmoving, with panic frozen on his face. Angie reached out her other hand, grabbed the barrels of the shotgun, and carefully twisted it out of the painter's hands.

"Jim, you know anything about guns?"

"Just to stay as far away from them as possible."

"Susie, would you unload this for me, please?"

"Yes, ma'am."

Susie took the gun from Angie, pointed it down to the floor, carefully eased the hammers down, flipped on the safety, broke the shotgun open, took out the two shells and put them on the table next to Angie's empty Coke can. At that point Jim saw Angie's finger ease up on the gadget. Suddenly the painter bent over, gasping for breath, clutching his chest. After a few shuddering staggers he made it back to the door and was gone. Angie calmly drained the last of the Coke and picked up the two shotgun shells.

"You know, Susie, I think we're going to have to come back for that French silk pie another time."

"Yes, ma'am."

Angie pulled a couple of twenty-dollar bills out of her jacket pocket as she stood and tossed them on the table.

"Keep the change."

"Thank you, ma'am."

Angie and Jim headed for the door at a deliberately slow walk.

"What you want me to do with the shotgun?"

"Hang it on the wall somewhere."

And they were out the door.

Once in the car, Angie leaned back in the seat as the car started and slowly drove back toward the office.

"I thought that went well, all things considered. I am going to have to try that pie though."

"What did you do to that guy?"

"It's just a little thing that paralyzes all the muscles."

"He couldn't breathe?"

"Couldn't breathe, couldn't move. Brain kept working though. It's not an experience he will want to repeat."

"I guess not. You realize everybody in the world will know there's an Alien in Sharon Springs within about an hour."

"Well, everybody in town, yes, but nobody will be able to post anything about me on the internet or make any phone calls about us that go outside the county. The construction workers will tell people when they get home, but television trucks coming to investigate will break down about fifty miles from here, conveniently near a diner but not a repair place; and satellite uplinks about me will mysteriously show I Love Lucy reruns."

"Sooner or later, a reporter with nothing but a notebook and a pen will get here, even if he has to walk."

"Well, we'll deal with that when it happens."

By then, they were back at the office building, and Angie's car glided into her parking space. As they got out, all the workers outside stopped working and stared. They entered the building and saw Mabel at her post with a look on her face that said Angie's electronic blocking had not included Susie's cell phone.

"You were right about that restaurant, Mabel. Very good hamburgers."

"I'm glad you enjoyed it, ma'am."

"Mr. King and I are going to be in conference discussing personnel matters the rest of the afternoon; please see that we are not disturbed."

"Yes, ma'am."

And they were past her through the double doors. Jim heard them lock behind him. Then the second set of double doors also closed and locked, and Jim suspected not even a tank could get through them now.

"You want to talk about some of the director candidates now?"

"Sure."

So they went into her office, Jim unfolded his tablet, and they discussed what other humans to invite to the lovely little town of Sharon Springs.

• • •

By 4:30 they had agreed on whom to interview for the director and deputy director positions, and Jim had sent emails asking to schedule teleconferences. He asked Angie if there was anything he could pick up for her from Miller's Food Store, but she claimed to be in good shape, foodwise. He went back to his office to grab the jacket he had yet to wear, waved to Mabel (who was on the phone again) on his way out, got in his car, and retraced his morning route down Main Street as far as Miller's.

Miller's, by any definition, was not Whole Foods. It wasn't even a Bi-Lo. But it did have an ATM where he got some cash, and it at least resembled a grocery store, so he was able to find some canned sweet potatoes, cans of black-eyed peas and green beans, a ham steak, Rice Krispies, marshmallows, real butter, eggs, Oreos, chocolate ice cream, tea bags, and (miracle of miracles) a box of grits. Combined with what he already had back at the house, he thought this would get him through a couple of days and give him time to develop a real shopping list.

As he came around the end of an aisle and headed to the only active checkout, he noticed that a man was hurriedly replacing the girl who had been checking people out. Jim wheeled up and began unloading his cart, and the man, who he noticed had a nametag that said "Manager, H. Miller," began running his items through the scanner.

"You the human one?"

"I guess you could put it that way."

"What are they like?"

"Think about the smartest person you ever met and make them just a little smarter. Then pretend that person taught themselves Chinese using one of those computer language programs. Then imagine that person gets dumped out in western China, where nobody speaks English, the Chinese dialect is a little different from what was on the computer, the customs and manners are really strange, and there's no way to get home again. That's how the Aliens feel."

"What did she do to that guy in the restaurant today?"

"Just put a little scare into him. He'll be fine."

"How'd she do it?"

"They really don't tell me the technical stuff."

"So what's the deal with the software company?"

"It will be almost all human, but the Aliens will tell us enough to give us a little edge on the competition. We make some money, you sell more groceries, the world gets better software. Win-win for everybody."

"And what do they get?"

"A place to live outside a spaceship."

"That'll be $43.95"

That seemed a little high to Jim for what he had bought, but he figured he better not complain about the only grocery store in town, so he swiped his new credit card, watched it process normally, took the offered receipt, picked up his two bags of groceries and went to the car.

• • •

Pulling into the driveway, he noticed his mailbox door was open and something was sticking out. He stopped, got out, and retrieved a copy of the Western Times newspaper, accompanied by a subscription form. He glanced at Angie's mailbox down the street and saw the same newspaper sticking out of her mailbox. He wondered if next week's paper would list her as a new arrival in town and if that would go on the front page or in the community news section. Considering that this edition's lead story was somebody retiring from the local farm agency after thirty years of service, he thought maybe Angie would either make the front page or not be mentioned at all.

Ignoring the number of curtains in houses across the street being pulled back a little so people could peek out, he continued into the garage, put the door down, carried his groceries into the kitchen and put them away. Unfolding his tablet on the counter, he listened, as he fried up the ham steak and microwaved the peas, to both the local and national news for any references to Aliens in Kansas, but heard nothing. He ate half the ham and the entire can of peas, then put the leftover ham in a baggie and into the refrigerator. After cleaning up, he walked a couple of steps out the back door and saw a door that appeared to go into the garage. It wasn't even locked, and a quick peek let him know it was a shed with a riding mower and other lawn care stuff. Again he wondered how much of this outdoor activity he was expected to do himself and how much could be contracted out to some thirteen-year-old.

Seeing nothing else but lots of dirt and a little grass, he went back inside and ventured down into the basement. The recreation room was concrete floor and walls, ceiling lights, a ping pong table with paddles and balls still in the boxes on top, and a couple of chairs. There was also a washer and dryer and rack to hang clothes on and a treadmill with lots of bells and whistles. Beyond that was a solid steel door that opened into a room with a couple of cots, two folding chairs, shelves stocked with lots of bottles of water and dried food, a camp toilet, a vent in the ceiling, several flashlights and stocks of batteries, and a big first aid kit.

Even knowing where the tunnel opening was supposed to be, it took him several minutes to find the place where a section of the shelves could swing back. After that, it was another minute of searching to find the hidden latch that had to be flipped open. Behind the shelves was another door with a metal plate indicating where to push. He pushed, but nothing happened. He looked for a lock, but there wasn't one. Going for the obvious, he put his hand on the metal door plate, looked straight at it, and said, "Jim King." The door swung open a little to his touch, he pushed, and it opened fully to reveal a well-lit corridor ending less than ten yards away in another door of the same type. Satisfied for now, he stepped back and the door closed on its own. He pushed the shelves back into place and retreated up the stairs.

The rest of the evening was spent reading the Western Times from front to back (all eight pages of it) and deciding that while the upcoming cakewalk at the Methodist church social sounded interesting, he thought it was a little early to show any interest in a religious affiliation. He went ahead and used his tablet to subscribe to the newspaper though. After that he moved on to reviewing resumes for the other positions he would have a say in hiring, then spent a few minutes reading what Wikipedia had to say about High Plains farming, semi-arid climates, and wheat. He then caught the ten o'clock news on the big-screen TV in the den before turning in for the night, wondering as he drifted off if this had been a good day or a bad one.

· · ·

The next morning he made it a point to arrive at work before eight o'clock. Taking the direct route up Carrie Avenue, he saw the large, golden wheat-colored apartment complex that appeared to have sprouted from a field a block to the west on the south side of 40. Arriving at the office building, he noticed that there were fewer painting trucks in the lot and more furniture trucks, but he wasn't sure if that was an indicator of the status of the construction or the starting hours of furniture suppliers. Mabel was not at her desk, so he went straight to his office and spent the first few minutes figuring out all the electronic controls to the various monitors and speakers. Just as he was thinking he understood what knob controlled what, Angie knocked and stuck her head in.

"We heard back from the top candidate for the Business Division job. You up for a nine o'clock teleconference?"

"Sure. While you're here, I noticed there was only one candidate for the secretary job."

"Executive secretary."

"Executive secretary, senior administrative assistant, deputy grand poohbah, whatever. Why only one?"

"A really good secretary that doesn't hate Aliens or the late king of the planet is evidently hard to find."

"This one seems very overqualified. Double major in English and theatre at Chapel Hill, ten years working her way up to an editor slot at UNC Press. What makes you think she would even want the job?"

"There are some personal factors that don't show up on the vita."

"Care to share?"

"Married straight out of college, two daughters. One evening the husband stops for a beer or twenty before picking the older daughter up from a friend's birthday party. Ran a stop sign. Crash. Older daughter killed outright. Husband spends two months in the hospital, three months on home care, another three in outpatient rehab. As soon as he can drive again, he sneaks out one night while the wife is tending the sick other kid, gets out on the interstate, cuts across the median and accelerates straight into the front of a semi-tractor-trailer doing eighty. Life insurance won't pay, of course. She's already up to her eyeballs in medical bills, even after the medical insurance pays what it will. The younger daughter has down syndrome. The Disappearance occurs."

"Damn."

"UNC Press has to reorganize. Budget cuts lay her off. She tries to sell the house to pay her debts, but of course there's a housing surplus, so she can't even pay off the mortgage. She ends up living with her mother in a little town named Mount Olive in eastern North Carolina."

"Tobacco country."

"Used to be."

"Anyway, we think she might be interested in making a move."

"That does sound like a possibility."

"Teleconference with her at, say, two o'clock?"

"OK."

"Lunch after the first interview? I think we need to go back to Stephens Restaurant."

"Do you like living dangerously?"

"I want to try that pie."

"Whatever."

"I'll be back a few minutes before nine."

She went back to her office, and he pulled out the vita for the first candidate and reviewed it.

• • •

At five of nine, there was a knock at the door and Angie entered.

"Ready?"

"If you are."

"Cameras work better if we sit on the sofa facing the monitors."

"Makes sense. Let me turn on a few monitors."

"We can do that from here."

He moved to the sofa and placed his tablet on the coffee table. She touched one of her gadgets to the side of the tablet.

"Little upgrade. Say 'Magdalena,' only sing it like this."

She demonstrated a four-note tune that went up in pitch on the third note and was twice as long on that note as the other three notes.

"You're kidding."

"You only have to come close."

He tried it. The tablet responded, "Yes, Jim?"

"Just tell her what you need. She puts the other computer voice recognition systems to shame."

"Really."

"Really," said Magdalena.

"OK, we need to start a teleconference with Dr. Pankaja Panda, the candidate for the director of the Business Division."

The office lights faded a little except for the ones aimed at the sofa. The monitors on the wall turned on, one showing the two of them sitting on the sofa, another showing the conference line connection status and the time the call started; then one brought up the face of an Indian woman of about forty with already greying hair.

"Dr. Panda, can you hear me?"

"Yes, I can see and hear you fine."

"Very good. Dr. Panda, I'm Jim King, this is Angie Winston, and we're with Sharon Springs Software. Thank you for agreeing to this interview at such a late hour in India."

"No problem."

"You read the details of the position that we sent you?"

"Yes. It looks like a very exciting position, somewhat similar to what I am doing now, though the products would be for a wider and more demanding market. I suspect I would also have to manage a more diverse group of people, but that would be an interesting challenge."

"You have a very impressive resume. University of Delhi, Cambridge, PhD from MIT, two-year post-doc at Stanford, ten years running a very successful software development company in New Delhi. There is no question you have the training and experience for the Business Division director position here, so we would like to talk a little bit about your personal situation, if you don't mind."

"I understand."

"Dr. Panda, our offices are located in a very small town in a rural area. Would that be a problem for you?"

"I admit that would be a change. Even when I was in America, I lived in big cities. But I did travel some, so I think I have some idea of what I would be getting into. I think I could adapt. There are suppliers of Indian spices on the internet that could ship me what I need for a home-cooked meal when I get the urge, if they are not available in any of the grocery stores there."

"It's grocery store, singular."

"Oh my."

"But I think Mr. Miller would consider expanding what he stocks if there turn out to be several Indian families living here."

"Yes. I'm sure. No doubt there would be a period of adjustment, but I'm sure I would enjoy living in the States again. Even in a small town."

"Is there a reason you want to leave your current position?"

"Mr. King, to be frank, when I finished my studies I did not want to return to India. I very much prefer the openness of the American society. But there were certain organizations and individuals who had provided financial support with the understanding that I would return. Certain obligations, if you will. A combination of circumstances—certain debts being paid, some family members dying, a set amount of time passing, the Disappearances, etc.—have recently allowed me to complete all my obligations here."

"I see."

"Mr. King, do you know much about Indian culture?"

"A few basics. I have worked in the past with Indians who have moved to the States."

"India is changing, but if I tell you that I am an unmarried woman from an upper-caste family who has adopted an orphan baby girl who probably is of the untouchables caste, would you have any insight into my personal situation?"

"Enough to understand that life might be much easier for both of you here."

"Yes."

"Which perhaps brings up another topic. This is confidential, but one of the reasons we believe we are going to have an advantage over our competition is that we may have some technical input from the Aliens. Would dealing with the Aliens be a problem for you?"

There was one of those long pauses where you thought at first that the screen had frozen. Then you noticed small movements around the eyes that said the wheels were furiously turning trying to figure out all the implications of the previous statement.

"You have contact with the Aliens?"

"Let's just say we have established a channel of communication."

"How have you managed to get anything out of them when no one else has?"

"That's proprietary information."

The good doctor said something in one of the Indian languages that probably should have been untranslatable. Angie glanced down at her tablet in her lap and smiled.

"Oh, excuse me."

"Doctor, I need you to be honest with me. I can't afford to hire you, move you all the way over here, then have you quit the first time you have to deal with anything Alien. Would working with the Aliens be a problem for you?" Jim asked.

"Well, to be bloody honest, it would be mixed emotions. Exciting, of course, to have access to some of their advanced technology. Challenging as well, no doubt. I understand why they did it. Even read several of the peer-reviewed papers by the human scientists, though some of the biology was beyond my training. I accept it had to be. But there is still a good bit of emotional pain involved. I had family, friends . . . Even the girl I adopted is an orphan because of—"

Angie spoke for the first time.

"All of that is very understandable, Dr. Panda. No one is expecting you to be their biggest fan. To try to put it in your terms, the Aliens are like a different caste, perhaps a higher caste with some unpleasant history. But this is a new day, a new set of rules still under development. Could you come here and help develop that new set of rules?"

Again, the screen seemed to freeze for a second.

"Yes, I could do that. Detachment is a virtue. I could do that."

"And if we did offer you the position, how soon could you be here?"

"Personally, I could leave within a few days, but it would probably take months to get the necessary visas and green cards. Especially for the baby."

"We have made some arrangements in advance with the State Department and the Indian government. If we offer you the job, you would receive all the papers you need within twenty-four hours."

"Then I could leave around the end of the week, depending on when I could get a flight. But I don't believe anyone could get all the legal papers that quickly."

"Give us a little time to talk and check recommendations."

"Certainly."

"Anything else, Jim?"

"No, I think that covers it. It was very nice speaking to you, Dr. Panda. You will hear from us again soon."

"Thank you."

And the connection was cut.

"Well?"

"I checked her recommendations by hacking into emails and phone calls. Both employees and competitors speak well of her, even in private. I'll forward you the highlights."

"Ah yes, no secrets from the Aliens."

"We needed to know what she really thought about us. In the process we found out what other people thought about her. Read what I send you and we can talk at lunch."

She went back to her office. He stared at the image on the screen still showing the live picture of the sofa. Coming back to the present, he sang, "Magdalena."

"Yes, Jim?"

"You can revert all the electronics to normal."

"Yes, Jim."

And she did.

"Magdalena?"

"Yes?"

"What am I going to do about her?"

"I assume you are referring to Angie?"

"Yes."

"I'm good at answering questions, Jim, but I'm not that good."

"OK, just show me all these hacked emails from Angie."

And she did, which kept him busy until lunchtime.

• • •

When they got back to Stephens Restaurant, there were two workmen in line waiting for a table who started to step aside. Jim lightly touched Angie's arm to get her to stop, then waved the two men back into line. He then leaned into Angie and whispered in her ear.

"You want respect, not fear."

Still, the wait was not long and nobody seemed to storm out.

Within a couple of minutes they were escorted to a booth. They both noticed the shotgun now bolted high up on the wall, over an old sign made of wood with "My country, may it always be right, but right or wrong, my country" burned into it. Susie quickly approached.

"I wasn't sure you folks would be coming back after yesterday."

"And not try that French silk pie? We had to come back for that."

"You just want the pie, or you want lunch in front of it?"

"I think I'll try the mushroom hamburger today, with fries, of course. And a Coke."

"I'll go for the grilled chicken sandwich, with coleslaw instead of fries, please. Iced tea to drink."

"And then two pieces of pie."

"You got it."

Susie moved away to put their order in, and the conversations at the other tables gradually resumed enough for Angie and Jim to talk quietly.

"The candidate this morning, you read the recommendations?"

"Yes. Very competent manager, highly respected, if you ignore the comments about her gender, marital status, possible sexual orientation, and possible background of the baby. It's a major achievement to get as far as she did in that environment. Technically excellent, of course. I can certainly see why she would want to move back to the States."

"I think she's a couple of cuts above the other candidates for that job."

"Are you suggesting that we go ahead and offer her the job without talking to the other candidates?"

"You've read their resumes; are they at the same level?"

"As far as technical expertise, no. Maybe not even as managers. But are you satisfied with her responses to the personal questions?"

"I think so. I'm not sure we're going to get much better responses that we can believe. At least she was very honest. Are you satisfied?"

"Well, like you said, I'm not sure I'd trust totally positive responses."

"So we can go ahead on this one?"

"Yes. One down, eight to go."

"I'll send her a full offer and get started on the government paperwork as soon as I get back to the office."

And the drinks arrived.

"Here you go."

"Thank you."

"My boss wants to know when the rest of the people at the software company will be arriving. He wants to be sure we keep enough food in stock."

"Some will be trickling in next week, but it will be two or three months before we get all the jobs filled."

"Is it really going to be three hundred people?"

"Three hundred employees. Probably twice that when you include the spouses and children."

"My God, no wonder they're moving all those trailers in behind the school. I'll go check your order."

When Susie returned, the mushroom burger turned out to be a double patty with an inch of mushrooms cooked in a brown sauce on top of the meat, with lettuce and tomato. The grilled chicken was almost an entire chicken breast between slabs of wheat bread with lettuce, tomato, mayo, mustard, and Thousand Island dressing. Jim began to wonder if it would be safe to take walks for exercise around town or if he needed to just cut out eating anything except lunch.

Just as they finished, Susie reappeared with two slices of French silk pie and poured a refill for Jim's tea. Jim asked Susie a question as she was setting down the pies.

"Susie, you mentioned the schools. Did you go to school here?"

"Kindergarten through twelfth. No other schools around here."

"You think you got a good education?"

"Well, they tried. My own fault if I didn't. It's just hard sometimes to see the point in some of it if you're not going off to college. And I got a little wild toward the end of high school. But the school is ranked pretty high, I hear tell. Classes are real small, so the teachers know who's getting it and who isn't. There were only twelve in my graduating class, and most of us had been in all the classes together all our lives. It's like the football team. We only have enough students to play eight-man, but everybody plays that wants to, and half the town comes to the games and knows exactly who does well and who doesn't. Nobody gets lost in this school, that's for sure."

"That sounds pretty good as schools go."

"Yeah, I guess it was. Enjoy your pie."

The pies were wedges about one sixth of an entire pie, black and smooth, with a rich chocolate taste that had a dark chocolate tang to it.

"Ohh, I love this pie."

"You love anything sweet."

"Yes, but I love some sweet things more than others."

After savoring the pie and the moment, they didn't wait for the bill, but Jim placed a couple of twenties on the table, and they headed back to the office.

• • •

A few minutes before two, Angie came back to Jim's office. Jim asked Magdalena to start the teleconference, and Becky Davis's face appeared on the big monitor screen. She was mid-thirties, brown hair, traces of youthful freckles, pretty, but lines starting to appear around the eyes.

"Ms. Davis, how is the connection?"

"Just fine, thank you."

"I'm Jim King and this is Angie Winston."

"Nice to meet you."

"Did you get the additional information we sent you about the position?"

"Yes, and I had a question about that."

"Yes?"

"Is that salary range right? It says $60,000-100,000 plus, depending on qualifications and experience."

"Let me answer that one. I think Jim might try to soft-pedal this a little. This is a very responsible position. It's not some nine-to-five answer the phones and take dictation. You work when Jim needs you to work. Jim and I basically are coordinating the work of three separate companies that need to feed off each other's innovations. He needs somebody who decides who gets in to see him, who gets a phone call, and who has to settle for an e-mail. You make sure he gets what he needs and that everybody else feels like they are getting what they need from him to get their jobs done. You also edit every document that comes out of his office, plug into all the gossip networks so he knows what is actually going on in the company, and deal with some very confidential and sensitive information with the best judgement and discretion possible. Believe me, you will earn every dollar you get."

"You understand that I know how to use computers, but I know nothing about programming them."

"That's not your job. There will be plenty of others who can do the technical tasks. We're looking for a people person who knows how to be loyal to her boss."

"Ah."

Jim took over the interview.

"Ms. Davis, let me pick up here. On paper, you are obviously overqualified for this job. But there are certain circumstances that might make you understand why we think you might be appropriate for this job. First of all, we are located in a very small town."

"Well, it would have to go some to be smaller than Mt. Olive."

"Sharon Springs makes Mt. Olive look like a metropolis."

"You're kidding."

"One grocery store. Five churches, but the Methodist preacher rides a circuit on Sundays. More cattle than people, more wheat than anything."

"But we are installing one heck of a Wi-Fi system," Angie added.

"No big cities for hundreds of miles. One of those old-fashioned small towns where everybody literally does know everybody else."

"That's not all bad."

"So, that would not be a problem for you?"

"Might be a little bit of a relief, actually."

"OK. I understand you are currently between engagements."

"UNC Press says they want me back as soon as funding permits."

"But you could relocate quickly if you were offered the position?"

"For the right salary I could be there tomorrow."

"We were thinking maybe next week."

"Not a problem."

"There is one other thing. This is confidential, Ms. Davis, but we have developed, shall we say, access to some of the Aliens' technology. This position might require contact with the Aliens. Would that be a problem for you?"

"You mean, like, talk to an Alien, on the phone or something?"

"Or something."

"Damn."

"Perhaps now you understand why we are looking for people who are overqualified. There are challenges to this job that we haven't even imagined yet."

"Holy s— Oops."

"So, again, and please be totally honest, would that be a problem for you?"

"Mr. King, my daughter was Disappeared."

"We all lost somebody."

"She was my precious."

"And I'm sure you will hold her in your heart forever. I'm not offering you consolation here. And I am definitely not offering an opportunity for revenge."

"Becky, what Jim is trying to say but saying very badly is that many people are still grieving and that's very understandable. But some people have been able to move past their grief, look at life as it is now, and start over. That's what we are offering here, a chance to start over. But starting over means not forgetting the past, but realizing that it is the past. There is a future here in Sharon Springs, but only if you can let the past be the past. That's what we are asking you. Can you come out here to the middle of nowhere, start fresh, leave the past behind like it's another country, and deal with the totally new?"

"I don't know how to answer that. I mean, I don't blame them anymore, not like it was personal. It was so impersonal. I mean, they didn't even decide who to . . . you know. They dumped that off on some poor dupe who sold out for money and women. I understand that I don't have to forget, I just have to forgive, and that the forgiving isn't for them, it's for me. I have to be able to forgive to stop the ache in my own heart.

"I learned that lesson the hard way when my husband was at fault in a car accident that killed my other daughter. I had to find a way to stop hating him, especially after he went out and killed himself. Oh, but that hurt like hell, forgiving him. But he was dead; hating him wasn't going to do anything to him, only to me. But these Aliens are still here, and my daughter isn't. I'm really not sure what I would say or do the first time I talked to one. Believe me, getting this job would solve a lot of my problems, but I'm not sure it would solve this one."

"Thank you for being so honest with us," Angie said. "It means more to me than I can say. But let's try this. Say I was an Alien. You can say anything you want to me. Say I am the first Alien you ever got to talk to, and you can say anything you want. Say it to me."

"I'm not sure I can do that."

"Please, try. Just whatever comes to you. If I was an Alien, what would you say to me?"

"OK, OK, uh . . . Do you have any idea what you did? She was just a little girl. So loving. So she wasn't quite normal; she loved me. She loved her sister and her father and she held me while I cried after they died. She loved me, and I loved her, and you left me so all alone. Do you understand that? Do you have any idea what that is like? Do you?"

"Yes, actually, I do. Our tears are just as salty as yours, Becky. There were many hard choices and heartbreaks and passings in that spaceship in all those generations, just like there were here. And there were just as many tears among us when we realized what had to be done as there were among you when it was over. We are having to live with this as much as you are. But we have gotten very good at doing what has to be done. So here we are, trying to find a way to move on, to find something better."

"You mean, you're a . . . ?"

"Yes. An Alien."

"God."

"Can you live with that, Becky? Can you sit at a desk not far from my office and help the very human Jim here find a way to deal with me and others like me? It's going to be a new world, Becky. Do you want to live in it?"

"Damn, damn, damn."

"Tell you what. Let Jim and me talk. If we're interested, we'll send you a written offer by e-mail today. But we would have to have a reply by the next day."

"I understand."

"Do you understand that my presence here is not something you are to talk about?"

"Yes. I get that."

"Thank you, Becky. You will hear from us one way or another very soon."

And the connection was cut.

"There is absolutely nothing in any of her communications that would indicate anything remotely approaching violence or revenge. She is just a very injured woman who would adapt quickly to a new situation."

"You seem very sure of that."

"We have profiled her extensively."

"More than the others?"

"It's very individualized. We have to do enough to be sure. Absolutely sure, when they will be this close to us."

"You really seem to want me to hire her," Jim said.

"We think she would be a good fit for the job."

"You're not giving me much of a choice."

"Another one of our bad habits, remember?"

"So, tell me about your heartbreak that made you able to empathize with her so much."

"It was when they told me I had to work with you."

"Human psychologists would say there is a certain amount of avoidance in that answer."

"Human psychologists don't know Aliens very well."

"So maybe we better hire one."

"When hell freezes over, to use the colloquial. So, I can make an offer to Becky Davis?"

"Better make it a good one; I think she just might tell us no."

"I think she just needs a night to sleep on it. I'll start setting up teleconferences for the other positions."

And she went back to her office for the rest of the day.

19.

THE VISITOR

It was that evening, after he had eaten the other half of the ham and the entire can of sweet potatoes for super and was finishing up mixing a big batch of Rice Krispy candy, that Magdalena surprised him by speaking without being spoken to.

"Hey, Jim."

"Magdalena?"

"Yes. There's a car turning into your driveway."

"Any idea who?"

"Hank Sweat. He owns a big wheat farm. He's also one of the Wallace County commissioners."

"OK. I wonder what he wants."

"You want me to guess?"

"No, I'm sure he'll tell us."

Jim quickly stuck the last pan of candy in the refrigerator and was washing his hands when the doorbell rang. Drying his hands on a dishcloth, he answered the door. Hank Sweat looked exactly like a Kansas wheat farmer, about sixty years old, well-weathered skin, real cowboy hat, dress coat over work shirt and jeans.

"Mr. King?"

"Yes."

"You're the normal person, right?"

"Well, I'm not sure how normal I am, but I'm a human being, if that's what you're asking."

"Yeah. Right. Mr. King, my name is Hank Sweat. I'm one of the local county commissioners. I was wondering if I could talk to you for a few minutes."

"Sure. Come in."

Jim stepped aside to let Hank enter, then closed the door behind him. A gesture at the seating in the living room got Hank to sit on the sofa, so Jim took one of the armchairs.

"I hope I'm not interrupting your supper or anything."

"No, no. Just finished cleaning up."

"I would have called, but I didn't have your home number and I didn't want to contact you at your office."

"If you're trying to keep this meeting secret, Mr. Sweat, you're out of luck. I suspect at least half my neighbors across the road already know you're here. I very quickly learned that there are no secrets in this town."

"Oh, call me Hank. Everybody does. And your neighbors across the street are not the ones I'm concerned about."

"Hank, I repeat, there are no secrets in this town."

"Well, whatever. Jim, to the point, some of the other officials in the county and the city, well, they sort of nominated me to talk to you, see if you could tell us what's really going on."

"Going on?"

"Yeah, sure. I mean, we all were informed about the software company moving in and saw the business licenses and things. We couldn't figure why anybody would put some computer company way out here, but we were notified about how many new families to expect and how some of them might be legal immigrants and that kind of thing. But nobody ever said anything about a bunch of Aliens moving in and taking over."

"Ten is hardly a bunch. And taking over is not what's going to happen. All the people running the county and the town can keep doing what they're doing. The Aliens are just going to be helping us develop some software and make a little money."

"Ten is it?"

"That's what I'm told. And I have no reason to doubt it."

"Well, Jayne Pearce, out at the Western Times, the newspaper, she says she tried to get an e-mail out to the Associated Press and the New York Times and several other papers about an Alien being here, and nothing would go. No text or even phone calls either."

"We're trying to keep a low profile right now. Anything that doesn't have to do with Aliens will go through fine."

"Still, you can't say that's not taking over, at least a little bit."

"We're just trying to keep this a quiet little town, not a media circus. You should appreciate that."

"All those construction workers from out of town, what happens to them? Some of them have started heading back where they came from as the work dries up."

"And they will tell their family and friends they saw an actual Alien in Sharon Springs, Kansas. And some people will believe them and others will ask them what they've been smoking. But sooner or later somebody will actually arrive here to see the Alien. We accept that."

"And then what happens?"

"Hank, do you remember Andy Griffith?"

"The TV actor? Sure."

"When he retired, he moved to the Outer Banks of North Carolina. Barrier islands; ocean, beaches, sand dunes, bays and marshes on the other side. Some places barely wide enough for one road. Two or three little towns, but no forest to hide a house behind. His house was right there, out in the open. But it wasn't marked on any tourist map, no sign out front. And when the tourists would ask the locals where Andy Griffith lived, they would give them directions, maybe even an address. And the tourists would end up at some restaurant or souvenir shop or maybe at the dead end of a road with ocean on the other side of the barrier. That prevented a lot of traffic jams."

"You're expecting us to protect them?"

"I'm expecting you to protect yourself. Unless you know what to look for, you can't tell an Alien just by looking. If they do a couple of things to blend in, you can't tell at all. Surely you've got a couple of people in this town that will try to make a few bucks pretending to be Aliens so they can get paid for interviews or having pictures taken with an Alien. And I'm sure some high school pranksters will be glad to lead some reporter on a merry chase looking for the Aliens working in the bean-processing company putting secret Alien beans in with the pinto beans. The alternative is to have five hundred reporters camped out on every lawn in town trying to take a picture of the Aliens."

"What about the government? Won't they send somebody out here?"

"Oh, they may want to, but I suspect somebody will talk them out of it. Aliens can be very persuasive when it comes to governments."

"And what are they going to persuade us to do?"

"Keep quiet. Go about your business. Don't freak out when they walk into a restaurant or grocery store. They might even show up for a high school football game, you never know. You might have to explain some of the rules to them, but they'll figure out which team to root for. You're going to be getting people from India, China, maybe even California, moving into town. Some of them will be more unfamiliar with the way things are done here than the Aliens are. Some of them will also look more different and have stranger accents. The Aliens are just a few really smart people with really neat stuff who want to help us improve our computer programs and get along. You're worried about the wrong people, Hank. It's the locals who can't accept that life here is changing that could cause the trouble."

"Well, maybe."

"The Aliens don't want to interfere any more than they have to in order to be safe. They're a little strange sometimes, but the ones I've met have been good people."

"Ten of 'em, eh?"

"That's what I'm told."

"And we don't get any say in the matter."

"We don't get a say in a lot of things, Aliens or no."

"Ain't that the truth. Well, Jim, I'll get out of your hair now, but let me know if there are any more surprises, OK? I've got an office in the courthouse on Main Street."

"I've driven past it."

Jim walked him to the door and flipped the switch for the outside lights. Hank got in his car and drove away. As soon as Jim closed the door, his tablet he had left in the kitchen beeped.

"Yes?"

Angie's voice came from the tablet.

"What was that all about?"

"County commissioner was fishing for information and expressing his concern about the Aliens."

"And?"

"And we need to be very good neighbors to all God's children."

"I think we can handle that."

"I sure hope so."

"See you in the morning."

"Roger that."

• • •

The next morning Jim got up a little early to cut the Rice Krispy candy into squares and load them into a couple of gallon baggies. On the way to work he took a left at the first intersection and took North Charlotte Avenue so he could drive by the apartment complex. It was big even by Atlanta standards, but he didn't think it had 300 units, so some people would have to move into other places around town.

Entering the building he noticed that Mabel had decided it was not good to get to work later than her bosses, so he stopped.

"Care for a Rice Krispy candy square?"

"Rice Krispy candy? I haven't had one of those in years."

"Angie loves them."

"That's a surprise."

"Why?"

"I mean, you know, with her figure and all."

"Oh, she's got a real sweet tooth."

"Well, good to know. And thanks."

Jim put the baggies on the coffee table in his office just as Angie came in.

"Oh, how sweet of you."

"I figured you might need something to keep you going."

"Well, I have lined up a lot of interviews."

"You saw that Becky Davis is driving in, pulling a trailer, and says she will be here Monday. I told her where the apartments are."

"Yes, and I booked Dr. Panda and her daughter on a Delhi to Berlin to New York to Denver combination of flights. She gets in to Denver Sunday afternoon, but I told her to stay in Denver a day or two to adjust to the time change and buy a car. I set up a line of credit for her. She asked about taking a Greyhound bus and I told her that was possible, but then she wouldn't have much choice when it came to buying a car here."

"Sounds right."

"OK, let's get to it."

So, over the next three days they managed to hire a certified genius as chief researcher, a Mao Xihong, who left Beijing at sixteen to attend UCLA, which she blew through in three years before moving to Cal Tech, where she had just defended her PhD dissertation on a new programming language that made it easier to program the multidimensional math the physicists exploring string theory needed. She seemed to be one of those nerds who weren't interested in what was going on in the world around them as long as somebody was handing her a programming puzzle to solve. She did say she was desperate to get out of the smog and had looked western Kansas up as having the cleanest air of any place that had job openings, even though the smog was drastically reduced in California already. They balanced her inexperience by snagging a former General Electric section chief named Henry Wengen, who had hit retirement age and was looking for a company that didn't believe in retirement, to be the director of the Research and Development Division.

For the director of the personal software line, they hired the unusually named Texas FitzGerald from Kent, Texas, a town almost as small as Sharon Springs. He had graduated from the University of Texas-El Paso, gone to the main campus in Austin for graduate work, dropped out to start his own company developing applications for laptops and tablets, grown it into a multimillion-dollar business, and sold out to Google. He was looking for something else to do that would get him out of the hustle and bustle of a big city like Austin, and while he really didn't care much for Aliens, he did like the idea of living in a small town again.

The position of deputy director under Jim was the one that gave them problems. Angie said she was worried that someone with a lot of technical expertise would think they could elbow Jim out of the way and take over the top spot, but Jim thought the sign of a good leader was hiring people smarter than he was. As it turned out, they didn't end up with much to fight about. The first two they interviewed just didn't cotton to the idea of a town so small there wasn't a bus line, and the third got as far as the question about dealing with Aliens before deciding this wasn't a pool they wanted swim in.

Option number four was a mousy-looking, fortyish woman of Arab descent named Olga Ali who had been born and raised in Sweden when her parents got out of Syria long before the troubles started. She had been a double major in business and computer science at the University of Gothenburg, gotten a job with the Norwegian oil company that was drilling in the North Sea, which led to a stationing in Aberdeen, Scotland, where some graduate studies in economics at the university there led to a job with Shell in the Netherlands, who sent her to New Orleans after the oil spill to manage some of the cleanup work, after which she took a job running the computer support division of Valero Oil in Texas rather than going back to Europe. She spoke five languages fluently and a couple more enough to get around in-country, had worked as a manager in some of the more male-dominated businesses in the world, and realized there wasn't much long-term future in the oil business anymore. She had grown up in a small town in Sweden, so while she didn't like the idea of a small town, it didn't send her screaming into the night either. As for Aliens, she didn't think they could be any more weird to deal with than some of the people she had met in the oil business. Her accepting an offer late Friday afternoon left just the three deputy positions in the divisions to deal with the next week.

During those three days they also, just to be fair, tried out the other lunch places in town, Penny's Diner and the restaurants at the two hotels. Nobody attacked them, and Angie's little gadget never detected anything wrong with the food, but nobody asked them how their day was going either. Not only that, the food just didn't have the pizazz or sheer bulk of Stephens Restaurant, so it was obvious what would become "the" lunch place.

• • •

When Saturday came, Jim got up early and climbed into one of the sweat suits he found in his closet so everybody who saw him would know he was just out for some exercise, and jogged and walked around a good section of the town. He noticed that the four townhouses now looked all ready for occupancy unless there was something on the inside that still needed work. The apartment complex on North Charlotte had an "Apartments for Rent, Furnished or Unfurnished, No Lease Required" sign out front and one car in front of the leasing office/clubhouse. The hardware store opened early on Saturdays, but he figured he already had the tools he needed, whatever they were. More "For Sale" signs were up in front of empty lots and houses in the middle of being renovated. There were even a couple of new houses being built by the wild real estate speculators of Sharon Springs.

Back home, he showered, dressed, carefully put together a grocery shopping list, and headed for Miller's Food Store, as had evidently everybody else in town. By sheer chance, as he wheeled his buggy into the first aisle he almost literally ran into Susie.

"Oops. Sorry."

"Oh, hi, Mr. King."

"Susie. Nice to see you."

"Haven't seen you for a few days."

"We tried out some of the other places, but I'm pretty sure we'll be back on Monday."

"Yeah, they're really not much competition."

"I think I'm going to have to agree."

"I hear Hank Sweat has been pestering you."

"No problem. He was just curious about some things."

"He and everybody else in town. 'Have you seen the Alien? What are they like? Are they going to take over the town?'"

"Well, you've met Miss Winston; what do you think?

"She's pretty, that's for sure. She'd be beautiful with a better hairstyle and a nice dress. So it's 'Miss'?"

"They have different words for marital status that don't quite translate into English. I guess 'Ms.' might be better, but that's not exactly the same either. They are a lot like us, but not exactly. Every now and then I get surprised."

"Well, she seems nice, at least as customers go."

"What about you? Miss, Ms., or Mrs.?"

"Just Susie, Susie Reynolds."

"Well, nice to meet you, Susie Reynolds."

"This your first time in Miller's?"

"I ran in a few days ago for milk and eggs, but this is the first time for serious shopping."

"Well, here, give me your list and I'll walk you through while I get mine. There's a lot more here than you think, but some things they only have one or two of, so they can be hard to find. Just stick with me and I'll take care of you."

So he handed her his list, and as they walked through the store she told him about her church (Baptist); her friends (one of the other waitresses, an elementary school teacher, and a clerk at the courthouse, all of whom she had known her entire life); the prospects for the high school football team for the coming season (they would probably do better in basketball); how the Strand Theater was only open on Friday and Saturday nights but always had a double feature, which she had heard was a rare thing now; how the Western Times had most of the official news, but either she or Mabel could fill him in on the unofficial stuff, if he was interested; and that the county fair in the fall was the big event of the year, so he better not miss it. After checking out, she waited for him to check out, then he helped her load her car and waved goodbye before loading his own car and heading home.

• • •

After a pimento cheese sandwich for lunch and a quick check of the news sites, he wondered if he should cut the grass, review resumes, or watch sports on TV. Then Angie called.

"Yes?"

"Could I come over for a minute?"

"Sure."

"Be right there."

Glancing out the kitchen window, he saw the gate between their backyards swing open, so he went to the back door and let her in.

"Want some iced tea?"

"Sure."

"Pull up a chair. What's up?"

"Well, I think I've got the financial system and all the employment regulations figured out, but I'm not so sure about this weekend thing. Am I supposed to be doing something besides getting ready for all the new people coming in?"

"Well, the thing about weekends is they're supposed to be the times you do things for yourself, not your job."

"Such as?"

"Such as catch up on a little sleep if you didn't get enough during the work week."

"Not necessary for me."

"Lots of people also do household chores: grocery shopping, laundry, yard work, minor house or car repairs, that kind of thing."

"I have plenty of food, clothes are clean. I hired Mabel's son to mow the grass, what there is of it. No repairs needed that I know of."

"People also play sports or get some kind of exercise. I took a little jog around town early this morning."

"I work out in my basement every day."

"There's also reading or surfing the internet or watching sports on TV; lots of the games are on Saturday or Sunday. Some people go out to eat sometime during the weekend, usually Friday or Saturday night or Sunday after church. That's another weekend thing, going to church on Sunday morning. You and I will probably be among the few heathens not in church tomorrow morning."

"Didn't you used to go to church?"

"Most of my life. In the South and in most small towns everywhere it's as much a social thing as religious. Church is where the potluck dinners are, where you meet your friends, where you flirt when you are young, where you talk politics when you get old, not just where you sing and pray."

"So should we . . . ?"

"Not yet. Let's get to know a few people first so we don't go in as strangers. Then we'll have to visit all the churches, just to be fair. And when your friends get here, we'll have to either not go to any or divide up and cover all the bases. Would not be good politics for all the Aliens to go to one church. I'm not sure you really want to do more than visit once or twice anyway; I have the sneaking suspicion that might prompt a little heresy. Most of these people believe Jesus died to save our souls, whatever that means, and if Jesus didn't also make an appearance on your planet, then either you don't have souls or you are in bad need of salvation. I suspect you might have a problem with either interpretation when it comes to getting along with poor old humans."

"I thought 'souls' was a Greek thing."

"It is. I'm a little bit of a heretic too."

"So, what do you think?"

"I think I am not now, nor have I ever been, God. Could we get back to weekends, where there are actual, real answers to questions, please?"

"Sure. So we scratch church tomorrow."

"People are also known to cook out, grilling meat and vegetables over hot coals on a grill outside to give them a different, smoky flavor compared to fried, baked, or broiled, and then eating outside. This usually only works part of the year, when the weather is not too cold or too hot."

"OK. Something to look forward to."

"People with busy lives have also been known to cook food for the rest of the week, big roast meats or something like cakes that take an hour or longer, so they can just pull them out of the refrigerator for a quick meal during the work week."

"Makes sense."

"Weekends are also times to visit friends, go out to a movie, go on a date, all the social stuff that is hard to squeeze in Monday to Friday."

"My friends are coming in late tonight, but they will probably be adjusting to the time change and getting organized for Monday most of tomorrow."

"Ah, so the adventure begins."

"Yes. I'll introduce you on Monday."

"OK."

"So what sports are in season?"

"Right now? Baseball, golf, tennis. Football will be starting soon. Do you have sports?"

"Sure. There were some back on the planet that we didn't have room for in the sphere, but I watched recordings. A thing with a big field and a ball, sort of like your lacrosse or soccer. Various things in big pools of water that we couldn't do on the sphere."

"So, on the sphere?"

"Imagine weightless handball in teams. Virtual races on exercise bikes. Weightless swimming in artificially dense air. Mostly we just did things for exercise, though. We're really not competitive like you. We just like to be our best self, whatever that is. There may be good and bad to that."

"Care to amplify that remark?"

"No. So, what were you going to do this weekend?"

"Well, I did my grocery shopping. Ran into Susie the waitress at Miller's and she told me all about how to find things in the store. I told her we would probably be back at Stephens on Monday."

"OK."

"I've got enough clean clothes to go another week, I will talk to Mabel on Monday about having her son cut my grass too, and I hope I don't need to fix anything about the house or the car yet. I'm lousy at fixing things anyway."

"Tell me before you try to fix anything. Not everything here is standard issue."

"I suspected not. I do want to do a little cooking, but that was planned for tomorrow so it would be fresher through the week. Eventually I guess I need to get on the internet and order a few decorations for the house, but I want to live in it for a while, figure out what I really want. So, I was down to reading a book or watching the baseball game on TV, then maybe rustling up a little supper. You ever watch baseball?"

"Just enough to know where 'striking out' came from before it meant not having sex with the girl. And the bases thing—'getting to first base,' etc."

"Yeah, baseball is the sexy sport. Hang out here for a while. I'll get the game on, zap us some popcorn, maybe figure out supper later."

"Sounds good."

So she stayed, and he spent the rest of the afternoon trying to explain baseball to an Alien while Kansas City beat the White Sox. Then he slipped a frozen pizza he had bought at Miller's that morning into the oven, and they sat around the kitchen table eating like life was normal. Then she went back through the fence to get ready for the Alien landing, and he looked up the infield fly rule and the definition of "foreign substance" in the baseball rule book on the internet.

20.

COME MONDAY

Come Monday morning he headed into work and noticed first that most of the construction trucks had moved west on 40 to the strip shopping center that was doing its best to appear overnight in the middle of a wheat field. The second thing he noticed was that there was a small, red pickup truck with North Carolina plates in the parking space next to his. Entering the building, he spotted Becky Davis, his new executive secretary, sitting in one of the lobby couches, dressed in business attire—green calf-length straight skirt and matching jacket over a white blouse. She stood as he entered.

"Mr. King?"

"Ah, Mrs. Davis. Welcome to Sharon Springs."

"Thank you."

"When did you get in?"

"Yesterday around noon."

"Did you find a place to stay?"

"Yes. Thank you. Like you suggested, I tried those apartments first. Evidently I'm one of the first; I got my pick of the one-bedrooms. They're very nice, very reasonable, and the manager had her two sons help me unload my trailer. I even had time to drive up to Goodland to turn in the trailer and get back before it got too dark."

"Good. Well, there's plenty to do, so let's started. First thing is an introduction."

They crossed over to Mabel.

"Mabel, this is Becky Davis, my executive secretary. Becky, this is Mabel Bently, the receptionist and expert on all things local."

"We sort of met when she came in," Mabel said. "Is she . . . ?"

"Becky is from North Carolina."

"OK, got it. Nice to meet you. Let me know if you need to know where anything is in town."

"Thank you. I'm sure I'll be asking dozens of questions."

"I'm not sure there are dozens of things to say about this town, but ask away."

He spied a big bowl of M&Ms on Mabel's desk.

"You thinking to get on Angie's good side?"

"Couldn't hurt."

"There may be some more sweet tooths coming in this week. If this gets expensive, let me know and we'll see what's in petty cash."

"OK."

"OK, Becky, let's get you started."

He guided her through the sets of double doors into the office area.

"This will be your desk. I'm right there, Angie Winston is just opposite. Her executive secretary will be in the desk across from you."

"Will she be a . . . ?"

"We haven't met, but I assume so."

"Oh boy."

"Not to worry. None of them have bitten me yet. Occasional awkward pauses in the conversations, but no biting."

"I just mean, you know, I'm still not sure how I—"

"As long as you don't bite or hit them, I think we'll be OK."

He walked around to the back of her desk and opened the middle drawer. Inside was a laptop computer. He placed it on the desk and stepped to the side so Becky could sit down.

"Open this up and see what happens."

She opened the computer and pressed the power button. A voice said, "Please place your right index finger on the scanner and say your name." Becky found the little fingerprint scanner and announced herself.

"Becky Davis."

"Welcome to Sharon Springs Software, Becky. We need to set you up in the system. For privacy, please use the headset in the drawer. I'll wait until you are ready."

"You go ahead and get set up. When you're ready, you will find a file of all the people we have hired so far under Personnel. Start with Dr. Panda and contact each of them and ask if there is anything we can do to help them with their relocation. Angie and I are going to be doing interviews most of the morning, but you can email me any questions and I'll reply as soon as I can."

"Uh, OK. Uh, Mr. King, I do have one question."

"Sure."

"I was just wondering when we get paid. The salary is great, it's just that—"

"It's the first of each month. Direct deposit to whatever bank account you designate, I guess when you set yourself up in the system this morning. If you don't have anything local, just ask Mabel which bank to use and enter what you can, fill the rest in later. And if you need a little advance to cover all those moving costs, just let me know. Not a problem. We're expecting several of the new hires to be tight until the first paycheck."

At that point, Angie entered, trailed by a young man. Angie was dressed a little better than usual in a blue skirt and matching shirt, but her hair was a little wilder, as if she was embracing her Alienness a little today with her compatriots arriving. The young man wore a blue business suit, minus the tie. He had dealt with the hair problem by getting a flat top, but two or three little black hairs akimbo even in the flat top gave away which planet his DNA came from. Otherwise, he looked exactly like a very tan Ricky Nelson when he first started singing a song at the end of each episode of Ozzie and Harriet.

"Oh, Becky, good, you're here."

"Hello, Ms. Winston."

"Jim, Becky, this is my executive secretary, Davey Jones."

Jim wasn't sure whether that was an allusion to the pirate with the underwater locker or the British singer in the TV show from the Sixties youth of his past life or not, but doubted anybody else would get the reference, so he let it pass by.

"Nice to meet you both."

"Welcome to Sharon Springs, Davey. I'm sure you and Becky will figure out how to manage us."

"I thought it was the other way—"

"He's using humor, Davey. Diffusing any awkwardness."

"Oh, right. Sorry. I'm still—"

"No problem. As Angie says, humor is always the last thing you learn in a new language. I'm sure Becky will help you keep your foot out of your mouth."

"Oh, unfortunate statements. I get that one."

"You know, Jim, I think we should take these two out to lunch with us today. Give Davey a little practice."

"Sounds good to me. Becky, maybe you can help Davey get started. Angie and I have an interview for one of the deputy director slots in a few minutes."

"I'll be right there."

And Angie went into her office and Jim went into his, leaving Becky and Davey staring at each other across her desk.

The morning turned out to be productive only in eliminating three candidates for deputy director jobs. Again, it was the small town that was the problem, and they never even got to the bit about the Aliens. After the third one withdrew his application, they headed out to lunch. Becky and Davey were waiting for them, so they piled into Jim's sedan and headed for Stephens Restaurant.

As they were driving off, Becky spoke up.

"I talked to Dr. Panda. She's in Denver and will be driving out this afternoon. I told her about the apartments, but she asked if there were any daycare agencies in town for her daughter. She's about three years old."

"I know there was a daycare room on the ground plan for the offices. Angie, any idea what the status of that is?"

"It's furnished, but we haven't hired any daycare staff yet. It's to be a local hire, if possible."

"OK, Becky, why don't you talk to Mabel this afternoon and find out if there is anything in town that could take a kid or two until we get up and running. Also draft a help wanted ad we could put in the Western Times and run that by me and Angie."

"Yes sir."

By then they were at Stephens. There was no line this time, but the only open seating for four was a table on the opposite side from where they sat the previous times. Jim spotted Hank Sweat and three other older men at another table nearby and gave him a nod of recognition, which was hesitantly returned. The hostess handed them menus and said, "Cindy will be with you in a moment." Davey looked a little confused by all the choices on the menu, so Angie helped out a little.

"It's faster to order off the lunch menu. I like the hamburgers, but Jim has tried the fish and the chicken sandwich. The portions are pretty big on everything we've tried."

"Drink refills only come with the coffee and tea. Otherwise, you just get a can. And this is on us, so get what you want."

They examined the menus for several minutes before Susie appeared.

"Sorry for the wait."

"Susie, this is my new executive secretary, Becky Davis, and Angie's executive secretary, Davey Jones. Susie Reynolds."

"Hi. Uh . . ."

"Becky is from North Carolina. Davey is not."

"Oh, OK. Well, welcome to Sharon Springs."

"Thank you."

"Aren't you a little out of your regular section?" Jim asked.

"Oh, Cindy is just a little uncomfortable serving . . . you know. I told her you were great tippers, but . . ."

Angie glanced up.

"Do you mean 'uncomfortable' as in scared out of her wits or 'uncomfortable' as in seething with rage?"

"Well, a little bit of both, but maybe not that strong. She lost a husband and a son."

Becky spoke up. "I lost a daughter. This is taking some getting used to for all of us."

"Yeah, I know. Listen, do you know what you want, or should I just get your drinks?"

Angie went with the all-American burger, fries, and a Coke. Becky opted for the chicken salad plate (chicken salad, sliced tomatoes, sliced cucumbers, and crackers) and tea. Jim experimented again, going for the ham and cheese sandwich with fries and tea. Davey decided to match Angie's order. After Susie left, Jim and Angie watched Becky and Davey try to read all the various sayings posted on the walls. Jim interrupted their rubbernecking.

"So, how have you two been getting along?"

There was a pause as they tried to figure out who would speak first.

"Becky has been very helpful."

"We're both kind of new at this. I think we're both set up in the system now. It even got me a bank account without having to go to the bank. It's amazing."

"Well, we are a cutting-edge software company; we better have a good computer system. How far did you get contacting the new employees?"

"We reached five of them. They're all on their way except for Mr. Wengen and Mr. FitzGerald. They are dealing with moving companies, so it's taking longer."

"Dr. Mao has one last meeting with her doctoral committee today, then will leave," added Davey.

At that point, Susie arrived with the drinks. As she put a glass of tea in front of Jim, she whispered in his ear, "Watch out for Hank Sweat; he and his buddies are up to something."

Jim managed not to react by looking directly at the table where Hank sat, instead just saying "Thank you" to Susie as if he were thanking her for the tea. Turning to Becky, he said, "It doesn't come sweet." Becky found the cup of sweeteners, took out a couple of Splenda, and passed it to Jim. He sweetened his tea with sugar and stirred it with the straw, then glanced up when the three men who had been sitting with Hank Sweat walked by the table. He looked over where Hank was still sitting, and Hank waved him over.

"Excuse me."

He got up and crossed to Hank, who signaled for him to sit down.

"Hank."

"Jim."

"What's up?"

"Those the Aliens?"

"Two of them."

"Which two?"

"Does it matter?"

"No, I guess not. Just curious."

"I'm sure word will get around."

"You know, I was just talking to some of the other men on

the council. Some of them still have a problem with these Aliens moving in."

"Send them around to my office. I'll be glad to talk to them."

"I'll pass the word. But it might take some convincing. You know how some people are, not liking change, still mourning, that kind of thing. You never know about some people."

"Yeah, I know how that works. But I'd still like to talk to them, one-on-one."

"I'm just letting you know."

"I appreciate it."

"Well, I'll let you get back to your lunch."

"Thanks. See you around."

"Yeah."

Jim got up and went back to his table just as the food arrived. Becky and Davey politely waited for everybody to be served, and this gave Angie a chance to discreetly scan the food with the little gadget hidden in her hand, but Becky seemed to notice something in the slightly longer than polite pause. Once Angie picked up a French fry, Jim, and then the others, began eating. Becky paused between bites of her chicken salad.

"For future reference, should I know who that was you were talking to?"

"Hank Sweat. Owns a huge wheat farm and is on the county commission. He at least pretends to be friendly, but I get the feeling he is not really our biggest fan."

"Oh."

"Even though we're bringing a lot of jobs and money into the town, not everybody is happy about us being here."

"That would probably be true even without the, uh . . ."

"Weird Aliens?" asked Angie.

"I wasn't thinking 'weird.'"

"We often think humans are weird. Why shouldn't you think we are weird?"

"Because I don't know you well enough to think you are weird."

"Ah. Well, give it time. How is the chicken salad?"

"It's good. It's not like the kind we have in Carolina, but it's good."

So the meal passed in conversation about the virtues of Southern cooking compared to the Midwestern fare. They passed on dessert this time, and Jim left five twenties on the table before waving to Susie as they left just as she was bringing the bill.

As they drove back to the office, Jim noticed a couple of little flashes off the side of the road that reminded him of flashes he had seen on Governors Island. He glanced at Angie, but she gave him a very small shake of the head, so he didn't say anything. He just wondered what would have happened if they hadn't been in the car.

In the parking lot, there were four more Mini Coopers parked side by side. Once back in the lobby, they ran into a crowd of eight people gathered around Mabel, rapidly emptying her bowl of M&Ms. Angie brightened up.

"Oh good, the rest of the gang of ten finally decided to make an appearance. Let me do the introductions."

To Jim's surprise, there were only two more males. The other six were women. They were all dressed in actually appropriate business attire in various shades of dark blues and blacks. Two of the women were brunettes, one of whom had slightly tan skin like Davey's. Another had black hair and olive skin like the royal physician. All the rest were blonds with blue eyes. Their hair had all been cut and styled to resemble something like you could see in Vogue or Glamour, but with a rebellious strand or two defying the convention.

In short order, Jim, Becky, and Mabel were introduced to Robert "Bob" Morris, Cecil Rhodes, Flo Nightingale, Rosalind "Rosey" Franklin, Mary Curie, Joan Clarke, Edith Wilson, and Barbara McClintock. Jim was so distracted trying to figure out the people the names alluded to that he didn't really listen to who went with which position and wasn't even sure he got the names and faces matched. Angie didn't seem to notice that she was overwhelming all the humans with too much information.

"OK, Davey, let's take these rookies back and show them their offices."

And the gang of ten headed through the first set of double doors, leaving Jim with Becky and Mabel.

"Anybody get all that?" asked Jim.

"Not even close," replied Mabel.

"Once they're in the system, there should be a picture to go with a name and title," said Jim.

"If they are like Davey, they are already in the system."

"OK. Well, I'll see how many names and faces I can learn before the next interview at two. Becky, I believe you have some questions for Mabel about daycare. She would probably also like you to set her up with about twenty dollars a week from petty cash for reception desk candy."

"No kidding. You'd think they never had candy before."

"Well, I'll leave you two to it."

And he went on to his office to call up personnel files and review resumes.

• • •

Ten minutes before the first interview, there was a knock at his office door and Angie entered. As soon as the door was closed, Jim asked, "Did I see what I thought I saw?"

"If you think you saw bullets being destroyed, yes."

"We seem to have a problem."

"We have taken precautions."

"At lunch, Hank Sweat asked me which of you three are Aliens. I asked him what difference it made, and he reckoned it really didn't make any. It's possible they may be willing to accept a little collateral damage."

"You think they would attack other humans?"

"I think they just did."

"The three that were with Hank?"

"That would be my guess. Susie tried to warn me that Hank and his pals were up to something, but I didn't think it would be this. I don't think she knew exactly what either."

"There are things we can do."

"Look, they've got us between a rock and a hard place. Aliens go chasing these guys down, it just proves their claim that the Aliens are taking over, converts more people to their side. But we do nothing and sooner or later somebody gets hurt."

"What about the local law enforcement? Surely shooting at a car with two humans in it is a crime."

"I'm not sure, but I think one of the guys sitting with Hank was the Wallace County sheriff."

"So what do you recommend?"

"Be careful. Use all the defensive tricks you've got and try to keep an eye on Hank and his friends. And let's get some more humans in here as quick as we can, people who work with the Aliens and can be another kind of outsider. And in the meantime, we need to figure out how to win over people like Cindy the other waitress."

"OK, go ahead and start the interview, and I'll send out a few instructions while you're doing the preliminaries."

She started tapping on her tablet. He gave Magdalena her cue, and the lights dimmed.

• • •

The afternoon interviews were not totally unsuccessful; they managed to hire a deputy for Dr. Panda in the Business Division. He was an Andrew Tutu, a distant relative of the famous bishop, who had graduated from the Cape Peninsula University of Technology in Cape Town, South Africa, then gone to Oxford in England for a graduate degree in technology before doing a post-grad at McGill in Montreal and starting his own company advising businesses on technology management. He had lived in a small town in South

Africa before going to the university, his business had dried up following the Disappearances, and he was desperate to move someplace warmer than Montreal.

It was after five o'clock before the last interview was over, and Angie hurried back to her office. Jim packed up and headed out, running into Becky and Davey in the parking lot. Davey seemed to be examining every inch of Becky's truck.

"Car trouble?"

"No, no. He just says he's never seen a pickup truck before, not close up, just pictures."

Jim thought that maybe there was more to it than that, but said nothing. He also noticed that four of the Mini Coopers were gone.

"You need a ride, Davey? I'm not sure how much longer Angie is going to be here."

"No. Thanks though. I'm going back in to help her. I just wanted to see Becky's truck before she left."

"It's old as the hills. Got over a hundred thousand miles on it. My husband used it for hunting and stuff, so it's all scratched up. Still runs though. It got me here."

"That's what counts. Let Davey have his fun. I'm sure he'll be finished in a minute. I'll see you tomorrow."

"Good night, Mr. King."

"Good night."

And, seeing no bullet holes, he got in his car and drove home. When he pulled into the drive, he hesitated a second before getting out to check the mailbox, but took a deep breath and did what normality required before driving into what he hoped was the safety of his garage.

21.

COME TUESDAY

The next morning a brand-new, burgundy Jeep Cherokee was sitting next to Becky's pickup in the parking lot. Entering the lobby, Jim saw Mabel at her desk, surrounded by Becky and a small Indian woman with a cute three-year-old girl plastered to her leg.

"Dr. Panda, I presume."

"Mr. King, so happy to meet you."

"And this is?"

"This is my daughter, Sonal."

Jim squatted down to the girl's eye level.

"It's nice to meet you too, Sonal."

The girl immediately hid her face behind her mother's leg.

"She's a little shy. And this is all very unfamiliar to her."

Jim stood back up.

"It's a little unfamiliar to all of us. She will probably adapt better than the rest of us, though. I assume that's your new Jeep out front."

"Yes."

"Angie's secretary, Davey Jones, is into cars and trucks. I'm sure he'd love to take a look at it when he gets in."

"Uh, certainly."

"Dr. Panda was just asking Mabel and me about the daycare options. The Catholic church has a 'Mother's Morning Out' thing on Wednesday and the Baptists have one on Thursday, but that seems to be about it."

"I've been calling around to see if I can get anybody to come in to our offices on a temporary basis. I might be able to get a couple of teenage girls for a few hours each day until school starts, if their parents don't object."

Before the conversation could continue, Angie and Davey entered from the parking lot.

"Oh, Dr. Panda. Welcome to Sharon Springs Software. This is my executive secretary, Davey Jones."

"Ms. Winston, Mr. Jones, nice to meet you. This is my daughter, Sonal."

"Becky and Mabel were just brainstorming about daycare for Sonal. I don't see a problem with her staying here for a couple of days while we get something set up. Mabel thinks she can get a teenager or two to come in and help out part of the time."

"That sounds good. There are a couple of places where they are still setting up furniture that we all need to stay out of, but otherwise we should be OK. Becky, where is the help wanted ad for the daycare staff?"

"I sent a draft to you and Mr. King last night."

"Angie, I've been thinking about that. If we can do it, it might be good to get as many of our local hire positions posted as possible. Let people see some of the ways we fit in to the community."

"That is a good idea."

"What else do we need that we can hire here?"

"The two or three daycare staff, a couple of maintenance staff, a cleaning crew that comes in after hours, maybe a gardener or two to get some green around the building. We can also advertise for administrative aides if we want to try to steal some clerks from the courthouse or the bank or somewhere. We were also thinking about trying to get a local as a liaison with the high school to get some internships or mentoring or something going."

"Could we open the daycare to the community? For a little fee the employees don't pay, of course. It seems to be a service they need," Jim suggested.

"I don't see any problem with that."

"And while I'm thinking about it, what would you think of a community garden for the employees in the land out back? I know we bought several acres back there we aren't using yet."

"How does a community garden work?"

"Several possibilities. Usually sweat equity earns a share of the crop. Or each person gets a different plot. Never done it myself, but they've worked in other places. We'd have to see if enough people are interested. I'm just tossing it out for future reference."

"OK, well, let's get started on the want ads."

"Western Times deadline for ads is Wednesday noon," said Mabel.

"Well then, it sounds like Becky, Davey, and Mabel have something to jump on first thing this morning."

"I thought Davey might like to look at Dr. Panda's new car."

"Davey checked that out on the way in. That's why we are a couple of minutes late."

"I'm sorry."

"Not a problem, Davey."

"Dr. Panda, unfortunately Angie and I are booked solid with interviews until lunch, but we'd like to take you and Sonal out to lunch around noon. In the meantime, Becky can help you get set up on the computer system. Once that's done you can access the personnel files for the Business Division. We just hired a Ralph Tutu out of South Africa by way of Oxford and McGill and his tech consulting company in Montreal to be your deputy, and you can review his vita. There are also vitas and job applications for most of the positions under you that you can start sifting through. You'll need to coordinate with Ralph, but we would like to hire staff as soon as possible. And you'll want to meet Cecil Rhodes and Joan Clarke, who are your liaisons in the Business Division, sometime this morning. Becky, why don't you show Dr. Panda and Sonal to their office and let them start getting settled in."

"Sure. Come on."

And everybody headed through the double doors, leaving Mabel to empty another giant bag of M&Ms into her bowl before the rest of the Aliens arrived.

• • •

The morning interviews resulted in three more turndowns, two because of location and one because of possible Alien contamination, but they were able to make one hire, a deputy for the research area. Bill Waller was a surfer from California who had managed to get through USC while surfing almost every day, then tried to support his surfing habit writing software for surfing equipment stores, including virtual reality programs for helping surfers pick the right boards in the stores. There evidently had also been a little hacking, but mostly white hat stuff for one government agency or another on the QT. Nothing that seemed to worry Angie, anyway. A bad wipeout four months ago resulting in some damaged vertebrae left him with a bad limp, strict doctor's orders to never even think about surfing again, and a decision to get as far away from an ocean as he could so as to remove temptation. Bill told Jim that Kansas seemed just barely far enough away.

When lunchtime came, Jim invited Becky to come with him to Stephens, but she said she and Davey were brown-bagging it today. Angie also begged off, with apologies to Pankaja and Sonal, saying there were some issues related to system security she had to deal with, but she sent Bob Morris, her deputy, in her place. They piled into Pankaja's Jeep since it already had the baby seat installed in the back seat.

At the restaurant the hostess, recognizing Jim but not seeing Angie, seated them at the first open table, which turned out to be in Cindy's section, and brought a high chair for Sonal. Sonal didn't seem real happy about the high chair, but didn't put up much fuss once Pankaja let Sonal hold her hand. Bob had evidently been briefed by Angie, since he hardly looked at the menu. Jim pointed out the lunch menu and the children's menu to Pankaja, and she worked her way through all the options while Jim saw Cindy and Susie having a brief, whispered discussion behind the counter.

Eventually a not very happy Cindy came over to their table, though the sight of Sonal in her high chair seemed to ease some of her distress. Cindy looked to be early thirties though maybe younger. She had evidently spent a lot of time in the Kansas sun, so the wrinkles around her eyes would not be true indicators of age. She carried a few more pounds than Susie on a slightly shorter frame, but looked like she might be pretty if she ever stopped frowning. As she approached the table, Sonal turned and gave Cindy a big smile, which Cindy almost returned.

"Well, aren't you a cute one. You folks ready to order?"

Cindy looked first to Pankaja, who was still examining all the options, so Jim ordered the fish and chips and tea. Bob then asked for the bacon-Swiss burger, fries, and a Coke, at which Cindy's frown returned. It was Pankaja's turn again.

"I would like a vegetable plate, if possible."

"No problem. Which vegetables would you like?"

"I believe I will have the creamed corn, the mashed potatoes, English peas, and green beans, please. And do you have hot tea?"

"If you can drink it when it's this hot outside."

"I'm from Delhi, India. We acquired a lot of English habits."

"No problem. And for the little girl?"

"What kind of oil is the grilled cheese sandwich grilled in?"

"Cook just uses a scoop of margarine on the grill."

"That's fine."

"It comes with fries cooked in canola oil and a carton of milk."

"That's fine. Thank you."

Cindy moved off.

"So, how is Sonal enjoying her first morning in Sharon Springs?"

"Sonal is doing just fine. She explored every nook and cranny in my office, then crawled up into my guest chair and took a nap. We're still adjusting to the time change."

"So, how is her mother doing?"

"My head is spinning. The resumes are starting to blend together."

"I know how that feels. I hear you got in just yesterday."

"We actually got to Denver Saturday night, actually very early Sunday morning, when it was too late to do anything except get a hotel room. Becky advised we buy a car in Denver rather than trying to buy one here, which I now fully understand, so we spent Sunday car shopping. Monday morning we visited one of the big malls to replace some of the things that didn't fit in the two suitcases each. Becky had asked the rental agent at the apartment building to stay open until we got there, so I was able to let a furnished two-bedroom and move right in."

"Well, don't feel you have to stay in the office all day. Talk to Mabel and Becky and then do what you need to do to get your life in order."

"Thank you. As long as Sonal cooperates, I'll keep plugging away."

"What about you, Bob? We really haven't had a chance to talk. Are you adjusting to Sharon Springs OK?"

"Angie is being a big help."

Nothing seemed to follow that as a topic for conversation, so Jim turned back to Pankaja.

"Did you get a chance to meet Cecil Rhodes and Joan Clark?"

"Yes, just very briefly."

Cindy brought the drinks, and this interrupted things while

Pankaja started her tea steeping, then set Sonal up with a straw in her milk carton. Jim sweetened his tea while noticing that Bob seemed to be scanning the drinks like Angie did; then Bob poured his Coke. Pankaja was busy for the next couple of minutes helping Sonal take a few sips of milk without spilling. By the time that process was under control, Cindy was back with the main dishes. Again, Bob scanned the food without Pankaja noticing, then he took a bite of his hamburger.

"Mmm, this is good."

The grilled cheese sandwich had been cut into quarters along the diagonal by the cook, so it was easy to handle for small hands. Jim didn't know if Sonal had ever had a grilled cheese sandwich before, but once she got a couple of bites she decided she agreed with Bob in liking this Kansas cuisine and could help herself from here on out. This left Pankaja free to deal with her own veggie plate. After downing the burger and fries, Bob got such a pleading look on his face that Jim decided they could take the time for dessert. Bob, of course, went for the French silk pie, Jim tried the apple pie, and Pankaja and Sonal decided to split a dish of vanilla ice cream. Cindy brought the bill before they were finished, but Jim didn't even look at it, laying four twenties on the table.

Exiting the restaurant, Bob took the lead and hesitated in the door a second, glancing around. Then they loaded back into the Jeep and headed back to the office.

"I think I can safely say that Bob and Sonal liked their meal. How was yours, Pankaja?"

"Well, it's not as good as Indian food, but better than what they serve in English pubs. The corn was especially good. I was afraid I wouldn't be able to find anything to eat, but I think this will work out."

• • •

The afternoon was taken up with more interviews, but they finally were able to hire the last top leadership position, the deputy in the Personal Software Division. Evita Krieger was from Buenos Aires, Argentina, but had gone to college at Smith in Massachusetts. She had returned home to work in the family electronics business, living with her widowed father and working her way up to VP of Technology. However, her father had backed the losing side in the last election a little too strongly, they had lost all their government contracts, and her father had gone out the back way just half an hour before some black sedans had pulled up in front. He father was now in Uruguay, and Evita was trying to hold the business together but realized it was a losing game.

When they started the interview, both Jim and Angie's tablets had silently flashed a warning that there was a third party on the line. Angie tapped a few buttons, and a fourth screen on the wall started showing an Evita that was almost identical to the real one, but that was being interviewed about a possible business deal in Argentina and giving very politically correct responses. Angie then filled Evita in on the situation and assured her the line was now very secure.

While Evita was not expecting black sedans to arrive for her any minute, she was also not put off by the idea of a little town or dealing with Aliens. Her only problem with taking the job immediately was that the men in the black sedans had taken her passport and she wasn't sure how long it would take to get it back. Angie wasn't so sure about the black sedans waiting around for Evita to get her paperwork if certain security people found out she was leaving the country, so Angie told her not to worry about getting her old passport back, to just go home and quickly pack a carry-on and wait until a messenger hand-delivered a large envelope to her with a new passport, visa, travel papers, and a plane ticket. Then go.

Jim and Angie then hung around the office, reviewing help wanted ad drafts and reports from Becky about Mabel's success in arranging for a teenage girl to come in for a few hours the next afternoon to help take care of Sonal, until Angie got a signal that

Evita was in the air on a plane to Brasilia with a connection to Miami, then on to Denver. By the time they left, everyone else had gone. Thus another day ended, they thought.

22.

COME WEDNESDAY

Jim was sound asleep in his bed when he felt someone shaking his shoulder.

"Jim. Jim. Come on, wake up."

He cracked his eyes open to see Angie, evidently wearing nothing except a thin, white, sleeveless T-shirt that seemed have been pulled on backwards and white cotton bikini panties, sitting on the side of his bed, shaking him.

"Angie? What's going on?"

He started to sit up, then remembered he was in the raw and rearranged the sheet to cover anything essential before coming half upright.

"Somebody tried to bomb the offices."

"What?"

"We're still doing analysis, but it looks like one of those crop-dusting planes flew over the office building and dropped some kind of homemade fertilizer and fuel oil bomb."

"Was anybody hurt?"

"No, the shield vaporized it, of course, but there was still quite a flash. Somebody will have noticed. What should we do?"

"OK, let me get this straight; there was no explosion, just the flash like on the island when a mortar came in?"

"Right, only bigger."

"And nobody got hurt?"

"Right."

"And no damage?"

"Not even burned grass."

Jim stared out the back window at his moonlit yard for a minute, wondering for a second when in the course of events he had become the go-to guy for handling emergencies, before considering the problem itself.

"Don't do anything. Just go back to bed and come in to work in the morning as if nothing had happened."

"Nothing? We know where the plane landed, which plane it was."

Jim turned back to Angie and managed to elevate his eyes back to her face.

"Can you imagine how frustrating it will be to them to work so hard and take all these chances, and we don't even notice? They'll feel like a gnat on a bull's back, not even worth swatting."

"I think I get that image."

"The worst thing we could do is make a big deal out of this. That would let them know they are bothering us, getting to us. Acting like it's not even worth noticing is the best way to make them face the new reality."

"OK, I'll go pass the word."

And she got up and walked out of the room, Jim watching her hips sway in the moonlight and trying not to think what he was thinking.

• • •

Jim pulled into the parking lot precisely at eight o'clock that morning, maneuvering around three Wallace County Sheriff's cars, which was probably the entire fleet, to get to his parking space. Mabel and Becky were standing by the front doors, which were blocked by two sheriff's deputies. As he got out of the car, the sheriff, in full uniform and badge, got out of his car and crossed to him.

"You Jim King?"

"Yes. Is there a problem?"

"I'm Sheriff Brooks."

"Yes, I believe I saw you in Stephens a couple of days ago with Hank Sweat."

"We got several reports of an explosion or some other kind of big flash of light coming from behind your office building last night, and I'm here to find out what your damn Aliens are up to."

"Sheriff, with all due respect, they are not my Aliens, they are not damn Aliens, and they are not up to anything that causes explosions."

"You sure about that?"

"Yes."

"Well, why don't we just go see."

"Fine with me."

Jim walked up to the front door, signaling Mabel and Becky to wait outside. The deputies parted to let him use his master key to open the door, then he and the sheriff entered. Using his key, Jim led the sheriff through both sets of double doors, then out an emergency door into the open field behind the building. He walked straight for about two football fields, until he came to a cattle fence with several cattle chewing their cud quietly on the other side. The sheriff had followed the entire way, looking somewhat surprised there were no bomb craters in the ground, no denuded trees, no scorched grass.

"Far enough?"

"What's inside?"

"Let's go see."

This time Jim angled across the acreage, coming to a door on one end of the complex. Using his key again, he entered the building and began walking down the hall, throwing all the doors open. He showed the sheriff the offices with their adjustable desks and lights; the conference rooms with their tables, chairs, and big-screen monitors; the break rooms with sinks, refrigerators, microwave ovens, and snack machines; the men's and women's restrooms, even opening all the stall doors; the daycare room with cribs and playpens; the closets for cleaning supplies; the electrical rooms; even the rooms housing the heaters, air conditioners, and water heaters. It took the better part of an hour before they doubled back toward the front doors.

"There is not a single thing in these buildings that you would not find in any office building in the world. There are no chemicals stronger than the bleach in the janitors' closet, no electrical equipment except what is necessary to heat or cool the building and run the computers. All that anybody, Alien or human, is going to do here is develop software to make businesses more efficient and make people's lives a little easier."

"Then how do you explain that big light in the night?"

"I don't. I didn't see it. I have no idea what it was. But nothing on this property caused it."

They were almost back to the front door when Jim stopped.

"Sheriff, in a few weeks this building is going to be full with about three hundred human beings, plus a few babies and toddlers. They and their wives and husbands will have come here from all over the world, China, India, South Africa, South America, as well as all over the United States. They are assuming Sharon Springs, Kansas, is a safe little town in the middle of America and that whoever is the law around here is here to protect them. They are going to shop at your stores, eat in your restaurants, live in your houses, go to your churches, and send their kids to your schools. Eventually they will vote in your elections, and then it will be their town too. Nothing is happening in here except writing lines of computer code. But if you think there is something going on out there that could put those three hundred people in danger just because there are ten Aliens here helping them write that computer code, then maybe you have a responsibility to protect them."

"If the Aliens weren't here, there wouldn't be a problem."

"But they are here, Sheriff. And they aren't going anywhere. They have nowhere else to go. It's a new reality; maybe you better catch up to it."

And Jim opened the front door and stepped out to see a little crowd gathered out front. Angie, Pankaja, and a woman he didn't recognize had found a blanket somewhere, spread it on the ground, and Angie was teaching Sonal a pat-a-cake game. Becky, Davey, and Bob had their heads under the hood of Becky's truck, with Flo in the driver's seat revving the engine when she got a signal. Cecil, Rosy, Mary, and Joan had put their tablet computers together on top of one of the Mini Coopers to create a big screen and were teaching Mabel to play some kind of computer game. Edith and Barbara had moved another one of the Mini Coopers over a little so the doors could be opened all the way, reclined the seats, and were grabbing forty winks, as if they had missed some sleep during the night. The two deputies were still sort of near the door, but were sipping soft drinks in a significantly more relaxed posture. Jim stopped in the door.

"Angie."

Angie passed Sonal back to her mother, got up, and crossed to Jim and the sheriff.

"Angie, I would like you to meet Sheriff Brooks. He says somebody reported flashing lights over our back forty last night."

"That's not exactly what I said."

"Well, it's still nice to meet you, Sheriff. I'm glad your office responds so promptly."

She stuck out her hand. The sheriff paused, then slowly extended his hand and completed the ritual of greeting.

"Well, you folks can go in now. We'll be moving on."

"Thanks again, Sheriff."

"Yes, thanks."

The sheriff crossed to his car, followed by his two deputies, and soon all three cars were driving out of the parking lot. Mabel approached Jim and the rest gathered around.

"What did Brooks want?"

"Somebody reported flashing lights in the sky last night. Probably some kind of UFO. You all know about those little green spacemen from Mars, the ones with the tentacles and the big heads, right?"

It took a couple of beats, but then Becky looked at Angie and grinned, then there were titters, then giggles, then laughs from everybody except the stranger, and they filed into the building with Bob moving his arm like it was a tentacle. Mabel pulled the stranger over to Jim as the others left.

"We may have a little problem."

Jim looked at the stranger, and the word "feisty" popped into his mind. It was a woman with leathered skin who looked somewhere between fifty and eighty years old. She was small and slim, but stood like people would get out of her way. She wore a cowboy hat that probably used to be white twenty years ago, one of those Western shirts that actually had snaps instead of buttons, worn jeans with a big silver belt buckle, and pointy-toed boots that were actually scuffed where the stirrups would have rubbed. She was a little bowlegged, and Jim wondered if she had a horse tied up somewhere in the parking lot.

"This is Jayne Pearce from the Western Times newspaper."

"Nice to meet you."

"Don't bet on it."

"Excuse me?"

"Uh, Jayne says she isn't going to print our help wanted ads."

"Oh really."

"It's my paper; I decide what gets in."

"And what's the problem with letting your fellow citizens know about some significant employment opportunities?"

"Well, first of all, I'm sick and tired of the goddamned Aliens blocking all my attempts to get the story of their being in town out to anybody. It's the biggest story of my life, and I can't even send an e-mail or make a phone call about it. And don't give me that line about all the TV trucks filling Main Street; they'd all be gone within a week. Second, there are a few high-falutin' muckity-mucks around here who are pretty determined to get rid of these Aliens. I'm not sure what all these lights were last night, but I suspect it had more to do with them pulling some stunt than the Aliens setting off firecrackers, and I'm not sure what they would do with their ad budgets if it looked like the paper was helping the Aliens. And third, I lost a granddaughter to that goddamned Disappearance thing, and I don't take kindly to that, whether it was necessary or not. I sure don't see any reason for me to help them."

"I see."

"Uh, I guess I better get inside now."

"OK, Mabel. Jayne and I will work this out."

Mabel went inside, leaving Jim and Jayne standing on the walkway.

"I appreciate your honesty."

"Don't start that psychobabble, bureaucratic bullshit."

"OK. One, it's pure self-defense. Behind all those TV trucks would be a wave of maniacs with shotguns and swords running around killing anybody they thought was an Alien, and in case you haven't noticed, it's not real obvious who is and who isn't. And believe me, it wouldn't be the Aliens who got killed.

"Second, we know Hank Sweat, the sheriff, and some of their ilk are not happy campers right now, but we think they've pretty much shot their wad and are coming to realize they can't do spit. And third, we all lost somebody. Yes, it hurt like hell. Yes, it's hard to get over. But it is over, and it could have been a hell of a lot worse. It could still be a hell of a lot worse. They're here, they can't go home, they can't go anywhere; it was a one-way ride. For some unknown reason they seem to think keeping humans around is a good idea, and I for one am trying hard to support that idea. They make a hell of a lot better friends than they would enemies. Now, woman up, get over it, and do what's going to get some of your friends and neighbors some damn good jobs."

And he turned and walked into the building, leaving Jayne standing on the walkway. On Friday the back page of the paper was nothing but Sharon Springs Software want ads. They were double the normal size, and the bill, when it came, was triple the usual cost. Jim saw to it that it was paid promptly.

• • •

Aside from waiting for the newspaper to come out, the rest of the week was busy for everybody except Jim. The rest of the new hires trickled into town, running Becky and Mabel ragged, especially getting some money to Evita Krieger so she could buy a car, clothes, and almost everything else she needed while she was still in Denver, then getting her set up in one of the furnished apartments when she actually got to Sharon Springs. Texas FitzGerald, Ralph Tutu, and Henry Wengen were almost the exact opposite problem, arriving with moving vans close behind and wanting to buy houses. Mabel complained that she needed a real estate license to do some of the things she was doing, but she got Henry into one of the newly renovated houses not far from the apartments, helped Ralph buy one of the new houses on 27 just north of 40, and convinced Texas that he needed to move into one of the unfurnished three-bedrooms and then take his time to find exactly what he wanted in a big farmhouse with twenty-plus acres around it.

Bill Waller showed up driving a U-Haul truck and was quickly helped by Becky, Davey, Bob, and the two sons of the rental agent to move into a ground-floor apartment where he wouldn't have to deal with stairs with his limp. Then he had to drive off again to turn in his truck in Goodland and try to buy a car there. Mao Xihong arrived at the office midmorning on Friday driving a ten-year-old Ford van that had already broken down twice on the drive out from California and asked if there were company dorms. Becky got her into one of the apartments, and Davey did something to her van that he said would keep it running until she could get a replacement. Olga Ali did not even come in to the office, just talked to both Becky and Mabel on the phone and then handled her own affairs somehow, renting a house a block off Main Street a little south of the schools.

Meanwhile, the Aliens, in addition to whatever else they were doing, were screening applications for the rest of the slots on the org chart and passing the approved ones on to the respective division directors and deputies. Pankaja was already working with Ralph remotely and Cecil and Joan on-site to do teleconference interviews with top candidates for system designer positions.

At any rate, Thursday and Friday were quiet for Jim, giving him a chance to get some policies and procedures written up, along with some orientation materials for personnel as they were hired. Thursday he ate lunch at Stephens with Angie, and they were actually served by Cindy, but it was otherwise an unremarkable meal, if you didn't count the huge slice of apple pie with ice cream that Angie tried and loved. Friday he ate lunch alone when Angie had to meet with Rosy and Barbara on some of the screening criteria for the research division, but business was a little slow at the restaurant without quite so many construction workers left in town, so he was able to have a long conversation in bits and pieces with Susie on the potential impact of the Chinese, Italian, and Mexican restaurants that were going to open in the little strip shopping center down the road, along with a dress boutique, a dry cleaner, and a health spa. He and Susie generally agreed that, while Stephen's might need to refocus their menu a little bit on typical American food and drop their versions of pizza and tacos, there should be enough people moving into town to keep all the restaurants busy.

Saturday Jim screwed his courage to the sticking place and took a morning jog around town, showered, changed, made a run to Miller's for milk and bread and a few other items, then tried out the washer and dryer in the basement and found them satisfactory. In the afternoon he did some internet shopping and ordered a few decorative items for the house, then took his tablet computer into the den and had Magdalena show him what she could do to augment the local cable TV system. That turned out to be just about anything anybody had ever put on TV or film, from pure porn to chess matches in Kazakhstan, but he settled for a Braves–Mets game. Once the Mets got ahead by nine runs, an idea came to him.

"Magdalena."

"Yes?"

"Can you show me things on the internet without leaving any trace or letting anybody know I've been to those sites?"

"I have that technical ability, but Angie would have to approve."

"Ask her if I can view the Facebook site with the wedding pictures of a certain woman. She will know who."

"One moment please."

There was a pause that seemed to drag on forever; then pictures began to appear on the big-screen TV. They weren't even professional pictures, just a few pictures of the bride and groom evidently taken by a friend at the wedding. But the bride was beautiful. She wore not a wedding gown, but a plain white dress. The groom wore a dark-blue suit. They both looked very happy. The wedding seemed to have been in somebody's living room. There was one picture of them cutting a small cake with white icing. There was no evidence of more than half a dozen people attending the wedding, including the minister. But the bride was beautiful. There were no pictures of a dinner or them driving off in a car, no pictures of a best man or maid of honor. But they looked very happy. And the bride was beautiful.

Jim just sat there and cried.

"Jim?"

"Yes, Magdalena?"

"Are you OK? Is there anything you need me to do?"

"No, I'm fine. Just very happy and very sad."

"Would you like me to save these pictures?"

"Yes. Wait. No, better not."

"Are you sure? Things don't stay on the internet forever."

"Yes, I'm sure. I shouldn't have looked in the first place."

"Why not? Who is she?"

"The daughter of someone I used to know, long, long ago. He's dead now. This just brings back memories. Let's not speak of it again, please. You can turn them off now."

"As you wish."

The screen went dark, but the images remained alive in his eyes. And he sat there for a long time before getting up and going to bed.

• • •

Sunday he slept late, made some giant batches of Rice Krispy candy to take in to the office Monday, and spent a lot of time reviewing the vitas of the new hires, the detailed org chart, and ideas for initial software products that would need to be discussed on Monday, when all of the leadership team should finally be in the office at once.

23.

THE CONFERENCE ROOM

Monday Jim got into work early. He went to the Executive Conference Room, which had a big conference table that seated twenty, shaped like a flattened football with the ends cut off, and set out the Rice Krispy candy on several plates and put name tents he had made in front of the chairs. On his way back to his office, he passed Becky at her desk explaining to Xihong that there wasn't a company cafeteria, only a break room, but that there were several good restaurants very close by.

After a few minutes there was a knock at his office and Angie entered, eating a Rice Krispy candy square.

"You ready for this?"

"I guess so. You?"

"Let's go over it one more time."

"OK."

• • •

At promptly nine o'clock, Jim and Angie entered the Executive Conference Room together. He noticed that the Aliens, Becky, and Pankaja were already chowing down on the candy squares, while the other humans seemed to be waiting for an invitation. There were small groups standing around talking and exchanging handshakes as people moved from group to group.

"If you would take your seats, please."

People quickly wound up conversations and took their assigned seats, with Jim and Angie seated together in the middle of one side. Olga was on Jim's other side, and Bob sat by Angie. Becky was at one end where the table squared off, and Davey was at the other. They were set up to take notes during the meeting. There was still one seat empty when Bill Waller hurried in and took the empty seat.

"Sorry. I'm from California; I didn't realize you actually started on time. Won't happen again."

Once everyone was seated, Jim stood up again.

"For those of you here for the first time, welcome to Sharon Springs Software. We'll get to all the formal introductions in a minute, but you need a little context to understand those introductions. First, if anybody hasn't figured it out yet, half the people in this room are Aliens. The other half are humans. I'll leave it to you to figure out who is who. At this leadership level, each of the humans is paired with an Alien who has an equivalent title and level of responsibility in the org chart. Below this level, all the employees will be humans. Basically, the Aliens will provide technical expertise and advice, and the humans will manage the development process and the personnel. This means you are going to have to work very closely with each other, making joint decisions.

"We have three divisions in the company, products for business, products for personal use, and a research division to advance the field of software development. As we told you during your interview, the idea is to leverage the Aliens' expertise to jump two or three generations ahead of everybody else, produce software products that make life better for everybody, make a lot of money, and have a professionally exciting time doing it. Now, we told all the humans during their interview that they would have to be in contact with Aliens. We understand that sitting next to them in a room full of them may be a little more than you expected, so if anybody is having second thoughts, now's the time to make your exit."

He paused. There were lots of exchanges of looks around the table. Texas and Henry looked like they weren't sure exactly what they had gotten themselves into, but they didn't move. Xihong looked like she was suddenly aware of life outside a computer and was trying to write a probabilities program in her head and run it mentally. Evita and Ralph seemed more interested in figuring out who was human and who wasn't. Olga's expression was unreadable. The pause dragged on.

"OK, haven't scared anybody away yet. Let me try again. As you may imagine, there are people here in the town of Sharon Springs and the surrounding Wallace County that are not pleased to have Aliens among them. Some of them are actively opposed. A few of them are willing to take action. There have been incidents. Precautions have been taken. Protections have been put in place. No one has been hurt. We have made some friends in town. We think the situation is changing, but this is not a change that occurs overnight.

"Your first task is to hire the rest of the staff as soon as possible, good people, people from all over the globe, to take some of the attention off the Aliens. Your Alien equivalents have already screened applicants for basic qualifications and lack of hostility to Aliens. There are lots of very good people on those lists, but many of them will not want to move to a little town in the middle of nowhere, and others will not want anything to do with a company associated with anything Alien, so you've got your work cut out for you. Your second task, to be done concurrently, is to create a list of proposed products to develop first. We have a few ideas as prompts to get you started, but don't limit yourselves to that. Angie and I would like to see your lists within two weeks. OK, second and last chance; anybody want out?"

He paused again. This time all eyes stayed focused on him.

"OK, we've got some very interesting people around this table, so let's get to know each other. We've also made arrangements to have lunch together in division groups, so we can be more informal then. As I'm sure you have noticed, you are seated by division, with the exception of my executive secretary, Becky Davis, down at one end taking notes, and Angie's executive secretary, Davey Jones, at the other end, who is available to call up any information we may need. And we can start with my deputy, who, frankly, I'm meeting today myself. Olga, tell us about yourself and your background for this job."

And so it started. The Aliens all had basically the same story to tell; they were born on the sphere, had worked low-level jobs, and had spent most of the past year learning English and human culture, and were very happy to be here where they could mingle with humans and feel the Earth beneath their feet. Jim suspected that it was all as much cow manure as anything Angie or he said about themselves, but he had no idea what the truth was.

The humans basically repeated what was in their vitas, with Pankaja adding a little about Sonal, who was being taken care of in the daycare room by a high school student Mabel had found. Bill Waller explained that his limp came from a surfing back injury. Texas had the good sense not to mention how many millions his old company had sold for, but explained that "Texas" was actually his legal name, not a nickname, given to him by his father at his birth, and that he actually was from Texas. Ralph said that his father had been Desmond Tutu's third cousin, but that neither he nor his father had actually met the bishop while he was alive.

Becky, Xihong, Evita, Henry, and Olga didn't add anything that wasn't directly related to the job, and everybody had the good manners not to mention anything about who they lost in the Disappearances. There were, of course, dozens of questions people asked of each other, especially trying to establish degrees of separation through colleagues from various universities, professional associations, and businesses. There were also hundreds of questions people wanted to ask but decided to save for a more private setting. Then there were questions about the hiring process; how much flexibility they had to negotiate salaries (some, but salaries were already high) and fringe benefits (not much flexibility), what to do if they ran out of applicants for a particular job (see if the other divisions had any extras who qualified; if not, the Aliens would screen some more). Then they moved on to discussing possible products; did "Business" include products for governments (no), where in the process would products coming out of the research division be made available to the other two divisions (only after beta testing), did "Personal" include entertainment products like games (no, but good graphics and user-friendly interfaces were high priority).

The whole discussion took them right up to lunchtime, at which time they figured out carpools to the restaurant, took a short break, and reconvened by division at Stephens, which had saved them two tables for six and two tables for four. Jim, Angie, Olga, Bob, Becky, and Davey occupied one of the tables, and Susie came over to serve them.

"OK, I know almost everybody."

"Susie Reynolds, this is my deputy, Olga Ali."

"Olga Ali? There's got to be a story behind that."

"I'm Swedish. I was born and raised in Sweden, but my parents are of Arab heritage."

"OK, I guess that explains it. Welcome to Sharon Springs."

"Thank you."

"Is keeping halal an issue?"

"I'm not strict, but steer me away from dishes with pork. Thank you for asking."

"We're big on beef around here, so it shouldn't be a problem."

"Susie, I'm proud of you," said Jim.

"I've been reading up. After helping Pankaja order, Cindy put the word out and we've all been boning up on all kinds of diets. Kosher, vegan, gluten-free; we know what's in all the dishes we serve now."

"Now, that's true Midwestern hospitality."

"OK, so let me get the drink orders, and we'll give Olga a couple of minutes to read the menu. Three Cokes, two teas, and a . . . ?"

"Iced tea would be fine."

"Three teas. Be right back."

Susie left and Angie turned to Jim.

"How do you think it's going?"

"So far, so good, I guess."

"Olga, what do you think?"

"As a Swedish Arab who has worked for Englishmen and Texans, so far you Aliens don't seem so weird. Has anybody had the mushroom burger?"

"Oh, it's great, lots of mushrooms in brown sauce, huge beef patty. You might want to ask them to leave off the onion, though, or grab half a dozen breath mints on the way out; it's a whole slab of onion. And the pies, you've got to try one of the pies."

And so it went.

• • •

The next day things seemed to be normal at the office until midmorning, when Becky buzzed his phone and told him he needed to go see what was happening outside. As he crossed to the lobby, Becky followed him to where Mabel was staring out the glass door. Angie soon joined them in the lobby. Outside, on the right-of-way between the highway and the parking lot, a group of about twenty people had appeared, walking in a circle, carrying signs saying things like "Aliens Out," "No Aliens in Sharon Springs," and "Aliens Go Home." When Mabel cracked the door open a little bit, they heard a chant of "Hey hey, ho ho, Aliens have got to go." Jim also noticed there were a couple of sheriff's deputies off to one side, acting like they were making sure the demonstrators stayed on the right-of-way. As he watched, Jayne Pearce drove up and parked, but she stayed in her car after rolling the window down.

The word spread fast, and the rest of the employees trickled into the lobby.

Angie asked, "Any ideas?"

Jim took a hundred dollars in cash from his wallet and gave it to Becky.

"You and Olga take your pickup truck and go to that little convenience store next to Stephens, buy a couple of big coolers, several bags of ice, and a bunch of sodas—you know, Cokes, Diet Cokes, maybe some Sprites, a variety of soft drinks, whatever they've got. Ice down the drinks in the coolers. Also get some snacks; candy, Moon Pies, the really sweet stuff. When you get back, park out in the middle of the lot, between the building and the demonstrators."

"OK. Come on, Olga."

"I take it this comes under 'other duties as assigned.'"

"They should know you two are not Aliens, so they shouldn't bother you."

Angie asked, "I take it you have an idea."

"We just need to wait for them to get tired and sweaty."

So Becky and Olga left and the rest of them waited in the lobby. Jim huddled with Angie quietly. After about twenty minutes Becky's truck pulled back into the parking lot and stopped between the groups.

"Angie, I think you and I should go out and offer our guests a cool drink. The rest of you stay here, at least at first."

Jim and Angie walked out to the pickup and pulled six-packs of cold drinks out of the coolers in the truck bed. Jim picked out the guy who seemed to be leading the chant and crossed to him, extending his hand.

"Hi. I'm Jim King. It's pretty hot out here; have a cold drink.

The lead demonstrator had to shift his sign pole to the crook of his arm in order to shake hands and then take the cold drink.

"You know, I want to thank you for coming out here today. We've been looking for some folks to give us a little feedback about the community's concerns. Why don't a couple of you come inside where it's cooler and we'll give you a look around and see what you have to say."

By now Jim had his arm around the demonstrator's shoulders and was guiding him toward the building, signaling a couple of others to come along and passing them the cold drinks. To say that this was not what the demonstrators had been expecting was obvious from the puzzled expressions on their faces, but they really didn't know how to object. Jim saw that Angie had corralled another couple of demonstrators.

"Olga, you and Becky make sure the rest of our friends get a cold drink and a little snack, and we'll be back in a little while."

Jim and Angie led the five demonstrators they had picked into the building, after they left their signs outside the door because they were too tall to take inside, passing between the little crowd in the lobby.

"Now, these are some of the people who are going to be working here. Eventually we hope to have about three hundred employees, almost all human. They'll be programmers and system engineers and all kinds of computer people from all over the world, but we'll also be hiring a lot of local people, as well as generating a lot of business for local companies. You probably saw the strip mall opening down the road that's also going to employ a lot of local people. And the schools are going to have to hire some more teachers, some of whom we hope will be local kids who went off to college but would come back if there were good jobs here. We also hope we can get some of the local kids to come back from college and work as programmers here. We do pay pretty well, so now there'll be reasons for the kids to move back. Come on, follow me and let me show you some of our offices and conference rooms. Angie, maybe you can explain about how our desks are adjustable so people can work standing up or sitting down and how that should be healthier."

"Sure, Jim, let's go into this office so I can demonstrate with one of the desks."

And so the demonstrators got the grand tour, with the big spiel about the types of computer programs they were going to develop, how they hoped to do things in such a way that it improved the whole economy of the town, even how the daycare center would be available to residents as well as employees. When they went back outside, they found the other demonstrators, the employees, and Jayne Pearce were gathered around Becky's truck, sucking down Cokes and Hershey bars, Sprites and Twix. Everybody sort of hung out for a little while, eating and talking baseball, the demonstrators filling in the newcomers on how life in Kansas was different from India or Argentina or even California or New England, at least from their point of view. Eventually the employees pleaded the need to get back to work, but left the coolers of drinks and food with the demonstrators in the parking lot. When Jim peeked out the door an hour later, all that was left were the two sheriff's deputies and two empty coolers.

24.

WORKING

The next few days were a bit of a blur to Jim, answering questions from the division directors, making up policy on the fly when necessary, sitting in on interview teleconferences and providing advice on how to handle questions about the town and the Aliens, approving job offers. He also got involved in the hiring of the locals, after Mabel found a retired elementary school teacher who was having trouble getting by on state retirement and Social Security and so was willing to come back to work for a year or two to get the daycare set up, in exchange for a decent salary, health insurance, and two all-expenses-paid two-week cruises each year.

The good part was that hiring her seemed to break a log jam. Not only was the retired teacher able to bring in some of her former students, now all grown up, to work a half-day here or there for significant pin money, but some of the young mothers in town started dropping off their kids for a day or half-day when they needed a break from being a parent. After all, it was their friends who would be taking care of the kids, and it didn't cost much, really. Sure, some of the kids of the employees weren't like their kids, but "Kids are kids, you know," they said to Jim when he dropped in on the daycare room.

Soon they had a farmer who had been injured in a wheat combine accident and couldn't handle the hard labor of farming applying his mechanical expertise to keeping all the heating, cooling, and plumbing equipment operating; then the wives of several of the Hispanic farmworkers were coming in right after they fed their husbands supper to empty the trash cans, sweep the floors, and clean the toilets, and earning more than their husbands in the process. They even hired two tellers from the bank and three clerks from the courthouse to be secretaries for the division directors and deputies before they had to start importing secretaries from out of town. Jim wasn't sure about the wisdom of hiring Hank Sweat's secretary to work for Texas FitzGerald, but she didn't seem to have any particular loyalty to Hank, and Susie put in a good word for her while serving lunch one day.

Within days there was a definite labor shortage in Sharon Springs as the restaurants and shops in the little strip mall started opening. The restaurant owners were all from out of town, but they needed to hire and train assistant cooks and waitresses for the Chinese, Mexican, and Italian restaurants opening there, and the locals who had been given loans to open the boutique, dry cleaners, and health spa also had to hire clerks and salespeople. The Mexican restaurant was able to hire a few Hispanics, but the owners quickly found themselves explaining the difference between a burrito and an enchilada to Kansas kids who thought Yucatán was an island in the Caribbean but needed a job after school to earn money for college. The Chinese couple from San Francisco at least expected to have to start from scratch, but the family opening the Italian restaurant was surprised all the job applicants assumed it was just a pizza joint, and ended up serving suppers to the new staff where they provided samples of all the different types of pasta and sauces, as well as everything else on the menu except pizza and spaghetti, so the servers would have some idea what to recommend to the customers who saw all those strangely named Italian dishes on the menu.

Jim and Angie and the others gradually tried all the new restaurants and kept one or two in a regular rotation or when looking for something new, but they became more dinner places than lunch spots. So it was at lunch at Stephens one day that Jayne Pearce slid into the booth beside Jim just as he and Angie were being seated.

"Mind if I join you?"

"I think you just did."

"I need to talk to your partner in crime, if you don't mind," Jayne said, gesturing at Angie.

"And it's nice to see you again too."

"What crime?" asked Angie.

"It's an expression. Somebody who's in cahoots with somebody else."

"I'm not sure 'cahoots' was in her English-Alien dictionary," Jim said.

"I get the idea."

"See, she gets it."

Susie appeared to take their order.

"Am I interrupting something?"

"The human Alien here was challenging my manners."

"Well, Mrs. Pearce, he wouldn't be the first."

"Susie, you are getting too sassy."

"He tips better, too."

"Well, bring me a fish and chips while the fish is still hot and maybe there'll be an extra quarter in it for you."

"Oh, yes ma'am. Anything to drink? We're out of Jack Daniel's."

"You've been out of Jack Daniel's since Prohibition started. Now you're just trying to make me look bad to these outsiders."

"Who, me? I just take orders."

"Well, take my order for the fish and chips special and an iced tea and get on with it."

"Yes ma'am. Anybody else want anything while I'm here?"

"Let me have an all-American burger, large fries, large Coke."

"The fish special and tea."

"Be right back."

"So, Mrs. Pearce, you needed to talk to me?"

"Call me Jayne, with a y in the middle to make it hard to spell. Susie was just being sarcastic with that Mrs. Pearce stuff."

"OK, Jayne with a y. I'm Angie. I think I saw you outside the offices the morning after the flash, but I believe you talked to Jim then."

"Yeah, we go way back, at least a week or two."

"And you would like to talk about . . . ?"

"I'm the editor of the Western Times, the local newspaper."

"Which I read every word of each week."

"Don't try to flatter me."

"Honest. I'm trying to understand as much as I can about this community."

"Well, OK, then you know we sometimes run stories about new people moving into the community."

"I saw the one last week about the Chinese couple who opened the new restaurant."

"Yeah, well, we've been holding off on anybody from Sharon Springs Software because, frankly, a lot of people hate your guts and we didn't want to draw attention to anybody in particular. Most people hear all about you guys anyway."

"And now?"

"Well, it's getting to be kind of ridiculous. Just plain bad journalism. You got a millionaire from Texas, an escapee from Argentinian death squads, an Arab from Sweden, and god knows what else. Not running something on these people is like promoting a big yard sale and not mentioning that the courthouse got blown up or the governor got shot or something."

"You seem to have done your homework."

"I'm a reporter. I may not be able to get anything with the word Alien in it to the printer, but my internet connection still gets incoming."

"So what do you want from us?"

"Can I print the stories if I don't say anything about Aliens? Just say a new employee at Sharon Springs Software, and not mention any connections to you folks?"

At that moment, Susie arrived with the food and drinks, handling Jayne's fish plate with a hot pot holder.

"Try not to burn your lips."

"I'll blow on it first."

And she put the food down and left.

"What do you think, Jim?" Angie asked.

"I think it should be up to the individuals. Evita may not want anything in print in case somebody unfriendly from Argentina is trying to find her or her father. I'm not sure Texas wants a big deal made about his previous success. And as she says, it might draw the unwanted attention of people who haven't adjusted to the new reality yet. On the other hand, it might help them adjust if they saw that most of us are just regular people doing a job and making a living. Let each person decide if they want to be interviewed or photographed."

"If somebody says no, will you leave them alone?" Angie asked Jayne.

"Well, they might have to say no two or three times, but if somebody has a good reason, like that Argentine girl, I'm not trying to get anybody in trouble."

"OK, I think Jim and I can live with that. Give us a day to pass the word that this is totally voluntary and not something the company wants or opposes."

"Great. And what about you?"

"What about me?" asked Angie.

"Can I interview you? Surely you've got some BS you can give me, whatever cover story you hand out."

"I've been very honest that I was born on the spacecraft and got this assignment because I was one of the ones assigned to learn English and Earth cultures and did pretty well. That's not the kind of thing we want delivered to every mailbox within a hundred miles."

"Well, you can't blame a gal for asking. What about you, Jim? You looked pretty bland on the internet."

"Bland Jim, the human Alien, that's me."

"I'm sure there's something sensational in there somewhere, or at least interesting. How you got this job must be quite a story."

"I made the mistake of applying. And I'm sure there are a lot more interesting people at the company than me."

"But you're the president."

"Co-president."

"Whatever."

"Your fish is getting cold."

"I'll take that as the first no."

"What about those Kansas City Royals? Did you see the game on Saturday?"

"You're right, my fish is getting cold."

Angie stepped back into the conversation, "Tell us about the Western Times, Jayne. What's the circulation? When did it start? Are you still printing offset?"

"OK, I got one yes and two no's, which is enough for now. I'll bite. The Western Times goes way back, long before I was even born."

And she told them a lot more than they really wanted to know before they finally finished eating, pleaded a meeting at work, and managed to escape.

25.

THE GAME

By the time the first football game of the season rolled around, they were about halfway to staffed up. As Mabel pointed out, supporting the high school football team was not only the only event on Friday nights, it was practically a patriotic duty. The problem was that there was only one set of stands to sit in, holding less than two hundred bottoms. This was fine when the school was less than fifty students and most of the high school was on the field as either players or cheerleaders, but with an extra few dozen families of recently hired programmers on hand, suddenly there were a lot more people elevated to prime sideline access.

As Jim walked down the sideline, he looked up in the stands and saw no open seats, but saw Becky trying to explain football to both Pankaja and Angie while Sonal discovered the joy of an orange popsicle. Texas FitzGerald was up in the booth on top with one of the assistant coaches, evidently helping Xihong and Bob learn how to keep track of the official statistics. Edith and Flo were with Mabel and some other women in the snack bar, selling Cokes, popcorn, hot dogs, candy bars, and popsicles. Continuing his stroll, he came up on Jayne Pearce.

"Well, the human Alien comes to football games. Will wonders never cease."

"You here to cover the game for the paper?"

"Nah, we have a couple of seniors write it up as extra credit for their English class. But I hang around just so I know if they don't stick to the objectivity of a good journalist."

"Looks like a good turnout."

"Lots of new folks in town."

"So I hear."

"Did you hire the new kid's parents on purpose?"

"What new kid?"

"A week ago a new kid from Alabama came out for the team. His parents are programmers at your shop. He's six feet two inches, two hundred and twenty pounds, and runs the forty in four point nine. The other team doesn't have anybody within thirty pounds of him except one lineman who weighs two fifty, but he's only five eight and they don't have a time for him in the forty-yard dash because he's never made it that far."

"This sounds interesting."

"I asked the coach how they were going to handle the new kid not knowing the plays, and he said they were just going to tell him to run right, run left, or go up the middle. He's also going to play middle linebacker, and his instructions are tackle whoever has the ball."

So, the game started, and suddenly the Wildcats actually were the greatest thing since sliced bread. The new kid gained about twenty yards a pop on the first two plays and broke loose for a touchdown on the third. Once on defense, the opposing team tried to block him with the center and lost yardage on their first three plays. When they got the ball back after another Wildcat touchdown, they tried blocking him with the center and one lineman, which resulted in two runs for no gain and a very hurried pass that was ten feet over the receiver's head and still rising when it went into the dark beyond the lights. A bunch of elementary school kids had to go scrambling off to find it since they only had three official game balls.

Back on offense, the new kid was chewing up yardage again when the opposing coach called time-out and had all his players just put all their focus on the new kid. That slowed him down for a few plays; then the quarterback called a fake run to the wide right, kept the ball himself after faking the handoff, and ran left into the half of the field that was totally empty between him and the goal line.

The Wildcats once more on defense, the opposing team now assigned all three linemen to block the middle linebacker, which slowed him down, but after three plays the defensive linemen figured out that nobody was blocking them at all and they could just run straight into the backfield and tackle whoever was upright.

On offense after receiving another punt, the Wildcats saw that the entire defense was still focused on the running back except for one safety who was now assigned to mirror the quarterback. Catching on to the possibilities now, the quarterback called another fake run to the right, but told the wide receiver to go ten yards and stop. Everybody on the field went to the right again, except for the quarterback, the wide receiver, and the other team's safety. The safety started to attack the quarterback, who calmly floated a pass to the wide receiver, who was so alone he had time to stand and wait for the ball, juggle it a little, finally tuck it away, and then turn and jog down the field for a touchdown.

By the end of the half, the score should have been fifty-six to nothing, but the Wildcats had missed two extra points, and the new kid wasn't even playing on offense anymore. He did play one series on defense at the start of the second half, but by then the opponents appeared to be a broken, dispirited mess. After a couple more touchdowns, the Wildcats coach was playing all second-stringers and probably would have put in the third string if he had had one. At the end of the third quarter, Jim heard the referee come over and ask if there was anything the head coach could do to hold down the score, but the coach was already calling nothing but running plays to help run down the clock. He told the referee he would have put in the student trainers and the ball boys if they had uniforms, and two of them were girls. Late in the fourth quarter the opponents did run back a kickoff for a touchdown and recovered a fumble close enough to the goal line to kick a field goal, so it wasn't a total shutout, but the final score was so embarrassing that the Western Times didn't even print it.

Walking off after the stands emptied onto the field in celebration, Jim ran into Jayne again.

"Well, that's going to make having all these software people in town more popular."

"You think so?" asked Jim.

"You bet your bippy."

"Wow, I haven't heard that saying in a while."

"What comes of getting old. You walking?"

"It's not exactly far."

"Come on, I'll give you a ride."

"That's OK; I know you go in the opposite direction."

"Humor me. I get cranky when people turn me down."

"OK. It would be my pleasure."

"You bet your bippy."

And so they turned around and walked back to the parking lot. Once inside Jayne's Ford F-150, Jim looked at the dozens of cars and trucks all trying to get out of the parking lot at once.

"OK, now that we're alone, what's this all about?"

"What makes you think I'm not just being neighborly?"

"You think your major ad buyers would support all this neighborliness to the human Alien, as you put it?"

"Maybe I'm trying to get you home and jump your bones."

"Oh, sure."

"Is that so unimaginable?"

"Well, you'd be the first woman to try it."

"You were married, weren't you? Widower, right?"

"Yeah, but all the bone-jumping was usually my idea, and it happened somewhere around the sixtieth date, not the first car ride. You may have noticed I don't make a great first impression, especially with women."

"Are you one of those male idiots who doesn't realize what women are thinking?"

"Probably. Let's just say I'm aware I have limited sex appeal, and then only among a very select number of women. I've learned not to expect anything."

"Well, for your information, for whatever good it does, Mabel says your secretary has the hots for you, but is so desperate to hang on to her job that she's playing it strictly hands off for now. And the rumor is that Susie Reynolds at the restaurant wouldn't turn down an invitation. She was a wild child in high school, but has calmed down a lot lately. She might have another fling or two in her though."

"I try to take rumors and gossip with a grain of salt."

"Just saying."

"Is that what you lured me into your truck for, to discuss my love life?"

"I thought it might be an amusing way to pass the time."

"Very funny."

"But what I really wanted to tell you is that you are wrong about the sheriff and Hank Sweat having shot their wad. They're up to something having to do with the Aliens; I just don't know what."

"You're kidding."

"God's truth."

"I guess some people just don't learn."

"You've got to understand. If we'd had any blacks in town before you guys got here, the sheriff would have organized a chapter of the Ku Klux Klan. He made it tough enough for the Mexicans coming in, but the big farmers made it clear they needed them for the rough farm work, so he had to back off. Now you've hauled in blacks, browns, yellows, and probably some greens and purples. He also lost a son who had HIV in the Disappearances, though he won't admit the HIV part to anybody.

"Hank Sweat, on the other hand, plays the good cop, and he's not so prejudiced, but he lost a daughter and two grandchildren. He understands farming, but he always thought all that stuff about climate change was bullshit, and when people started throwing around words like 'ecosystem collapse' and 'oxygen deprivation' he leaped for the nearest conspiracy theory. He's a bitter man with a few self-delusions and maybe more dangerous than the sheriff. They've been nosing around for a few people to sign up for something, but I can't get a line on what."

"So why tell me? Aren't you just making enemies?"

"Probably. But I don't hold with shooting people in the back either. Especially ones with enough grit to stand up to me."

"I just needed my ads run."

Jayne pulled into Jim's driveway and stopped.

"Well, it's been a pleasure talking with you, Jim King."

"I guess this is probably not the time to invite you in for a glass of tea."

"Probably not. I don't jump men's bones after the first car ride. I usually wait until about the sixth. You got five to go."

"I'll keep that in mind."

"You do that."

"Goodnight, Jayne, and thank you."

"Goodnight, Jim."

And he got out of the truck and went inside his house as she backed out and drove off.

• • •

The next afternoon, Angie came over through the backyard and knocked on his back door. Jim came into the kitchen and let her in.

"How's it going?" he asked.

"Nothing's shaking."

"What did you think of the football game?"

"Well, I see what you mean about it being an adolescent contest to demonstrate male fitness to reproduce. But watching the people was fun; Sonal and I got a big kick out of that. And I've decided I love snack bars. Pankaja wouldn't let Sonal have a hot dog, of course, but the two of us tried just about everything else they had to eat."

"Jayne Pearce from the Western Times gave me a ride home after the game."

"Oh really. I wasn't expecting that."

"She wanted to warn me that Hank Sweat and the sheriff are up to no good again. She claimed not to have any details, but evidently the sheriff has problems that go beyond hating Aliens, and Hank Sweat is a bitter man who doesn't always accept reality."

"Well, as long as they communicate electronically and keep using bullets or explosives or anything that has even the simplest computer chip, I think we've got it covered. I'll pass the word, though."

"Sounds good."

"What you up to today?"

"Well, chores are done. Want to watch a game?"

"What's on?"

"Got your choice of college football or pro baseball."

"Let's go with the baseball; I don't like seeing people get hurt."

"Fine with me. You want some popcorn?"

"Of course."

The Atlanta Braves weren't playing, so they watched Kansas City play the Sox.

26.

AND SO IT WAS

A nd so it was the following Monday at the restaurant when another warning came. Jim was eating with Angie, Bob, and Olga when Susie whispered in his ear again while serving tea that Hank Sweat was up to something. Jim casually looked around the restaurant. Hank and the sheriff were sitting with two other men Jim didn't recognize at a table near the door, just sipping coffee. Becky and Davey were at another table with Texas and Flo, and Bill and Xihong were with Rosy and Mary over in Cindy's section. Jayne Pearce was not far from the sheriff's table meeting with what looked like some church women's group at one of the tables for six.

After the meal, Jim and Olga slowly finished their teas while Angie and Bob savored their new favorite pies, lemon meringue and coconut cream. They all laid some cash on the table, waved to Susie, and headed for the door. Just as they approached the area of Hank and the sheriff, all four men sprang to their feet. There was no thought, no contemplation of alternatives, no heroic resolve in facing danger. Jim simply took one step to the left to be in front of Angie and felt a sharp pain somewhere in the middle of his body. He grabbed at the pain and instead wrapped his hands around an arm and held on. He saw a pitcher of unsweet tea slam into Hank's head, felt the cold tea splash into his face, and then life slowly went dark.

. . .

When light returned, he blinked and suddenly felt a strong hand on his chest and heard a vaguely familiar voice saying, "Don't try to move. You're going to be fine. Everything is OK, but it will hurt if you try to move."

Jim managed to focus his eyes and saw Doctor Harvard sitting next to the bed and leaning over him to keep him from sitting up or twisting.

"Just hold still and let me do my doctor stuff, OK?"

Jim nodded slightly, and Dr. Harvard took out one of his Star Trek whizbangs and held it an inch above his midsection. Jim looked up and saw several medical-looking gizmos arranged around his bed at home. He glanced to his left and was surprised to see Angie lying beside him, looking very pale and tired and still, but with an IV dripping something red into her and other tubes and wires hooked to the gizmos. It took him a second to see a slight movement under the sheet covering her chest and know she was sleeping.

Over by the side window Bob sat at a table, bare-chested but with a big bandage on his left shoulder, his left arm in a sling, and a set of straps holding his arm tight to his chest. He was sitting in front of a dinner plate with a humongous steak on it, and Susie was there holding a knife and fork as if she had been cutting the steak into bite-sized pieces for him. Harvard leaned back, and Jim looked out his back window at one of the Alien spheres parked in his backyard. In front of the window sat Jayne and the Dragon Lady, each with some playing cards in their hands, as if waiting for somebody else to play a card. Harvard sat back down, and Jim could now see Becky, Mabel, and Davey hovering in the doorway.

"What happened?"

"Well, from a strictly medical point of view, you were stabbed with an eight-inch-long hunting knife, which sliced through your liver, penetrated your diaphragm, and punctured one lung, severing one major and a couple of minor arteries in the process. Fortunately, you didn't allow your assailant to pull the knife out, so when the aptly named Florence Nightingale got to you, she was able to reduce the bleeding somewhat and jury-rig a transfusion directly from Angie to keep you alive until I could get there. I just happened to be in the hemisphere, so within thirty minutes I was performing major surgery on a table in the restaurant, which was a novel experience for me.

"We just about bled Angie dry, but she was the best blood match and we really didn't have time to be switching donors, so that is the reason I have given her a mild sedative while building up her blood again. She will be fine, though it will take two or three days for her to recover fully. As for you, you will also recover, though we are talking a couple of weeks, not days, for you. I have bound the surgical area rather tightly, but I also applied one of our wonder drugs to spur the healing process, which includes making the nerves regenerate. One unfortunate side effect of that is making it hurt like hell if you twist or stretch along the incision for the first couple of days. In short, old friend, you very nearly died, but you are going to totally recover. However, it will not be a totally pain-free process, especially for the first two days."

"How long have I been out?"

"I kept you sedated for about twenty-four hours to give your body time to regenerate. You challenged my medical skills a little more than I like."

Jim noticed that Jayne and the Dragon Lady had moved to stand at the foot of his bed.

"OK, that's the medical report. What's the news report?"

"How much do you remember?" asked the Dragon Lady.

"I remember Hank Sweat having something in his hand, then a pain, then seeing a big pitcher of tea whack Hank in the head. After that it gets fuzzy fast."

"As best I can piece together the various accounts, Hank, the sheriff, and the other two men all had knives and each one tried to stab a different Alien. Hank was going for Angie and you got in his way, for which I will be eternally grateful. The pitcher of tea was in Susie's hand. Did you know they still use the old heavy glass pitchers at Stephens? I would have expected plastic, but it was glass with a thick bottom so it's difficult to turn over. Susie actually managed to get in two whacks to Hank's head, the second one as he was collapsing and had the corner of a booth on the other side of his head. Dr. Harvard can go into the details about intercranial hemorrhaging and traumatic brain swelling, but the result was fatal brain injuries.

"While all this was going on with you, the good sheriff managed to get his knife into Bob's left chest and shoulder a couple of times, missing his heart by about an inch, until my new friend Ms. Pearce here managed to pull the sheriff's pistol out of his holster from behind, step to the side, and put three bullets into his chest, persuading him to drop his knife, fall to the floor, and die. The other two men had further to go to reach their targets, so Davey, Rosy, and Mary had time to pull out their little muscle paralysis units before they reached anybody. The owner of the restaurant and a couple of other humans there ripped the knives away, threw the two men on the floor, and tied them up like hogs. Becky managed to persuade Davey and the others to turn their units off before the men died, and they are now locked up in the jail in the basement of the courthouse. There are rumors the key has been thrown away.

"Meanwhile, Harvard here came whipping down in his sphere, landing right in front of the door and dashing out with his arms full of medical equipment. Gathered quite a crowd in the parking lot checking out the Alien's hot rod. It also created a stir inside the restaurant when first Flo and Angie, then the others, reverted to our own language to deal with the medical and communication emergencies. The church ladies Jayne had been meeting with started praying out loud and singing 'Amazing Grace,' so it turned into quite a scene, I am told."

"Well, talk about an exciting lunch."

"Exciting, perhaps, but I'm afraid it means our little experiment has failed. I'm just sorry you and Angie and Bob have suffered for it."

He glanced around the room again.

"Failed? Look around the room, Lady. You call that failure?"

The Dragon Lady looked down at Jim lying next to Angie, then at Susie still holding the knife and fork for Bob, to Jayne standing beside her with playing cards still in her hand, then to the door where Olga, Pankaja, and Flo had joined Becky, Davey and Mabel in peering into the room.

"Perhaps you have a point. Perhaps we should not rush to any conclusions."

At that point the doctor asserted his authority.

"Perhaps you should all get out and let these patients rest now that you know they will survive."

"Becky, I think you'll find all the fixings for Rice Krispy candy in my kitchen. I'm sure the Dragon Lady here would love the recipe. Maybe some iced tea for everybody."

"Yes, sir. Just so you know, I think half the town brought casseroles. We've been eating the ones we couldn't get in the fridge. Food is not a problem. Come on, Mabel; let's show these Aliens how it's done."

And gradually everybody straggled out with smiles and shy waves, Susie carrying the plate of steak for Bob, until only Harvard and Jim were left, other than the still sleeping Angie.

"There is one other medical thing I guess I need to mention."

"Uh-oh."

"Well, maybe yes, maybe no. It's just that we've never transfused a human with Alien blood before, and you got a lot of it. Angie really was the best match, and we think there shouldn't be a problem, but, you know, you're never really sure until you actually do it. If it makes any difference at all, it could just as easily be a good thing as a bad thing. You really are a little bit Alien now. I remember you don't like me keeping secrets, so I wanted you to know."

"Thank you. For everything."

"That's my job. Now, you get some more sleep. I'll come back in a couple of hours to torture you by getting you up and moving, no matter how much it hurts."

"That gives me something to look forward to."

"I'll send Flo in to keep an eye on you while I get some of that candy."

The doctor left, and he was alone with the sleeping Angie beside him. She shifted in the bed, and he slowly turned his head to look at her. She blinked, then slowly opened her eyes.

"Ohhh."

"Angie? You OK?"

She turned her head to look at him.

"Just really tired. You?"

"They say I'll live."

"Good."

"Thanks for all the blood."

"Least I could do. Where is everybody?"

"In the kitchen making Rice Krispy candy."

"Then it sounds like we will be OK."

"We'll live to eat another day."

Angie's eyes began to close again.

"Hope you don't mind me sleeping with you," she murmured.

"I don't mind at all."

And her eyes closed and there was a faint snore. Flo came in and sat in the chair next to the bed. Jim closed his eyes and drifted off with the image of an Alien sphere sitting in his backyard.

EPILOGUE

Three weeks later, Jim was eating lunch at the restaurant with Angie and Jayne. He still had a small bandage over the incision under his shirt, but it was more to help the scar fade than to protect anything. He hadn't recovered all his weight and his iron was still a little low, so he was indulging in a bacon-Swiss hamburger, wondering if his appetite had been affected by all the Alien blood. Sharon Springs Software had just launched its first product, a computer-optimization software that doubled hard-drive speed and memory. At first people thought it was too good to be true, but then the rumor got out that it was ripped off from an Alien computer, and now it was selling like ice cream in August.

As they were eating, a stranger carrying a bicycle helmet and a small backpack was brought in and seated in the booth next to them, behind Jim. The stranger wore bicycling shorts and a windbreaker, and looked to be around thirty years old, very lean, black hair and glasses. Susie came over to take his order.

"Just a big glass of ice water to start with, please. I just rode a bicycle all the way down from Goodland, and I'm pretty thirsty."

"Sure. But why on a bicycle?"

"Because if you're a reporter, that's the only way to get here, except maybe walk. Anything with an engine or electricity with a reporter in it stalls as soon as you turn south on 27 from the interstate."

"You're a reporter?"

"Yeah. New York Times."

"What are you doing here?"

"Looking for the Aliens. There's rumors flying around from person to person, but a real blackout on anything hooked to a computer anywhere, like the internet or cell phones, that there are Aliens in Sharon Springs, Kansas. So, I was sent to find the Aliens, even if I have to ride in on a bike. You know anything about it?"

"Which aliens you talking about?"

"Which Aliens? What do you mean?"

"Well, we got aliens from China, we got aliens from India, we got aliens from South America, we even got one alien from South Africa, but he's nice. We got a few people from California and Oregon that aren't aliens, but some of them are a little strange."

"I'm not talking about immigrant aliens, I'm talking about Alien Aliens—you know, the ones from another planet, the spacemen."

"Oh, them. No, they're not weird. They're actually pretty nice. Let me get you that water."

And Susie winked at Angie as she walked by. By then, the restaurant had grown strangely quiet and everybody seemed to be listening to see what would happen. Jim turned in his seat to face the reporter.

"You really a reporter from the Times?"

"I've got my employee ID if you want to see it."

"No, that's OK. Why don't you come join us? This is Jayne Pearce, the editor of the Western Times, the newspaper that covers western Kansas and eastern Colorado."

The reporter moved over to the booth and sat by Jim.

"Pleased to meet a colleague. Randy Smith."

"My pleasure. My friends are Jim King and Angie Winston from Sharon Springs Software, the major business in town."

"Nice to meet all of you. Maybe you can help me with this Alien thing."

"You know, even if you find an Alien and get a story, you're not going to be able to print anything. I've got Pulitzer Prize copy sitting on my desk that I keep writing on an antique typewriter, because my computer won't take it, and I can't get it up on any wire service or anything. It's basically turning into a manuscript for the archives."

"I suspected as much."

"So why'd you come all the way out here?"

"I'm a reporter. I want to know what's really going on. And I guess I'm a little more pig-headed than the rest of my colleagues. Or maybe more stupid. Pick one."

"Anything against the Aliens?"

"Me? No, nothing personal. I lost a cousin, a couple of acquaintances, but I get it. Probably the best they could do. Even Aliens have limits."

"Well, while you're here looking for Aliens, maybe Jim and Angie could give you a tour of Sharon Springs Software. They're doing some really cutting-edge stuff. There might be a story there that you could actually print."

"Sounds good. Any Alien employees?"

Jim replied, "Actually, they're all in management."

Susie came back with the ice water and put it in front of Randy.

"Special today is the Alien burger plate. It's two, third-pound, all-beef patties; four strips of bacon; Swiss and cheddar cheese, lettuce, tomato, onion, pickles, and mushrooms on a sourdough bun. It comes with a large order of fries, plus coleslaw or a salad, a twenty-four-ounce soft drink, and a slice of pie and a square of Rice Krispy candy for dessert."

Angie said, "It's what I'm having. If you want to be an Alien, you have to eat like one."

And the reporter just sat there with his mouth open, but with no thought of putting food in it.

THE END

ACKNOWLEDGMENTS

Thanks to Sam and Molly Elkind and Jim Gray, who read an early draft and gently pointed out my errors. Also thanks to Drs. Ketty Gonzalez and Roger Vega for medical input.